D1431037

SECRETS IN THE STORM

PATCHWORK MYSTERIES

SECRETS IN THE STORM

SUSAN PAGE DAVIS

Guideposts

New York

Guideposts.org
(800) 932-2145
Guideposts Books & Inspirational Media

Cover design by Wendy Bass
Cover illustration by Joyce Patti
Interior design by Lorie Pagnozzi
Typeset by Aptara, Inc.

Printed and bound in the United States of America
10 9 8 7 6 5 4 3

PATCHWORK MYSTERIES

SECRETS IN THE STORM

 ## CHAPTER ONE

Maggie Hart drove carefully around a large tree limb lying in the street. Her Tahoe crunched through six inches of new snow that swooped in heavy drifts from the storm the night before.

"Maybe we should have waited until the plows got around to all the residential areas." Sarah, Maggie's mother-in-law, tried not to be too obvious as she clung to the armrest.

"I'm sure we'll be fine. But it's my fault for talking you into going out this morning. You can blame me if we get stuck."

Several people were out shoveling their walks, and more tree branches lay on the sidewalks and lawns.

"That was quite the wind we had last night," Maggie said. "Our neighbor had a tree branch fall on her cable TV line and take it down."

"I'm glad it's not so gusty now," Sarah said. "Do you think the twins will be okay at home?"

"Oh yes. They're thrilled to have a day off from school. Audrey asked if they could make brownies this morning, and I left them with a mix. And we'll be home before lunch. They can go sledding this afternoon if they want."

"They're resourceful girls." Sarah reminded herself that Audrey and Amy were thirteen now, perfectly capable of taking care of themselves for a few hours.

"I think I'll open the store while we work, even though I don't expect anyone to come in this morning." Maggie waved to a man who was clearing his driveway with a snow blower.

"If no one comes in, we'll get more done," Sarah said. "What is it we're unpacking?"

"Three boxes of china and one of antique linens. I need to catalog them all, check them over closely for flaws, and price them. Then we can do the fun part—deciding how to display them."

"Sounds great."

Maggie guided the SUV onto Park Street, the street that ran beside the public library, and conditions improved. The plow had cleared the streets in the center of town. Brilliant sun sparkled on the snow, and a drift had formed around the war memorial in the park. Sarah was glad to see there wasn't much damage in the town. She waved to Eugene Briggs, who was walking toward the bank. They rolled toward the green and Maggie's antique shop.

"Wait! Stop!" Sarah reached over and touched Maggie's sleeve.

"What is it?" Maggie pumped the brakes, and the Tahoe shuddered to a halt opposite the side door of the Maple Hill Public Library.

"Look." Sarah pointed toward the imposing stone building.

"What—" Maggie sucked in a breath. "Oh no!"

Sarah stared bleakly at the library's sidewall. Where a beautiful, century-old stained glass window should have been, letting shimmering rays of light in over the library's stairway landing, was only a gaping hole.

Sarah took out her phone and called the librarian. She and Maggie waited in the vehicle. Sarah had a vague feeling that they were guarding the site, making sure no one else came along and disturbed things.

"You're active in the Friends of the Library group, aren't you?" Maggie asked.

"Yes. I was elected secretary at the January meeting." Sarah eyed the broken window. "This is terrible. Maybe the club can do something to help."

Spencer Hewitt drove up fifteen minutes later and climbed out of his car. He trudged up the snowy sidewalk, not seeming to notice that his shoes were completely covered in snow. Pain radiated from his eyes as he stared up at the hole in the library wall.

Sarah jumped out of the SUV. "Spencer, are you all right?" She and Maggie hurried toward him.

"Yes, I'm ..." He shook his head, still gazing at the black emptiness before them.

The arched frame of the stained glass window was intact but almost empty. Around the edges, a few pieces of yellow, red, and green glass hung tenaciously from the metal edging. Several larger pieces stuck up at the bottom of the framing.

"I can't believe it. How could this happen? I mean, I know it was windy last night, but we've had lots of worse storms before."

Sarah's heart went out to the librarian. Spencer loved the library, and he was obviously shocked by the destruction of the lovely window.

"Would you like Maggie and me to go in with you?" she asked.

"Thank you. It would be good to have someone else along. I'd like to see what the damage is inside, but let's go around to the front door." He started toward the street corner, then stopped, frowning. "Oh, great. Of course the walk's not shoveled, and the shovel's inside in the closet."

"I have a shovel in the back of my Tahoe," Maggie said. "Let me get it."

She hurried to the back of her vehicle and pulled out an aluminum snow shovel. "Jason won't let me go anywhere in winter without a shovel, a blanket, and a bag of sand."

"Thanks, Maggie. Let me get that." Spencer took the shovel from her.

"I wouldn't think any books would be damaged," Sarah said as they walked along the edge of the plowed street until they were even with the sidewalk that ran in front of the library. The small sidewalk plow hadn't been here yet, and she stayed at the edge of the snowy street.

"Let's hope not," Spencer said as they rounded the corner. "I guess it depends on how much snow blew in. But that window was unique, like the Palladian window up there." He glanced upward, toward the three-sectioned, arched window above the front entrance. "I don't know if it will be possible to replace it."

Sarah knew the window well—it was a landmark in the town, like the steeple of the Congregational Church and the courthouse on the hill. "It's a shame," she said.

"You're right though. Some snow probably did blow in, but there aren't any books close to the window. I hate to think of the heat we've lost through that hole." Spencer took a deep breath. "Well, ladies, this will take a couple of minutes. I'll dig through the ridge the plow left, and then it shouldn't be too bad."

Most of the flat expanses, like the library lawn, were covered by several inches of snow. On the windward sides of buildings and fences, deeper drifts had formed. The wind still blew, though not too fiercely. It was enough to lift swirls of loose snow and fling it across the open areas, and to make Sarah shiver and put up the hood on her jacket.

Spencer attacked the higher ridge of packed snow that the town's plow truck had pushed aside and soon had a narrow path through it, onto the sidewalk.

"Here, let me take a turn," Maggie said.

"No need."

"Come on, you did the hardest part." Maggie reached for the shovel. "Take a minute's rest, and then I'll give the shovel back."

He handed it over with obvious reluctance. Maggie made quick progress along the walkway, carving a path one shovel blade wide through the looser snow for them to walk along.

Spencer looked plaintively at Sarah. "What am I going to tell the trustees? The windows in this building are the pride of our architectural detail."

Sarah patted his shoulder. "Wait until we get a look inside, Spencer. It may not be as bad as it looks from out here."

He shook his head. "I don't know how it could be any better. I was just reading up on the construction of the library a couple of weeks ago. This building is a hundred and ten years old. How can we replace a window with such history?"

He followed Maggie's path. She was halfway to the steps. "Here, let me finish."

Maggie gave him the shovel and waited behind him with Sarah, inching toward the steps as he cleared the way. He scooped the white fluff off each step and scraped down to the stone. Sarah and Maggie followed him up toward the door, until they stood under the overhang of the entrance.

Spencer leaned the shovel against the wall and took out his key ring.

"The man who designed the building was a famous architect from Boston, and they hired a master craftsman to do the molding and the window frames," he said as he fitted his key into the lock. Swinging the door inward, he looked down at their feet for the first time.

"I'm sorry, ladies. Here I am dithering on about the architecture, and your feet are probably soaked. You must be freezing."

"It's not too bad, actually, thanks to your hard work with that shovel," Sarah said.

"Don't worry about us, Spencer. Sarah and I both have boots." Maggie drew him inside. They all wiped their feet on the mat inside the door.

Spencer peered about the large room. "Can you see any damage in here?"

"No," Sarah said. She looked over at Maggie.

"Nope, I can't," Maggie said.

"Me either." Spencer hauled in a deep breath. "So far so good. Let's take a look at the stairway."

They walked past the circulation desk and around the ends of several rows of shelving until they came to the bottom of the curving staircase. They all stood silently gazing at the hole in the wall halfway up. Where the stairs turned gracefully at a triangular landing, the multicolored rose window had always let the sun in. It cast colored shafts of light on the library patrons as they went quietly up the carpeted stairs to the Massachusetts Room or the upper stacks.

But today, only a big hole in the wall greeted them. Through it they could see the gray sky. Wind blew in, sweeping down upon them in icy gusts and whistling eerily around the broken edges of the window frame. Spread over the stairs, from the landing down to the main level floor at their feet, splinters of colored glass glinted at them. No one spoke for a long moment.

Sarah eyed the dusting of snow that lay on the landing and the two steps beneath it. The snow seemed not to have found its way farther down, into the reading room. "We need to cover that hole and sweep up the glass."

"Can we sweep that snow up too, before it melts?" Maggie asked.

Sarah realized how cold it was in the room, even though it was significantly warmer than outside. Some of the snow may have melted already. "We could scoop some of it up with a dustpan, but we'll have to be careful."

"Yes." Spencer unzipped his jacket. "I should get a move on."

"I'm just glad I've got my warm coat and gloves on," Maggie said. She crouched and touched an almost perfect circle of yellow glass. "I can't imagine what did this. There aren't any trees close enough for a limb to smash the window."

"No, and if one did, we'd have found it here or seen it on the ground outside," Sarah said.

Spencer knelt and touched part of a metal strip that had separated the colored pieces of glass.

"Be careful," Sarah told him.

"Better keep your gloves on," Maggie added.

"This will take some time to clean up. I'll have to notify the trustees right away." Spencer stood. "I'll get a broom from the storage room. I think there's a tarp in there too."

"I'll start picking up the bigger pieces," Maggie said. "Sarah and I will help you, right?" She looked expectantly at Sarah.

"Of course. And if we need more help, maybe the Friends of the Library could come."

"I don't know," Spencer said. "It may be better not to get too many people in here until all the glass is taken care of. I can do it myself. What a shame." He shook his head as he gazed at the mess, then turned and walked back toward the circulation desk. Sarah followed him.

"Maggie and I don't mind staying awhile to help."

"You don't need to do that," Spencer said. "I wasn't planning to open today, anyway. The schools are closed because of the storm. A lot of roads aren't passable yet, and most people are staying home."

"Let us give you a little of our time," Sarah said. "It won't take long with all three of us working."

"Thanks, Sarah." He went through a swinging gate in the counter and opened a drawer. "Let me get the key to the storage room."

"You don't carry it with you?"

"No, I have too many keys on my key ring as it is. I leave the storeroom and restroom keys in here." He closed the drawer. "We don't keep anything important in there, but I can't leave it open because of the toxic cleaning supplies."

Sarah nodded, thinking of all the children who came to the library.

He held up a key with a pasteboard tag attached. "This way."

Sarah followed him around a corner to a doorway between the two restrooms.

"You must turn the heat down at night in here," she said.

"Yes, we run it at about fifty degrees overnight to save fuel. I come in at least an hour before opening time and turn it up." Spencer glanced at her. "Maybe I should turn it right off until we get the window covered."

"It shouldn't take us long," she said. "I know you don't want to lose too much heat out that hole, but you don't want it to get too cold in here, either."

He nodded and fitted the key into the lock. "The trustees will be unhappy over next month's fuel bill. It will probably be sky high."

"Well, we have trustees for a reason—to deal with problems like this."

Spencer turned the knob and opened the door, then flipped on the light. He entered first, with Sarah on his heels.

The small room had gray steel utility shelving on two sides. Along a third wall, cartons were stacked and neatly labeled.

"There's a stepladder over here," Spencer said, pointing toward a corner. "We'll need that."

Sarah eyed it doubtfully. It was only a folding step stool, like she had in her hall closet. "It may not be tall enough."

"I've got the broom and dustpan, but I'd better get a box for the glass." Spencer poked about in some bins on the metal shelving. "Here's a roll of sheet plastic. It's not as heavy as a tarp, but it will work until we get something better. Now, what can we fasten it with? I don't want to damage the wall or the molding."

Sarah looked around, curious. She had never been in this room before. She stepped away from Spencer and closed the door part way so she could see into the corner behind it. Beside a stack of three cardboard boxes, a dark mound lay on the floor. She stooped to examine it.

"Spencer, what's this?"

"*Hmm?*" He turned his head and blinked, squinting toward where she stood in the shadows.

"It looks like a blanket," Sarah said.

Spencer walked toward her, frowning. "A blanket? Where did that come from?" He joined her in the corner and lifted it, turning it about, staring at it.

Sarah reached out to touch it. "It feels like wool."

"That's very odd," Spencer said. "Why would it be in here?"

"And here's another." Sarah nodded at the floor, where a second blanket—this one a deep red plaid acrylic fiber—lay in an untidy heap. "And a flashlight and ... "

"How on earth did this stuff get here?" Spencer asked.

Sarah stooped and picked up a small cardboard box. "*Hmm*. Crackers. Is it possible someone used this for a hideaway? A clubhouse, maybe?"

"Kids, you mean?" Spencer frowned and shook his head. "I don't see how. I keep the key in the desk drawer all the time."

"Is there a second key?" Sarah asked.

"Not that I know of."

They looked about for a moment, thinking.

"Who else comes in here?" Sarah asked at last. "Do you have someone who cleans the library?"

"Yes, but I always unlock the door for her and lock it again afterward. She cleans during our regular hours, not at night."

"I guess that rules out the janitor."

"Well, let's get what we need, and then I'd better call the trustees." Spencer dropped the blanket and moved toward the step stool.

"All right," Sarah said. "I'll carry the broom and dustpan."

Spencer glanced down at the blankets in the corner. "Maybe one of those would give better insulation than the plastic."

"I don't think you should use them," Sarah said. "You should bundle all of that stuff up and look it over closely. There may be clues here as to who's been using this room."

"Do you think I should call the police?" Spencer's worried frown told Sarah that he would hate to have police officers tramp through the library all day.

"You probably don't need to do that. Just get the lock on this door changed and make sure you don't leave the new keys lying around. Problem solved."

"Hey, Sarah," Maggie called from the reading room. "Spencer, come here!"

Sarah and Spencer looked at each other, then hurried out to the staircase carrying the cleanup gear.

"What is it?" Sarah asked.

"Over here."

Maggie stood on the far side of the staircase, on the floor below the railing.

"I found this on the floor here, by the wall." She held up a squarish brown object, a little bigger than her fist.

"What is that?" Spencer asked.

"I'm not sure," Maggie said. "It looks like part of a brick."

Sarah set down the broom and dustpan and moved closer. "Spencer, doesn't that look like the bricks in the walkway out front?"

"It does."

They all looked at each other.

"Okay," Spencer said. "Now I'm calling the police."

CHAPTER TWO

Officers Hopkins and Pratt arrived a few minutes later in a squad car, though the police station was less than a block away. They had to park in the street, as the library's parking lot hadn't been plowed. Both came in through the front door. Spencer met them there and led them around to the bottom of the stairway.

"We were going to clean up the broken glass," Spencer said, "but we quit after Maggie found a piece of a brick."

Both officers gazed up at the window frame and then at the colored shards scattered on the stairs.

"It couldn't be an accident," Sarah said. She pointed to the half brick Maggie had set down on the third step. "It seems likely this was used to break the window."

Maggie stepped forward. "I'm sorry I touched it, but I did have my gloves on. We all wore our gloves so we wouldn't cut ourselves on the glass."

Officer Pratt bent over to study the brick. "Did you find it right there?"

14

"No. Over here." Maggie walked around to the side of the stairway, below the railing, and pointed out the exact spot near the wall.

Some slivers of glass had flown over the railing or between the balusters and landed on the hardwood floor below. Not many pieces of any size had survived down there, but the slivers caught the glint of the overhead lights and shone little rainbows on the off-white wall.

"Do you know anyone who'd want to break the window?" Officer Hopkins asked, pulling a small notebook from his pocket.

"I can't imagine anyone wanting to destroy something that beautiful," Sarah said.

Spencer, however, stroked his chin and grimaced. "I don't like to say it, but there is someone who's upset with me."

"Oh?" Hopkins asked. "Can you tell me about that?"

"Yeah. One of the library trustees was in here a week or so ago. He made some copies and just looked around. Then he asked for the key to the men's room. We keep the restrooms locked, and patrons ask for the keys when they need them. I told him I'd just given it to a young man, so I guess he went over there to wait." Spencer nodded in the direction of the restrooms. "Well, a couple of minutes later he came back as mad as a wet hen without a towel. He said someone was smoking in there. He could smell it."

"What did you do?" Officer Hopkins asked.

"I went over and knocked on the door. I told the kid to open up. He did, and the air was just blue in there. I asked him if he'd been smoking. Of course he said no, but there was all the smoke, and the trustee found some ash on the sink. The boy had a pack of cigarettes in his shirt pocket." Spencer shrugged unhappily. "I had to call his folks. The kid was fourteen, and the board of trustees would have made a huge fuss if I hadn't."

"What was the boy's name?"

"Jacob Hull. His folks are good people. I wish it hadn't happened."

Officer Hopkins wrote it down. "Anything come of that?"

Spencer sighed. "The trustees also made me revoke Jacob's library privileges, but that came later. When I confronted him that first day, Jacob was very angry. He tried to run out, but Mr. Danvers held onto him and wouldn't let him go."

"Mr. Danvers being the trustee?"

"That's right. I called Jacob's mom. She was at work, but she said she'd ask his grandmother to come right over and pick him up. She wasn't mad, just sad, I think."

Sarah felt sad too. She knew Julie Hull, the boy's grandmother, and she was sure this incident had grieved Julie and her husband, as well as Jacob's parents.

"But Jacob was sure upset." Spencer shook his head.

"What did he do?" Officer Hopkins asked.

"He yelled at me. Used some colorful language. Then he took out his library card and tore it up and threw it at me. It was not a scene I'd like to repeat."

"What would you have done if Mr. Danvers hadn't been here?" Officer Lisa Pratt asked.

"I would have given him a stern talking to, and I probably would have called his mom, but I would have waited until I didn't have an audience. The way it was handled was humiliating for Jacob." Spencer looked a bit upset, just recalling the incident.

"Okay, we'll talk to the boy and his parents," Officer Hopkins said. "And we'll take the brick. I'll even help you tack up that plastic before we leave."

"Thanks," Spencer said, and Sarah nudged him. "Oh, and there's something else."

"Yes?"

"We found—that is, Sarah found—some things in the storage room when we went to get the broom and the ladder. Somebody has been in there and left some blankets and things. Only thing is I keep that room locked too."

"Could you show it to us, please?" Officer Pratt asked.

"Sure." Spencer took the two officers around to the storeroom.

"Doesn't Jacob Hull have a brother in the twins' class?" Sarah asked Maggie.

"Yeah, Michael. I feel bad for his folks."

"Me too." Sarah looked at the mess on the floor. "I wonder if it's okay to get on with the cleanup. They didn't tell us not to."

"I thought maybe they'd take pictures," Maggie said.

"Perhaps we'd already disturbed the scene too much." Sarah hated to think she had made the police investigation more difficult.

"Well, I took a few with my cell phone while you and Spencer were getting the cleaning stuff."

"Good thinking," Sarah said. "Maybe send those to me later?"

Maggie smiled. "I had a feeling you would say that."

A few minutes later, Spencer and the two officers returned. Officer Pratt held two plastic bags with the flashlight and cracker box inside them. Officer Hopkins was carrying the two blankets Sarah had found, and in the brighter light of the reading room, Sarah noticed a white bedding tag on the border of one.

"I didn't notice anything when we came up the walk," Spencer was saying, "but we just made a narrow path so we wouldn't get our feet wet. Of course, there's another brick walkway leading to the side door. That's closer to the window."

"I didn't see any footprints in the snow out there," Sarah said, trying to recall exactly how the ground had looked when she and Maggie had first spotted the damage.

"We'll check into it," Officer Hopkins said.

He and Spencer managed to cover the window frame with plastic, using thumb tacks and masking tape to hold it in place. Meanwhile, Officer Pratt searched the carpeted stair treads and the floor near the stairs carefully.

"You'll want to get something else over that hole soon," Officer Hopkins said as he descended the ladder.

"Can we go ahead and clean up?" Sarah asked. "Or do you need any of the pieces of glass?"

Hopkins looked over the stairs again. "I guess you can keep the glass. Since the window was so high up and was broken from outside, it's doubtful we'd find anything useful on the pieces."

"So, we can go ahead and sweep it up?" Maggie asked.

"Sure." Officer Hopkins turned to Spencer. "When does the library open?"

"I was going to keep it closed today. I closed early yesterday, and I doubt many people would come in today because the roads are still bad."

"All right. Let us know if you find anything else unusual. We'll talk to this Jacob Hull."

"And probably some other youngsters who've been connected to vandalism in the past year or two," Officer Pratt added.

Sarah said nothing, but the thought put her a little on edge. She figured that list of suspected vandals would include Ian Carper, her best friend Martha's grandson. Ian had had a brush with the law a year or so earlier, but he had caused no trouble since. Still, the police would probably question him. She tried not to worry about it.

As Officer Pratt picked up the folded blankets, Sarah caught a flash of white.

"Did you notice that tag?" Sarah asked.

The policewoman stopped and looked down.

Sarah pointed to the white manufacturer's bedding tag attached to the edge of one of the blankets. "There's something written on it."

Officer Pratt took the blankets over to the circulation desk and set them down. She took hold of the two-inch-long tag and flattened it out. Sarah and the others moved in closer so they could see it.

"Looks like someone wrote on the tag with a permanent marker," the officer said.

Sarah read the large block letters inked in black over the fainter printed message on the tag. "W.D.S. Could those be initials?"

"It's possible," Officer Pratt said. "We'll check into it."

"What about the flashlight?" Sarah asked.

Officer Pratt held up the plastic bags containing the cracker box and flashlight. The crackers were a common brand sold nationwide in any market. The flashlight, however, looked rugged.

"That looks like a nice one," Sarah said.

Officer Pratt examined it closely. "Yes. Not rechargeable but not a cheap one. I don't see any initials or other identifying marks though."

Sarah sighed. "I suppose they're widely available."

"I'd think so, but I'll check on the brand to be sure," Officer Pratt said.

She and Officer Hopkins soon left with the brick and the items from the storage room. Spencer joined Maggie as she stooped and resumed picking up fragments of glass with her gloves on. Sarah took an empty wastebasket and a dustpan and scooped what snow was left on the landing into the basket, but at least half of it had melted since they came in, leaving the carpeting on the stairs and landing spongy.

"Do you think we should keep the glass?" Maggie asked.

"Let's," Spencer told her. "Maybe someone can use it to help reconstruct the window. If not, we could have someone make a small piece as a keepsake and hang it in here somewhere."

"That's a good idea," Sarah said.

Maggie set the cardboard box on the bottom step and carefully lifted the stack she had made of large shards of glass. As she set it inside the box, she said, "I hope the window can be fixed."

"Me too." Sarah took the broom and dustpan around to the floor below the railing and swept up the bits of glass that had fallen there.

When they had gotten all the glass that could be easily picked or swept up, Spencer stood and stretched.

"Leave the rest, ladies. I'll get the vacuum cleaner out after I make myself a cup of coffee. Would you like some?"

"Thank you, but we ought to get on with the errand we originally set out for this morning," Sarah said. "Is there anything else we can do for you before we go?"

"Well, we'll need someone to give us an estimate on replacing the window. You're an officer of the Friends of the Library, aren't you?"

"Yes," Sarah said. "I'm the secretary. I'd be happy to make a few calls about that." She took her duties seriously, and this sounded like a job she could grab hold of, relieving some of the responsibility for Spencer.

"Thanks. It would be nice if I could suggest someone to the trustees."

"I'll work on it later today. And I'm sure the Friends group will do anything possible to help out."

"Great. They've always been wonderful when I needed support. And thank you too, Maggie, for all your help."

"Any time, Spencer," Maggie said. "I'm glad it's starting to warm up in here."

"You know, if you've got a fan, you might want to put it over there to blow toward the landing," Sarah said. "It might help dry the carpet quicker."

"Thanks. I'll try it."

The two women headed out the front door. The sun shone brilliantly outside, glinting off the snow. Trees had begun to drop the clumps from their branches to the ground below.

Officer Hopkins was brushing away snow on the brick walkway. "Ladies," he said as they passed him.

They walked down the edge of the street to the corner and along the side street toward Maggie's Tahoe. Officer Pratt stood on the snowy sidewalk near the path to the library's side door. She stooped and picked something up and dropped it into a bag she held in her other hand.

"Have a good day, ladies," she called.

"Picking up litter?" Maggie asked.

Officer Pratt held up her bag. "So far I've got a cigarette butt, a bottle cap, and a candy wrapper. But I think I'll have to come back after the snow melts." She glanced up at the broken window with the cloudy plastic filling the gap. "You never know what people leave behind."

A few minutes later, Maggie found a parking space directly in front of her store. The plows had cleared the streets around the common, and the sidewalk plow was busy in front of the Galleria. A few people were venturing out.

"Yes, I think I'll open," Maggie said. She unlocked the door and flipped the light switch. "Oops. Nix that idea. The power's out."

"Spencer had electricity at the library," Sarah said.

"He's on the other side of the park though." Maggie sighed. "It's cold in here too. Can you stand to work for a while under these conditions, or should we just go home?"

"I'm game for a little while," Sarah said. "Why don't you call the power company and report the outage, and I'll go in the back and make us some hot tea."

"Great." Maggie set down her purse and rummaged through it for her phone.

Sarah went to the back room, where Maggie had an office area and storage. The one window over the desk let in enough light for her to work.

Maggie's tea things were neatly washed and waiting. Sarah loved the antique teapot and cups Maggie used at the store. For a moment she thought she was stymied, as it occurred to her that the water probably wasn't running either, if the electric pump was off. Then she spotted a case of bottled water on the floor and grabbed two pint bottles.

"Perfect!" She hummed "Amazing Grace" as she went about filling the teakettle and setting it on the burner. "Oops. Now how will I heat it?"

Maggie came in from the store. "The power company says there's a line down between here and the bank. Just a few shops are without electricity, and they're working on it. It should be fixed within an hour."

"Good," Sarah said. "I thought I was doing well to make tea from bottled water, and then I realized the burner won't work."

Maggie grinned. "We're so dependent on technology! Well, we don't have a wood stove in here—at least not one that works. I do have that small cast-iron one out in the store. But why don't we run across to the café and get some coffee if they're open."

"Good idea, but I think I'll call first and see if anybody's over there."

Liam Connolly answered on the second ring. "Spotted Dog," he said in his cheerful Irish brogue.

"Bless you," Sarah replied. "It's Sarah, and Maggie and I are at her store with no electricity. We're going to invade your store for hot tea."

"I wasn't going to open until noon, but for you, me darlin', I'll break out the scones and shortbread."

"Sounds wonderful."

Sarah and Maggie pushed against the wind as they crossed the common. The bell rang brightly as Sarah pushed the door open. Liam came toward them smiling.

"Top o' the blustery mornin' to ye."

Murphy, his spotted corgi, gave a happy yip and danced around them, wagging his tail. Sarah gave him a pat.

"You silly thing. Were you afraid no one would come to see you today?"

The warmth of the café tempted her and Maggie to stay, but they took their tea in disposable cups, along with a small bag of scones.

"The treats are on me," Liam insisted. "I wouldn't like to think of you over there shivering and starving while you work. Just don't tell anyone else how generous I am, or I'll be overrun with people wanting free scones."

They laughed and thanked him. Sarah and Liam had become special friends over the past year or so. His upbeat mood and lilting voice never failed to cheer her. She and Maggie called good-bye and plunged out into the icy cold again.

"Brr," Maggie said as they entered her shop. "I hoped it would feel warmer in here, but it doesn't."

Sarah had to agree. "Let's work for half an hour. If it's too cold, we'll quit then. We don't want to get frostbite."

"Deal," Maggie said, cradling her warm cup in both hands.

They set to work, removing new merchandise from cartons. Sarah brought each piece to Maggie at her desk, and she entered its description, condition, and price into a notebook by hand.

"I'll have to put these in the computer catalog later, but if I have the listings ready, it will go faster then," Maggie said.

Her cell phone rang, and she pulled it out and looked at the display. "Jordan."

Sarah took away an empty box while Maggie talked to her part-time assistant.

"No, don't even try to come today," Maggie said. "I'll be ready for your help tomorrow, though, when the power's back on."

She hung up, and Sarah set another box on the desk and opened it.

"I wish we had a better chance to look over those things from Spencer's storage room before the police took them away." Sarah took a sip from her cup of tea, then delved into the carton of linens.

"Yeah," Maggie said. "What was there, besides blankets? That looked like some kind of snack crackers Officer Pratt had bagged."

"That's exactly what it was. Cheese crackers. And a flashlight."

"*Hmm,*" Maggie said. "The person who left them must have planned to be back inside the library before dark. Otherwise, he'd have taken his flashlight with him, right?"

"Maybe he comes in during the day, while the library is open," Sarah said.

"Only it wasn't open today."

"Right." Sarah frowned. "I didn't see any footprints leaving the library in the snow."

"That's true," Maggie said. "The surface of the snow was pretty even when we got there. Of course, with the wind blowing, snow had drifted all night. Anyone could have gone in or out late last night or early this morning, and their footprints would probably be gone now."

Sarah thought about that as she handed Maggie a tatted doily. "That supports the window being broken last night too. Maybe the person who used the storage room doesn't stay there every night. Maybe they just go in there once in a while."

"Yeah, when they need a place to hide. Like..." Maggie shrugged. "I don't know. Like after they've robbed a convenience store?"

Sarah laughed. "I don't think we have any convenience store thieves in Maple Hill," she said. "But yeah, something like that. Maybe some youngster goes there when his—or her—parents are angry with him. Or I suppose it's possible the person only used the room once."

Maggie nodded and spread the doily out on her desk. "Or maybe they never stayed there at all. Maybe they just hid their stuff there, where it was out of the way—or so they thought." She blew on her fingers and picked up her pen.

"I can imagine that scenario. It could even be one of the part-time helpers, if he knew where the key was kept, which seems likely. He came to work with that stuff and needed a place to stash it during his shift, then forgot to take it home."

She and Maggie looked at each other, and at the same time they said, "Nah."

Maggie smiled. "Who goes in to work carrying two blankets, a flashlight, and a box of crackers?"

"Right. But it would probably be a good idea for Spencer to ask all the employees about it."

The light overhead flickered. Sarah caught her breath and looked up. After a second, the fixture glowed.

"Hooray!" Maggie rolled her chair sideways so she sat in front of her keyboard. "I'll reboot the computer."

"And I'll heat water for more tea," Sarah said. "But you know, the real question about the mysterious library lurker is this: Did the person who left that stuff there also break the window?"

CHAPTER THREE

The twins met Sarah and Maggie at the door of Maggie and Jason's house.

"Mom! Wait until you see our snow elephant." Audrey was practically dancing as she let them in.

"A snow elephant?" Sarah said. "That's different."

Amy smiled sheepishly. "Well, it started out to be a snowman, but it sort of got out of shape, and we decided to change it a little."

Maggie and Sarah followed the girls out the back door and gazed at the four-foot snow sculpture gracing the back lawn.

"What do you know," Maggie said. "It really does look like an elephant."

"Well, of course," Audrey said.

"It's charming," Sarah said sincerely. "Too bad it's not out front where all the neighbors can see it."

"I can smell the brownies," Maggie said as they went inside. "Did you put the casserole in the oven?"

"Yes, and it should be done soon." Amy hurried over to the stove and peeked inside the oven.

"It's been in like half an hour," Audrey said, "and we have the table set."

"I must say, you girls have been busy this morning." Sarah removed her jacket and let Maggie take it.

"Dad's here," Amy called from near the window.

"Perfect timing," Maggie said. "Fill the water glasses, please, girls."

Five minutes later they all sat down in the dining room of the old Victorian house. This had once been Sarah's grandfather's home, and she had always loved it. Jason and Maggie had bought it about two years before, and had spent all the time and funds they could on restoring it. The dining room had the elegance of the 1890s, with its long maple table and spindle-backed chairs. The windows held the original sashes with small, beveled panes, flanked by forest green drapes. Sarah could remember decades of Thanksgiving and Christmas dinners served in this room.

"We had quite an adventure this morning," Maggie said after the blessing.

"Oh? No trouble with the SUV, I hope." Jason took Sarah's plate and dished out a substantial helping of the casserole.

"Actually, it's a new mystery for your mother to work on." Maggie's eyes twinkled as she passed the conversational ball to Sarah.

Sarah shook her head. "I'm sure the police can handle it."

Every eye was on Sarah now.

"What happened, Mom?" Jason asked.

"Maggie and I discovered that the stained glass window at the library has been broken."

He handed her the plate. "You mean the one over the stairway?"

"Yes."

"Aw," Audrey wailed. "I love that window."

"Me too," Amy said.

"Well, somebody didn't. They pitched a piece of a brick through it." Maggie helped herself to a roll and passed the plate to Amy.

"A brick?" Jason frowned at her. "It wasn't storm damage?"

"Apparently not," Sarah said. "We found the brick inside, along with the broken glass. The police are looking into it. It looks as though someone did it last night during the storm."

"Somebody must be awfully mad," Audrey said. She sneaked a glance at her twin.

Amy grimaced at her, and Audrey looked away.

"That's not all we found," Maggie said. "Your grandmother spotted something really odd in the storeroom where Spencer keeps his cleaning supplies."

"What?" Amy asked.

Sarah brushed a hand through the air, as though it wasn't important. "Somebody left a few things in there, is all. Blankets and a flashlight."

"And a box of crackers," Maggie added. "And Spencer keeps the room locked all the time."

"Who cleans the library?" Jason asked.

"I thought of that," Sarah said. "Spencer lets her in and locks the door when she's done. He would have known about those things if the cleaning lady took them in and left them."

"Mom, just be careful, you hear?" Jason eyed her severely, and Sarah had to hold back a laugh. Her father had given her that same look many times over the years.

"I mean it," Jason said.

"I know you do." Sarah looked across the table at the twins, who were strangely quiet. "There was an interesting clue on one of the blankets."

"Yes," Maggie said. "Do you girls know anyone at school with the initials WDS?"

Amy and Audrey looked at each other. At the same moment, they shrugged.

"Don't think so," Amy said. "There's a Wendy in our class, but her last name is Glover."

"There's a kid named William something in the fifth grade," Audrey added.

"Well, it was just a thought," Sarah said. "I was thinking that if kids have been sneaking into the library somehow, maybe one of them left that stuff. But those letters might not be initials at all."

"And the stuff in the storeroom might have nothing to do with the broken window," Maggie added. "It could have been in there for weeks."

"True enough." Sarah took a bite of her casserole, thinking that Spencer, while very intelligent, was not always observant. "Oh, this casserole is very good. Perfect for a cold winter day."

"Thanks," Maggie said.

"Hey, Mom," Audrey said, "do you think we need to buy valentines this year?"

"What do you mean, honey?" Maggie paused with her fork in midair.

"Well, last year the teacher had a decorated box for everyone to put their cards into, but this year our homeroom teacher hasn't said anything about it."

"Oh yeah, I remember dashing out to buy a box at the drugstore the night before Valentine's Day," Maggie said.

"That was so lame," Amy muttered.

"Yeah, I hope we don't do it again," Audrey said.

"Why don't you just ask the teacher?"

Amy's eyes widened. "No, Mom! We don't want to give her any ideas if she hasn't thought of it."

"Maybe she realizes we're too mature for that now," Audrey said.

"Well, your father and I are mature, and we're celebrating Valentine's Day." Maggie smiled at Jason.

"That's right," he said. "I made a reservation for two at the Old Mill."

Amy scrunched up her face. "That's different."

"Very different for us," Maggie told her. "We haven't had a date in ages. I'm thinking of buying a new dress."

"I think you should," Jason said. "Though you'd look beautiful in a potato sack."

Sarah smiled. It must feel good for him to be able to tell his wife to indulge in a little "extra." For the first year after they moved to Maple Hill, his law practice ran on a shoestring, but business had picked up a lot in the last six or eight months.

"If you want a grandma's opinion," she said to the twins, "maybe you should ask your friends about the valentines. If everyone is going to trade cards, you don't want to be the only ones who don't."

Audrey glanced over at Amy. "Well...I suppose."

"We could ask Pru and Trina," Amy said.

Sarah smiled. "Sure. See what they're going to do and follow their lead."

"What are *you* doing on Valentine's Day, Grandma?" Audrey asked.

Sarah chuckled. "Just being Grandma, I expect." Although Liam Connolly came to mind, she didn't expect an invitation from him. Not that she would mind, but she wouldn't expect anything.

She finished her lunch while listening to the family's chatter, thankful to have them around her. She knew right then that she would do something special for the girls for the holiday, and she wouldn't ask them if they thought it was lame for a grandmother to send valentines.

When Sarah got home, she called Irene Stuart, the town's historian. Irene had already heard about the library window.

"What a shame," she said. "Is there anything I can do to help?"

"Yes, thanks," Sarah said. "I'm trying to find out who made the stained glass window. Spencer had some records about when the library was built, the name of the architect and the man who did the woodwork, but I don't think the same person who made the window frames would have done the glass, do you?"

"I'll look and see what I can find," Irene said.

"Thanks. I believe it was made in 1902."

Sarah spent more than an hour on her computer, researching stained glass artists. Her own church didn't have any stained glass windows, and she wasn't sure where to start looking. She scoured Web sites for artists in New England, and when she found a trade site that listed several professionals, she checked out the artists' personal pages to see their work.

By the time she had viewed a few dozen bright, kaleidoscopic images, her brain was beginning to feel numb. She went to the kitchen and fixed herself a cup of tea.

She thought of sitting down to start an article for her monthly column in *Country Cottage* magazine, but instead went back to the computer, determined to fulfill her duty for Spencer and the Friends of the Library.

A few minutes later, Irene called her.

"I'm not sure this is what you want, but I found records of some payments the town made in 1902. I figure some of them were to people who worked on the building, but not all of them say what the money was for."

"Okay, it's a start."

"I'll e-mail you the list," Irene said. "Records and receipts weren't always as clear and detailed then as they are now."

"At least you have receipts."

A couple of minutes later, Sarah pulled up the e-mail with a list of six names. One of them was the architect, whose name Spencer had given her. Sarah had no idea who the other five were.

On a long shot, she searched each name along with "Massachusetts" on her computer. Fifteen minutes later, her diligence was rewarded. "Robert Hutchins" matched the name of a stained glass artist living about forty minutes from Maple Hill. Sarah clicked on the Web site, intrigued. It seemed more than a coincidence that this artist had the same name as a man to whom the town had paid several hundred dollars the year the window was made.

Her interest grew even stronger when she learned on the Web site that the artist restored vintage windows. His work reminded her of the library window. Each piece had a classic grace and proportion, and the vibrant colors melded into scenes of such beauty she itched to copy them for quilt designs.

Sarah clicked on the tab for contact information and jotted down his name and telephone number. Of all the artists she had investigated so far, Robert Hutchins lived the closest to Maple Hill. The bio on his Web site said his craft had been passed down in his family. She snatched up the phone and placed the call.

Mr. Hutchins answered her cheerfully, and Sarah explained why she had called.

"Somebody broke that window? Now that's a real shame," he said. "Great-grandpa loved that window, and so did I."

"Your great-grandfather wasn't by any chance the artist who created it, was he?" Sarah held her breath.

"You bet."

Sarah smiled.

"He died sixty years ago," Mr. Hutchins said, "but he was a master craftsman. He did a lot of windows in that area. There's one in a church in Piedmont. I've been over to Maple Hill to see the one at the library a couple of times. It was a good example of his work."

"It was dear to my heart too," Sarah said. "We hope it can be restored, but of course that depends on so many things, one of them being price, as compared to the town's budget."

"Oh, I understand completely."

"Tell me a bit about how you got into this type of work yourself."

"Oh, I learned the trade from my dad and his father—it's kind of stayed in the family."

"I've looked at your Web site," Sarah said. "Would you be interested in giving us an estimate for restoring the window, Mr. Hutchins?"

"I'd love to."

"That's just what I hoped you'd say."

"Sure thing. And call me Bob. Of course, it's impossible to get exactly the same materials these days, but I believe I could make the window look the same as the original, or very close. I'd have to see it, of course. Did you save the broken glass?"

"Yes, we saved all the pieces bigger than a kernel of corn, I think. There are quite a few large ones, but hardly any of them held together. It was quite a mess."

"It will help me to see the original glass and the dividers between the pieces."

"We kept all of those," Sarah said. "How soon could you come?"

"Not tomorrow—I'll be working all day. How does Friday morning sound? Is nine o'clock all right?"

"Perfect. I'll meet you at the library. Of course our librarian, Spencer Hewitt, will be there, and I'll alert the board of trustees as well. I'm sure the chairman will want to meet you and hear what you have to say after you see the damage."

"All right, I'll see you then," Mr. Hutchins said.

Smiling, Sarah turned to her next task. She loaded the pictures Maggie had sent to her cell phone onto her computer. Fortunately, Maggie had snapped the photos soon after they got to the library. Sarah pondered over them for quite some time, noting where the glass had fallen, and how much snow had come in through the window on top of it. However, Sarah was unable to draw any new conclusions from viewing them.

She went to the living room and took out a couple of her older photo albums. Trying to recall dates, she sat down in her oak rocker to browse through them. So many of the old pictures of Jason and his sister Jenna caught her eye that she was soon immersed in memories.

She was sure Gerry had taken some detail photos of the window back in the 1990s. After twenty minutes of slowly leafing through the albums, she located them. As she turned the pages, she sighed. That beautiful window—smashed. Why would anyone do such a thing?

Sarah lightly touched the plastic that covered a close-up of the vibrant rosette in the middle of the window. Each piece fitted exactly to those bordering it, with strips of lead between them. How many hours had it taken Bob Hutchins's great-grandfather to complete this gorgeous work of art?

The design was simple, but the combination of colors and shapes gave it a timeless look, classic yet always stylish. The colored rose that burst against the lighter mosaic of the background always lifted her spirits. At one time she had even considered stitching a patchwork quilt in a similar design. She wished now that she had done it. But she could still copy the design from Gerry's photographs and enlarge it for a quilt pattern now.

She sat back and rocked slowly, thinking about the steps that would entail. Gerry had been gone six years now, but she almost felt his presence as she sat in the chair he had crafted for her and gazed at the pictures he had taken. What would Gerry say if he were here now?

Sarah smiled. That was easy. He would say, "Go for it!"

CHAPTER FOUR

S pencer stood behind the circulation desk when Sarah entered the library Thursday morning. He left the stack of returned books he was checking in, picked up a folder, and joined her in the middle of the room.

"Good morning," Sarah said. "We're all set for tomorrow. Bob Hutchins will be here at nine to see the window, and Edward Winsor says he can come too." Her call to Edward, the chairman of the library's board of trustees, had given him an opportunity to vent his anger over the senseless vandalism, and Sarah had endured quite a lengthy monologue from him. Apparently she had called him not long after he learned about the damage, and the news was still sinking in.

"Good," Spencer said. "Let's go up to the Massachusetts Room. Do you mind? My office is a mess right now."

"That's fine."

As they rounded the corner toward the stairway, Sarah could see that the hole was now neatly covered with a fabric curtain, and all the glass had been cleaned up. Not a single shard glittered on the stairs or the floor nearby. The snow, of course, had also disappeared.

"You've done a good job here," she said.

"Thanks. Dave Diamond came by and brought that quilted material to go over the plastic sheeting. He called it a 'window quilt.' Said they were popular before triple-glazed windows. He used some laths to tack it in place so we'd have a better seal and not lose so much heat, and he said when we're ready to take it down, he'll fill the nail holes so no one can tell."

"That was thoughtful of him."

"No kidding. I'm glad he finished before Edward Winsor sees it. He's a fanatic about saving fuel."

"How did the carpeting turn out?"

"I think we're all right there. I used fans, the way you suggested, and that helped a lot. And the heat came up as soon as we had the hole covered. I was afraid the rug would take a long time to dry out, and that it might even have to be replaced, but now I think it's going to be okay. Can you smell any mildew?"

Sarah mounted the first few steps and sniffed. "No, I don't smell anything."

"Great."

A middle-aged woman bustled in wearing a navy woolen coat and a cheerful red scarf and matching hat.

"Good morning, Spencer. Sorry I'm late. My car didn't want to start."

"It's chilly out," Spencer said.

"Good morning, Mrs. Hart."

Sarah smiled at Spencer's part-time helper. "Hello, Madeline. Good to see you. And please call me Sarah."

Madeline pulled off her gloves and stuck them in her oversize purse. "What should I work on this morning, Spencer?"

He nodded toward the circulation desk, where a young man was standing holding a couple of books. "If you could check that gentleman out, it would help me a lot. I'd like to talk to Sarah for a few minutes upstairs. Can you just hold down the front desk for a little while?"

"I'd be glad to."

"Great. We'll be in the Massachusetts Room."

Madeline hurried toward the desk, unwinding her scarf as she walked.

Spencer held out a hand toward the stairs like an usher. "Shall we? It's usually quiet up here."

As Sarah walked with him up the curving stairs, she cast another rueful glance at the covered frame. The whole library seemed shadowy without the light pouring through the colorful window.

She loved the small reading room on the upper level, where Spencer had moved the local interest books, including Massachusetts history and genealogy. She had spent several hours there herself doing research. Spencer had hung antique maps and prints on the few stretches of wall without shelving, and an oak library table had four chairs grouped around it. In one corner two padded chairs and a small wicker table made a cozy spot for two friends to discuss books—or windows.

They both sat in the comfortable chairs.

"So tell me more about the window man," Spencer said.

"Well, I started looking online for stained glass artists in the Northeast. And I asked Irene if she could help me find out who made that window. She came up with a list of people the town had paid money to in 1902, and one name was on both lists—Robert Hutchins. I contacted the *artist* Bob Hutchins, and it was his great-grandfather who made our original window."

"Really? That sounds like a promising connection."

Sarah nodded. "I think so. Bob says he learned the craft from his father and grandfather. I was delighted to find the great-grandson of the man who made the window. It seems to me that it would be fitting to have him reconstruct what the other Mr. Hutchins created."

"If he's as good as his ancestor," Spencer said.

"Well, I did make a couple of other phone calls, and he comes highly recommended. One of his most recent projects was a window for the new chapel at the hospital in Peabody. And he restored three windows for a church in Southwick. I saw pictures of them online, and they're gorgeous. The folks there are very happy with his work."

"We'll see what he says about price," Spencer said. "He may be out of our league. You know there's no money in the budget for something like this."

Sarah sighed. "There never is extra money for the unexpected."

"True. I called the town office this morning and talked to Linda Rowell—you know, the town clerk."

Sarah smiled. She did indeed know Linda and her family—in fact she had helped them iron out a long-standing grudge not too long ago. "What did she say?"

"She's going to talk to the insurance company and see if the window is covered. For a new stained glass window, I mean. She wasn't sure if that was considered a work of art. If there wasn't a separate rider on it, we might not get back what it will take to replace it. We might have to make do with plain, clear glass."

"That would be a pity."

"I agree." Spencer opened the folder he had been holding. "I pulled these out this morning, but I haven't had a chance to do more than glance at them. They're old architectural drawings from when the library was built."

"Let's go over to the table," Sarah said.

They moved to the oak chairs, and Spencer spread out several large sheets of paper on the tabletop.

"Oh, a detail of the Palladian window." Sarah picked it up and studied it for a minute. The window over the front entrance was as beautiful as the stained glass one, in its own way. The three gracefully arched sections contained many small panes of clear glass.

"I used to wish that was lower so people could see it better," Spencer said, "but not anymore. If we've got a window-smashing vandal in town, I'm glad that one's not so easy to get at. Here's the stained glass one."

Sarah took the sheet from him. "This is something. I wonder if Bob's great-grandfather drew it."

"Could be. I can make a photocopy for Bob. It may be helpful to him. It has all the measurements, see?"

"Yes. I'd love to have a copy, too, if it's not too much trouble."

"Sure," Spencer said.

"That reminds me." Sarah reached for her tote bag. "Last night I pulled out some photographs Gerry took of the window about fifteen years ago. We both loved it, and I had been thinking of using the design in a quilting project. He took a lot of pictures for me, and he got some great detail shots." She handed Spencer the envelope of prints.

He took them out and sorted through them. "Wow, these *are* good. We have a few in a scrapbook, but these are better. I just hope that if the insurance company won't pay for a replacement, the town doesn't tell us the restoration is too expensive."

"Well, maybe the people in town would be willing to raise the money," Sarah said. "The Friends of the Library are scheduled to meet tomorrow night. Maybe by then we'll have more information. I'm sure the group will do anything it can to help."

"We definitely should bring them in on this. I'm sure there's a lot they can do."

They heard footsteps on the stair landing outside, and Madeline Crosby appeared in the doorway. "Excuse me, Spencer, but the police chief wanted to see you. I hope you don't mind—I brought him up."

"Not at all. Welcome, Chief." Spencer rose and extended his hand to Nate Webber. Madeline ducked out the doorway and left.

The tall, lean man entered and shook Spencer's hand. "Hi. Thought I'd touch base with you on our investigation." He nodded at Sarah. "Morning, Mrs. Hart."

"Hello. I'll leave you two alone." Sarah started to rise.

"No, that's all right—if Spencer doesn't mind." Chief Webber glanced at Spencer.

"I don't mind if Sarah stays," Spencer said. "She was the one who discovered that the window had been broken."

"So I understand. Well, we have a few developments." They all sat down, and the police chief folded his hands on the table. "My officers have talked to the boy who was caught smoking in the men's room here—Jacob Hull."

Spencer and Sarah nodded.

"It's true he was upset about what happened, but enough time has passed that I think he sees things more clearly now. He was willing to take responsibility for his actions. Officer Hopkins said he seemed genuinely remorseful. And he said his anger was directed at Mr. Danvers, not at you personally, Mr. Hewitt. He claims he would never do something like breaking the library window."

"I know his family," Sarah said. "They seem like good-hearted people."

"Yes, I think they are," Chief Webber said. "Jacob seemed credible and contrite, according to Officer Hopkins, and his alibi is likely to hold up. He'd been to visit a friend Tuesday evening. The storm got so bad, he called his father and asked if he'd come and pick him up. So his father was with him during the time he'd have been most likely to throw the brick through the window. The parents confirm that, and we'll check with the friend's parents to be sure he was at their house as long as he says he was."

"It certainly sounds as if Jacob is innocent," Sarah said.

"Yes. There's still one black mark against him though."

"What's that?" Spencer asked.

"Mr. Danvers's tire was slashed a week or so after the smoking incident. We have no proof that Jacob did it, and my people are looking into his alibi for it. But he says it wasn't his doing."

"So he could be lying about both cases of vandalism," Spencer said.

"It's possible—he might have been able to break the window before his father picked him up. But we're looking for other suspects, especially on the window."

"Thank you, Chief," Spencer said.

"What about the blankets we found in the storage room?" Sarah asked. "Have you learned anything about the lettering on that tag?"

"Not yet. I've put an officer on it, but we're just getting started on this case. It may be a while before it's solved."

"If there's anything I can do to help, please don't hesitate to call on me," Spencer said.

Sarah nodded. "I feel the same way."

"Thank you both. I know you'll let us in on any discoveries you make."

Sarah thought that last remark was directed at her as Chief Webber's brown eyes seemed to warm even as he gave her a stern look. She and Spencer walked downstairs with the chief and said good-bye to him in the main room.

"I'm supposed to meet Martha at the café this morning, so I'll head out now, Spencer," Sarah said.

"Can I make copies of those drawings for you first?"

"Oh, I'd like that."

Sarah waited while Spencer copied the architectural details for her. He stacked them neatly and handed them to her.

"Thanks, Sarah. I'll see you back here tomorrow." He headed for the circulation desk, where Madeline had three patrons lined up and waiting.

Cars filled most of the parking spaces along the snow-covered green. Sarah was glad to see that so many people had come out to shop downtown. The pavement had been sanded and she got good traction as she drove along downtown. The severe storm was only an unpleasant memory.

At the Spotted Dog, Liam and Murphy greeted her as she walked in.

"Welcome, me dear," Liam said. Murphy just snuffled her shoes and licked her hand when Sarah stooped to pet him.

"Looks like Maple Hill has nearly recovered from the storm," Sarah said as she stood.

"Yes, but it was quite a storm. You know I don't close often because of the weather, but yesterday was an exception."

Sarah smiled. "Did you open at noon yesterday?"

"Sooner, actually. After you and your charming daughter-in-law were in, I was inspired to get to work. And did you get your electricity back?"

"We did." Sarah pulled off her gloves. "There always seems to be at least one good storm in February, doesn't there?"

Liam smiled. "Now, speaking of February, you know what's coming up in a couple of weeks."

"*Hmm*, let's see. Not your birthday?"

He laughed. "No, I was referring to Valentine's Day." He gave a sweeping gesture that encompassed the bookstore side of his business.

Sarah surveyed it with appreciation. Red hearts hung from the ceiling, and a sizable rack of romance novels was prominently displayed near the entrance.

"I see you've been busy decorating."

"Oh, that's Karen for you," Liam said, mentioning his star waitress. "She insisted. And we have heart-shaped cookies in the café."

"Nice touch," Sarah said.

"It's part of what I did yesterday, while business was slow," he admitted.

Sarah smiled. "I'll have to try one."

"Well, speaking of Valentine's ..."

She laughed, but her pulse picked up a little at his words. "We're 'speaking of' lots of things today."

"No one I'd rather be speaking *to*," Liam said with a heart-stopper smile. "I was wondering if you have plans that evening. If not, I thought we could perhaps do something special."

Sarah let the happy feeling his attention brought wash over her for a moment. "That sounds lovely."

"Well," Liam said with a bit more confidence, if possible, in his tone, "there's a restaurant in Pittsfield where they'll be presenting a murder mystery dinner." Before Sarah could speak, he held up both hands. "Now, I realize that's an odd choice for a Valentine's Day production, but I thought to myself, there's nothing Sarah would enjoy more."

She couldn't hold back her smile. "I would be delighted to go with you."

He nodded with satisfaction. "Well, then, that's settled."

The bell on the door behind him jingled as Martha entered.

"There you are, Sarah. Hello, Liam! Am I late?"

"Not a bit," Sarah said. "And guess what they're featuring today?"

"What?" Martha asked as she dropped her keys into her purse.

"Valentine cookies."

"Fun!"

Once Karen had brought their chai tea and cookies, Martha took out her crocheting, and Sarah filled her in on the developments in the case of the broken window.

"If the Friends of the Library ends up doing a fund-raiser, I'd be happy to donate an afghan," Martha said.

"That'd be super. If it comes to that, I'll call you. Or are you going to the meeting tomorrow?"

"Planning on it."

"Good. Of course, we're hoping the insurance company will pay for the window." Sarah picked up one of the sugar cookies and laughed. The heart was frosted in pink, and red icing spelled out "BE MINE."

"I love holidays," Martha said.

"Me too. You know, I was going to make treats for the girls. I think I'll make some cookies for the folks at Bradford Manor too."

"They'd love that." Martha took a bite of her white-frosted heart.

"Leland has quite a sweet tooth, I'm finding. And he's so tickled when we remember him on holidays." Sarah and Jason's family had "adopted" Leland Mercer after Sarah's father died. He had been a friend of William's, and though he had been abrasive at first, the family had come to care about him and welcome him into their circle.

Sarah enjoyed the rest of her visit with Martha and then headed home. She went to her sewing room and got out a fresh spiral-bound notebook and the local phone book. She opened the notebook and wrote on the first page, "Broken Stained Glass Window at Library."

Below it she jotted down what she knew of the evidence and the police investigation into the matter. On another page, she listed all the things found in the storage room. On the next, she described the partial brick Maggie had found among the shards of glass. Still another page she headed "Jacob Hull" and wrote a brief account of why he had made the top of the officers' suspect list.

Finally she turned to the phone book. There must be several people living in Maple Hill who had the initials W.S. Matching them with the middle initial D might be harder, but at least she would have a place to start. Of course, only adults were listed in the phone book. If youngsters were responsible for the items left at the library, she wouldn't find them in the phone directory.

One glance at the tiny print sent her off for a pair of reading glasses. After twenty minutes of painstaking work, she had a list of more than twenty people with the initials W.S. She sighed, pulled off her glasses, and rubbed her eyes. What other ways could she find public lists of people living in Maple Hill, so she could check on the initials? Young people especially might be difficult to track down.

School yearbooks, she thought. They had helped her more than once in the past. She would mention them to Spencer when she saw him again. The library had quite a few in its stacks. Perhaps the police could ask the school administrators to check their enrollment lists for the initials too. She jotted a note so she wouldn't forget to ask and laid the notebook aside.

Liam's invitation had started her thinking about making a special Valentine's Day gift for him. Baked goods were a bit ordinary for the café owner, and she decided to make a pieced pillow top instead. If she kept the project small, it wouldn't take her long. She had seen a pattern for a block containing four shamrocks. The heart-shaped leaves made the plant perfect for a Valentine's Day gift. Maybe she would create the shamrocks in red instead of green. She looked up the pattern in one of her books and put a sticky note on the page. She probably even had enough fabric on hand.

Next she gathered items that would help her start her window quilt project—the drawings Spencer had copied for her, Gerry's snapshots, and a pad of graph paper. Carefully she drew the window's outline to scale and sketched in the main parts of the design. A quilt would be the perfect complement to the colored glass. She could match the colors of the patchwork pieces to the glass components for the most part. Some pieces in the window had textured glass, and she could use textured or patterned fabrics to simulate that. Her mind flitted off as she imagined the decorative stitches and vibrant materials she could use. This was a project she definitely wanted to do.

CHAPTER FIVE

Sarah dressed carefully the next morning in navy blue slacks and jacket, along with a cranberry blouse and a silver necklace and bracelet set Jenna had given her for Christmas. She wanted to look nice—and competent—when she met with the library's head trustee and the stained glass artist. At quarter to nine, she set out for downtown.

Edward Winsor was talking to Spencer when she arrived. The two welcomed her and drew her into the reference room. No patrons were in there yet, and Edward turned to Sarah with a smile.

"Sarah, I'm glad you got here before Mr. Hutchins. I wanted to tell you and Spencer what the town clerk has learned. The insurance company's response to her inquiry isn't quite what we'd hoped, but they will share the cost of replacing the window."

"Oh?" Sarah asked. "But they won't cover the full cost."

"Right. Unfortunately, the town never sought extra coverage for unique architectural details and artwork at the library. At the time it was built, that may not have been as common as it is now. So the insurance will pay to put in a modern, energy-efficient window, but it won't cover the cost of restoring the stained glass."

"I see."

"I'm guessing you both saw the article in this morning's *Monitor*," Edward said.

"Yes, I saw it." Sarah had enjoyed reading it over breakfast. "I thought Abby McCormick did a good job of reporting on the case."

Spencer nodded. "She came in yesterday afternoon—I think she heard about the broken window when she went to the police station to get the latest entries in the police log. I gave her the basics, of course."

Neither he nor Sarah mentioned the items found in the storage room—they hadn't been revealed in the news story, either, and Sarah figured he hadn't told the reporter. Just as well. She would as soon keep that quiet—it probably had nothing to do with the broken window, and there was no sense getting people upset about it.

Spencer peeked past her, toward the main entrance. "I think that's Mr. Hutchins now. Madeline's bringing him this way. I guess we'll see what his estimate is."

Edward nodded. "If it's higher than the cost of a new window, the insurance company will expect us to put in the modern one or pay the difference."

Madeline brought a tall man with graying hair into the reference room. "Mr. Hutchins is here."

He looked toward the group and advanced smiling. "Mrs. Hart?"

"Yes. Pleased to meet you, Mr. Hutchins." Sarah held out her hand.

"Oh, call me Bob."

Sarah introduced Spencer and Edward Winsor.

"Let's go out to the stairway," Spencer said. They all walked out to the main room and he led them to the bottom of the staircase. "The window was right up there, over the landing."

"Yes, I saw it a couple of times. Over the years, I've tried to get around and see all the windows my great-grandfather made—that is, the ones that are still intact. And I saw the damage from the outside just now. Pity." Bob walked up to the landing. Spencer followed and picked up a small hammer from the floor beneath the window. He used it to carefully pull off the lath holding the quilted material in place across the bottom.

Bob peeked under the edge and shook his head. "Just went all to smithereens, didn't it?"

"I'm afraid so," Spencer said. "There are only those lower cross members left. We didn't find it until the morning after the storm, and there was a fierce wind that night. If it wasn't all splintered when the brick went through it, I suppose jagged pieces could have blown out after. We saved as many pieces as we could though."

"Great," Bob said. "Sometimes it's possible to reuse old pieces, even if I have to cut them down to fit a smaller spot than the one they were in before. And studying the original glass will help me decide what to use to replace it if I have that privilege."

He lowered the material and fitted the lath with its protruding nails back in place. Spencer gave a few light blows with the hammer to secure it. Next, he showed Bob the box of shards, and the artist pulled out a pair of gloves. He put them on and picked up a few of the pieces. After examining several closely, he held up a yellow one and frowned at it.

"Mr. Hewitt, did you notice this?"

Spencer leaned in and eyed the piece of glass. "What am I looking at?"

"That brownish stain on the edge. It's small, but you see what I mean?"

Spencer caught his breath. "What is that—blood?"

"Could be. I've cut myself on glass a lot of times, and that's what it looks like to me."

"May I?" Sarah asked.

"Of course." Bob held it for her and Sarah stepped closer to scrutinize it. "Oh dear. We surely didn't see that when we cleaned up." She glanced at Spencer. "Should we take that to the police?"

"I'd say so."

"Do you have a clean bag we can put it in?" Sarah asked.

Spencer went over to the circulation desk and came back a minute later with an envelope. "Best I can do."

Bob eased the shard of glass into it.

"I guess we'd better take them all of the glass," Sarah said. "I hate to have it tied up as evidence, but if that's blood, the more they get the better, I'd say."

"Are you sure none of you got any small cuts while you cleaned up the floor?" Edward asked.

"I know I didn't," Spencer said.

Sarah shook her head. "Me either, and if Maggie did, she'd have told me."

"There was no one else here but the police officers," Spencer said. "At least, not after we found the damage. I'll call the police as soon as we're done here."

Bob put the envelope in the box and handed it to Spencer. "I think I could use quite a few of those. That is, if the police don't keep them too long."

The four of them went down to the main reading room and sat around one of the oak tables.

"Mr. Hutchins, I'd appreciate it if you'd tell us a little more about your family and how you learned the art of stained glass," Spencer said.

"I'd love to hear that too," Sarah added. "I think it's wonderful that we might be able to have the window rebuilt by the original artist's great-grandson."

Bob smiled at them. "Well, as you know, my great-grandfather, the first Robert Hutchins, made the window in 1902 when the library was built. He was a highly skilled craftsman, very meticulous, and he passed the trade down in the family. My grandfather worked with him, and he in turn passed the skill on to my dad and his brother. I'm actually the fourth Robert, and I'm honored to bear Great-grandpa's name as well as carry on the business.

"Stained glass is a tedious art form in some ways, but I've come to love it. When I was little, my dad used to take me to the workshop where he and Grandpa worked. Of course, I couldn't touch the glass back then, but I would sit and watch them by the hour. Then my dad started me on making mosaics with little tiles. When I got older, he showed me how to use the tools. But it took years to master cutting the glass and making the strips that hold the pieces of glass together."

"Do you still use lead?" Sarah asked.

"Copper foil came into use a hundred years or so ago, and it's considered safer for the artist, but the solder still contains some lead. Handled correctly, it's not a problem."

Sarah nodded. "Fascinating."

"There are other, more modern methods too," Bob said. "Some don't use any metal between the glass pieces—it just depends on the project. I've made lamps and other three-D artworks—trinket boxes, for instance—and I usually use copper foil for those, but I've seen some with overlapping glass that don't have any metal joints. However, with a window like this, you need a framework strong enough to bear the weight. Did you notice the steel rods that went across the window frame?"

"Yes," Spencer said. Sarah and Edward nodded.

"Those are there purely for support. For a vintage window, I like to do things the way they were originally done whenever possible. Of course, the ideal restoration would be done while the window is still intact. Sometimes people will notice a church window sagging, and the joints starting to buckle. If we catch it at that stage, we can remove the window in one unit, lay it flat, restore the joints, and put it back in place. That's comparatively simple—unlike what I'll have to do here."

"And are you able to give us an estimate today?" Edward asked.

"Well, seeing the glass you've collected is helpful in guessing approximately how much I'll have to provide. If I had no materials to work with, it might run ten thousand dollars."

Spencer winced.

"But, since you have a lot of the pieces, and since this is a sentimental project, I'm thinking less than half that."

"We have the original 1902 drawings of the window and some very detailed photographs," Sarah said.

"That will be a tremendous help. I found a few photos in my father's files, and I took some myself on one of my visits here. If we share all the information we have, it should help move things along quickly. If the town decides to pursue the project, of course."

"And where do you get glass for a project like this?" Edward asked. "Obviously some of the pieces were shattered beyond reusing."

"Yes, I'd have to replace those. I have quite a supply of glass in my workshop, and I do business with several suppliers. It would be nice to find period glass to supplement what you have. I think I'll be able to. If not, I'll look for the modern glass that best matches the old pieces."

"Oh, I empathize with you there," Sarah said. "I restore old quilts, and I've spent many an hour searching for vintage fabrics to match the ones in a worn quilt."

"I expect that part of your work is similar to what I do with old windows." Bob smiled at her. "One thing I can pretty much guarantee: when the window is finished, it will look virtually the same as the one my great-grandfather made. Only an expert will know that it was made a hundred and ten years later."

"That's wonderful," Edward said. "Unfortunately, we'll have to wait and see what the town officials say when they meet. I assure you, Mr. Hutchins, I'll call you the minute we know whether or not we can hire you."

They all shook hands with Bob and thanked him for his time.

"You know, the Friends of the Library may be able to raise the extra money to hire him if the town can't afford it," Sarah said as Bob left the building.

"Yes." Edward looked toward the covered hole where the window had been. "I would hate to see it replaced with a plain, functional window."

"I agree," Spencer said. "Let's wait and see what the selectmen and trustees think, but I'm sure the Friends of the Library would be happy to help out."

"Will you be able to come to the meeting tonight?" Sarah asked. She had expected her job as secretary for the group to be somewhat sedate, but now she was in the middle of this exciting turn of events. She could hardly wait for the meeting.

Spencer nodded. "Wouldn't miss it."

"Well, I need to get to work," Edward said. "Spencer, would you call me after the meeting and let me know what they say? It may help in persuading the selectmen."

"Sure."

After Edward had left, Sarah turned to Spencer. "We should let the police know about that glass right away."

"Agreed. I'll call them now."

"Wouldn't it be wild if it is blood, and it belongs to the person who broke the window?"

Spencer's brow puckered. "I don't see how that could happen."

While he went to the desk and placed the call to the police station, Sarah tried to think of ways it might have happened. The most logical was that someone had received a cut during the cleanup, but again she couldn't see how. They would all have known it and commented on it at the time.

The person who had thrown the brick from outside wouldn't get his blood on pieces of the glass inside the library. Had someone been in here when the window was broken? Or was it possible someone else had handled the glass after they put it in the box?

Spencer came back to the table. "They're sending some-one over for it."

"Good," Sarah said. "Has anyone else had access to that box for the last couple of days?"

"No. I locked it up."

"In the storage room?"

Spencer gritted his teeth. "Yeah. Oh man, you don't think the person who left the blankets could have gone in there again, do you? I'd hate to think someone went in there in the last forty-eight hours and cut himself handling the glass."

"Let's not get too worked up until we at least know if it's blood," Sarah said. "You know, I had an idea last night that might possibly help us learn who left the things in that room."

"I'm open to any suggestions," he said. "That really both-ers me—that I didn't have a clue someone had been in there."

"It's not your fault, Spencer. At this point, I'm assuming the letters on the blanket tag are initials. I looked through the phone book and began a list of names. Maple Hill resi-dents with the initials WDS."

"Good thinking, but it's going to be hard to sort through those, isn't it?"

"It's quite a list, and I'm sure I've missed a lot," Sarah said. "If kids are involved, their names wouldn't show up in the phone book. So I thought maybe I could go through some of the recent school yearbooks. They would list nearly all the high school students."

"True. It's worth a try." Spencer glanced around. "It's getting busy here. I'd better touch base with Madeline. Why don't you go up to the Massachusetts Room? I'll bring up some yearbooks, and if she doesn't need me right away, I'll help you."

A few minutes later, Spencer came up the stairs with an armful of recent yearbooks.

"Officer Pratt just came to get the box of glass."

"That was quick," Sarah said.

"Yeah. She says they'll send it to the lab, and I told her we want it back for the artist. She said she'd find out if we can have the pieces without blood back soon."

They spent half an hour leafing through the yearbooks, and Sarah added another five names to her list.

"How are you going to check on those?" Spencer asked.

"I'm not sure yet. I know some of the people, or their families. I might just call some of them and ask."

"But would they admit to stashing stuff in a locked room?"

Sarah sighed. "I don't know. Maybe I should just turn the list over to the police."

"Well, I'm just saying, if you call and ask whether they were poking around in locked rooms at the library after hours…" Spencer's eyes focused on something outside the reading room.

"What is it?" Sarah asked.

"I'd almost forgotten. The oddest thing happened a week or so ago. I'd gone home for the night, and I got a call about eleven o'clock. I was still up, but barely. It was a woman, and she said she'd seen a light inside the library."

"Had you left a light on?"

"No, I was sure I hadn't, and besides, she said it was kind of flickering around—like a flashlight, maybe."

"That *is* odd," Sarah said. "What did you do?"

"I drove down here. I checked everything, but there were no lights, and I didn't see anything wrong. The doors were all locked. I decided she must have seen a reflection on a window pane. But now I wonder." Spencer's eyes narrowed as he thought about it.

"Did you look in the storage room that night?" Sarah asked.

"I...don't think so. I may have tried the knob, but if it was locked...To tell you the truth, I'm not sure."

"And you don't know who made the call."

"No. She didn't give her name. When I checked things out and didn't find anything wrong, I wondered if it was a prank, but it didn't sound like one. I had the impression she was an older woman."

"Did she call your cell phone?"

"Yes." Spencer reached for his breast pocket and took out the phone. "I don't have a land line at home."

"How did she get the number?"

He shrugged. "You have it, don't you?"

"Well, yes."

"I give it to a lot of people," Spencer said. "Since I don't have a home phone, I give it every time I need to list a contact number. It's even on my library business cards that a lot of patrons take. It's no secret."

"I guess not." Sarah was a lot more particular about her mobile phone number. "Anyway, I was thinking—you could check 'received calls' if it wasn't too long ago."

"That's a thought." Spencer pushed a few buttons. "*Hmm* . . . there's one late on the twenty-eighth."

"That was last Friday," Sarah said.

"That seems about right." Spencer read off the local number, and Sarah copied it down.

"Do you mind if I pursue this?"

"Go ahead." Spencer pushed back his chair and stacked the yearbooks. "I'd better go relieve Madeline. It's time for her break. Thanks a lot for all your help, Sarah."

That afternoon, Sarah went to her computer, where she pulled up a reverse phone directory. The anonymous caller had a listing—the Reed residence on the other side of town from Sarah. She went to her kitchen phone and punched in the number.

"Mrs. Reed?" she asked when a woman answered. "This is Sarah Hart." She explained briefly why she was calling.

"Why, yes, I did call Mr. Hewitt that night," Mrs. Reed said. "I was driving home late from a committee meeting, and I saw that odd light moving about inside the library."

"Are you certain it was inside the library, not a reflection on the window?" Sarah asked.

"I'm sure. It was moving around in there. I saw it through one of the side windows. I thought it was odd, so I called the librarian. I thought it was probably him, but he said he was at his house. So I was glad I'd called and let him know. Of course, I don't know if he checked on it."

"Oh, he did," Sarah said. "He thought it was strange too, and he went right down to the library. But he told me he didn't find anything wrong, and nobody inside."

"Well, that's good, I guess," Mrs. Reed said.

Sarah reassured her that she had done the right thing and said good-bye. She decided not to lose her momentum in investigating. After noting her conversation with Mrs. Reed in her notebook, she called several people on the list she and Spencer had made—people with the initials W.S., starting with those she knew. She told each of them that a blanket had been found at the library with the initials "W.D.S." on it, and she and Spencer were trying to locate the person who had left it there. She left out the part about it being found in a locked storeroom with some other items. None of them admitted to having misplaced a blanket. Sarah checked five people off her list of names.

That evening she picked up Martha for the meeting of the Friends of the Library. The group supported the library by hosting book sales and author events, as well as raising money for special purchases. Sarah had joined the group years ago, but this was the first year she was serving as an officer. She didn't mind keeping minutes of the meetings, and the position gave her an added feeling of responsibility. Because of it, she felt more than willing to ask people questions about things like initials and late night phone calls.

They met in their usual place—the main reading room at the library. More members turned out than Sarah had seen in several months, and quite a few newcomers joined them. Several people were gathered at the foot of the stairs, gazing at the covered window frame. The news story about the window must have stirred public interest.

Aiden McLean, the local jeweler who was the group's current president, called for order, and the people found seats facing the officers' table. After opening the meeting, Aiden invited Spencer to address the group.

Spencer stood and faced the gathering of about two dozen people. "Thank you all for coming. I know you all love the library and have given your support to many projects here in the past. Now we have a big need. As I'm sure you all know, the stained glass window was broken during the storm Tuesday night or Wednesday morning. The library's trustees and I hope that we will be able to see the window restored."

A murmur of approval rippled through the crowd.

"Sarah Hart took on the job of looking up an artist for us," Spencer went on, "and she contacted Bob Hutchins, whose great-grandfather built the original window in 1902. Bob is a master craftsman, and if the town approves the expenditure, he'll be the one to restore the window for us."

Everyone clapped.

Spencer continued, "We won't know until tomorrow whether or not the town can pay Bob to do the work. They've contacted the insurance company already, and it seems the insurance will only cover the price of a new, energy-efficient window."

A soft murmur ran through the audience.

Spencer shrugged. "We hope the selectmen will decide to go ahead with replacing the stained glass anyway. That would mean extra money, and that's where you come in."

"Sure, we'll help," Martha called.

Spencer smiled. "Thank you, Martha. It's basically a waiting game until after the selectmen meet tomorrow afternoon. They're holding a joint session with the library's trustees, and they hope to make a decision then. It was good of them to call an emergency meeting so that the window question can be settled as soon as possible. Now, with the president's permission, I'd like to ask Sarah to tell you a little about how you can help."

Everyone applauded again, and the president pointed his gavel at Sarah. "If you please, Mrs. Hart."

"Thank you," Sarah said as she rose. "I must say it was a delight to meet Bob Hutchins this morning. He was very enthusiastic, and he took the time to explain to us how he would do the work if the town hires him. He certainly seems to be the person best qualified to restore the window, and I hope the town agrees to take him on. Spencer and I thought the selectmen might be more inclined to do so if we could present them with a plan to help raise the money."

"Good thinking," called Irene Stuart.

"We could have a big fund-raiser," said accountant Neil Lawton. "Let the whole town get involved."

Sarah smiled at their enthusiasm. "Thank you. This is the attitude I was hoping for. If we had one large event to raise money, we could also incorporate smaller projects."

"How about a silent auction?" Hannah Grace asked. "That worked well for the fire department last summer."

"That's right," Neil said. "They raised a lot of money. We could ask local businesses to donate merchandise."

"Or we could have a bazaar," Martha added. "We could rent table space to organizations."

Sarah nodded. "Maybe we should form a committee to head up an event, whatever it turns out to be. And I wondered if any of you would be interested in helping me make a special quilt to commemorate the window. I've been working on a quilt pattern based on the design of the stained glass window."

"Oh, that will be so pretty," Hannah said. Sarah smiled at her, knowing Hannah was a skilled quilt maker.

"I'll help," called Cate Goodman from the back row.

"Thank you all," Sarah said. "I thought that by making and selling a quilt patterned after the window, we could raise some money and maybe get some publicity for the whole fund-raising campaign."

"Great idea!" Irene beamed at her from the front row.

Sarah looked out over the room full of smiling faces. "Terrific. Maybe those interested in the quilt project could see me afterward. I'll make a list and call you after the selectmen's meeting tomorrow. If the project is a go, we can set a time to meet and get started."

Sarah took her seat, and Aiden rose with his gavel in his hand.

"It sounds to me like we need a committee to plan the fund-raiser," he said. "Or should we decide what type of event we want first?"

After some informal discussion, the group voted to hold a silent auction if the town officials agreed to the restoration. The committee nominations followed. Sarah declined to be a member, as she would be in charge of the quilting project, which was much more to her liking anyway. Irene Stuart protested when she was nominated for chairman of the auction committee.

"I'm not sure I'll have the time."

"Oh, but you did such a great job on the fire department auction," Neil said.

"Thank you, but that only reminds me of how much work it was."

"How about if we elect a committee, and we choose two people from among the committee members as co-chairmen?" Aiden suggested.

That idea met with approval, and a roster of committee members was soon completed.

"So when will the auction be held?" asked Cate Goodman, one of those nominated to serve.

Aiden said, "We'll need to get the funds in hand as soon as possible. Could we do it at the end of this month?"

"That would be pushing it," Irene said.

Martha pulled a pocket calendar from her purse and opened it.

"Still, that may be wise, if we can pull it together that quickly," Cate said. "Then we'd have the money in plenty of time to pay Mr. Hutchins. How about the last Saturday of February?"

Martha called, "That's only three weeks away. The twenty-fifth."

Cate looked around at the group. "Can we do it?"

A chorus of "yeses" answered, and she nodded with a grin.

"I nominate Cate for cochair of the committee," Martha said.

Applause broke out all around the room.

"Well, Cate, what do you say?" Aiden asked.

"I'll do it if Irene is the other cochair."

Everyone looked expectantly toward Irene. She held up both hands in surrender.

"Okay, I give in. But I'm warning you, Cate, we're in for a wild and woolly time. This is really short notice."

Aiden tapped his gavel on the table. "All right, provided the town officials are in agreement, we'll hold our silent auction on the twenty-fifth. I believe our last item of business is to select someone to present our plan to the board of trustees and the selectmen tomorrow."

"Sarah," several members called out.

"Sarah, would you be willing to attend that meeting on our behalf?" Aiden turned a hopeful gaze on her.

"It would be an honor."

When the group disbanded for refreshments, people deluged Sarah with promises to help with the quilt. Even a couple of men offered to help cut out the pieces or give money toward the supplies.

Mavis Hoyt came over to speak to her, carrying her paper cup of punch and a small paper plate bearing cookies. "Sarah, that quilt is going to be gorgeous. I'll help."

"Thank you," Sarah said, jotting Mavis's name on the list in her pocket notebook. "I appreciate your offer."

"Anything you make is top quality." Mavis winked at her. "I'm sure a lot of people will bid on it."

That is, Sarah thought, if they could get the selectmen to approve their plan.

CHAPTER SIX

The town's selectmen were a tougher sell than the Friends of the Library had been. Chairman Jack Handelman welcomed Sarah and Spencer, along with thirty or so other people, to their meeting and then opened discussion about the library window among the joint boards. While the library's trustees favored restoring the stained glass for aesthetic reasons, the selectmen focused more on the cost. One selectman in particular—Jim Brooks—had a list of objections that he seemed unwilling to give up.

"I know it was pretty," he said when one of the residents in the audience voiced a plea for art, "but have you seen what we're paying for heat on that building?"

Edward Winsor asked to be recognized and rose to address Jack Handelman and the other selectmen. "Mr. Chairman, it's true the library takes a lot of fuel to heat, but that's a separate issue. The restored window wouldn't lose any more heat than the old one did."

"But a modern, energy-efficient one would save us—"

Jack Handelman brought down his gavel on Brooks's interruption. "Mr. Winsor has the floor. Let's let him speak."

"Thank you," Edward said. "I don't deny we could probably save a little in the future by going with a triple-glazed model, but look at what we've lost artistically."

Another selectman looked over at Jack and said, "Mr. Chairman, maybe we should entertain suggestions for other ways to fill that hole in the library wall. Perhaps there's a compromise that would save energy and still satisfy the public's desire for art."

A woman in the second row spoke next. "I'm a library patron, and I loved the stained glass window. Maybe if you put in a high-efficiency window, you could hang a decorative stained glass piece in front of it."

"Or brick up the hole and hang a picture in front of it," Jim Brooks said.

Jack tapped with his gavel again.

Aiden McLean rose and was granted permission to speak. "These ideas should all be considered. However, as president of the Friends of the Library, I ask that the board consider our proposal as well. Sarah Hart is our secretary, and the group appointed her to bring our offer to you."

"Then let's hear what Mrs. Hart has to say," Jack said with a smile.

Sarah rose, her knees shaking a bit, and faced the selectmen and the library trustees. "Ladies and gentlemen, the Friends of the Library offers you its support in fixing the window. In fact, we have voted to hold a fund-raising event to help defray the cost. We are willing to raise the difference between the insurance company's payment and the cost of restoring the stained glass window. We've found an artist who can do the job, and we'd love to see the town hire him to create a new window for us."

All of the selectmen listened as she told them about Bob Hutchins, his relationship to the original artist, and his estimate for the restoration. When she finished and sat down, the audience clapped—that is, except for Jim Brooks. Sarah sighed deeply, trying not to second-guess herself, but she couldn't help wondering if she should have said they would *try* to raise the money, instead of stating flatly that they would.

Other members of the audience spoke in turn, mostly in support of the plan Sarah had outlined, and Spencer added his plea to Sarah's. The men and women serving on the two boards threw comments back and forth for a good twenty minutes. Finally Jack Handelman called a halt to discussion.

He consulted a sheet of paper in front of him as he said, "We have a motion on the floor to hire Robert Hutchins to restore the stained glass window at the library, with the Friends of the Library assisting by making up the difference in cost between Hutchins's price and the amount the insurance company will allow. All those in favor?"

All but Jim Brooks said, "Aye."

"Ladies and gentleman, the motion carries," Handelman said. "Despite the higher cost of the window and the decrease in energy efficiency, Maple Hill has spoken in favor of beauty."

The audience applauded heartily.

"We'd spend a lot less on fuel with a plain window," Brooks muttered.

As they left the meeting, Spencer told Sarah, "Looks like you and the auction committee have your work cut out for you."

"Yes, and we'd better tell Irene and Cate right away," Sarah said. Irene had been unable to attend the board meeting because the historical society was open that afternoon, and Cate Goodman had a previous commitment. "Maybe I'll drop by and tell Irene in person."

"Great. I'm heading back to the library," Spencer said, "and I'll call Cate."

They separated, and Sarah drove to the Maple Hill Historical Society, where Irene received her news with eager approval.

"Wonderful. I've already started a list of businesses to ask for donations for the auction, and I'm getting more volunteers today. I have a copy of all the donors from the firemen's auction, so that will help. Cate called me an hour ago with the news that the DAR ladies are going to donate something and help with the canvassing."

Sarah smiled. "Sounds like you and your cochair have things under control. I hope you have fun."

She went next to one of her favorite shops in town—Wild Goose Chase. The bell on the door rang as she entered, and the owner—her friend Vanessa Sawyer—walked toward her with a grin.

"Well, hello! Glad to see you."

"You too," Sarah said. "I've got an exciting new project in the works, and I need your help."

"Just what I like to hear on a slow Saturday afternoon." Vanessa's cheerful attitude was contagious, and Sarah smiled.

"Mrs. Hart!"

Sarah turned to greet Vanessa's seven-year-old daughter Lena. "Well, hello, Lena. Are you helping your mom today?"

"Yes." Lena's big brown eyes studied her.

"She's been a big help too," Vanessa said. "So what's the new project?"

Sarah took a folder from her tote bag and quickly outlined the quilt she planned to make with the group of volunteers. She pulled out her sketches of the design and a photo of the library window and laid them on the counter.

"It's pretty," Lena said as she looked at the photograph.

"It sure is." Vanessa's eyes sparkled as she glanced at Sarah. "Ambitious though."

"Well, I have some skilled volunteers who'll help me," Sarah said. "Hannah Grace, for one, and Cate Goodman. I'm going to round up as many experienced quilters as I can. I have some amateurs on my list too, and they can certainly help with the quilting."

"Great. The more people learning to quilt the better." Vanessa compared Sarah's quilt diagram to the color photo of the window. "I think we can find the perfect fabrics for this. Or are you going to use vintage fabrics?"

"No, I thought I'd use new material. I want it to be nice and sturdy. Jewel tones mostly, like the window."

Vanessa nodded. "Do you want to use any prints, or all solids?"

"Maybe some tiny prints to give us the nubby texture that was in the glass leaves." Sarah pointed to the photo. "I have some close-ups in here somewhere." She opened her folder and flipped through it. "Here we go. Gerry took these for me years ago."

"Oh, that's nice. I can see what you mean about the textured glass. Now do you want all cottons for this?"

They walked through the store as they talked, and Vanessa pulled out several bolts of material for Sarah's consideration.

"I like this pink one," Lena said, stroking a polished cotton material with one fingertip.

"So do I." Sarah stooped down to Lena's height. "I think we might be able to use that for some of the flower petals in the design."

"It's almost a perfect match to the color in the photo," Vanessa said. "Is the color true in these?"

"For the most part. Some of the pieces on the left side of the window look darker." Sarah pointed. "But I think that was because of the position of the sun when Gerry took the pictures. See this one here? It looks almost like a forest green, but I believe it was actually the same shade as this one." She pointed to a triangular piece on the opposite edge of the design.

"Uh-huh." Vanessa handed her the photo. "And are these pieces clear?" She indicated a few sections at the edge of the design.

"I think they were, but I'm not positive. I'm going to look through the pieces of glass we picked up and see if there are any clear ones." That reminded her that the police had taken away the box of glass shards, but she decided not to mention that. She wasn't sure how much Chief Webber would want the public to know about the investigation.

Vanessa nodded. "And where are you going to do the quilting?"

"Hadn't thought about it yet. My house, maybe?"

"How about here?"

"Really? That would be wonderful."

Vanessa smiled. "It would be good for both of us. You wouldn't have to keep having all those people over to your house, and it would bring a lot of folks into my store."

"I think that's a fantastic plan, if you have the space and the patience," Sarah said. "We hope to have it completed in three weeks, though that may be a little optimistic. Still, we're going to stitch the top together by machine. It would take way too long to do it by hand. And if I get several of those experienced quilters in on it ..."

"I can send out the word to all the people who take part in my classes and fabric swaps."

"Would you?"

Vanessa laid her hand on Sarah's shoulder. "Between the two of us, we can get this thing done in grand style. Do you have time for a cup of tea? We can rough out the strategy."

"Sounds good," Sarah said.

Lena tugged on the hem of Vanessa's sweater. "Let's have a tea party, Mama."

Vanessa laughed. The bell over the door rang as two women entered. "All right, you and Mrs. Hart go put the kettle on while I help these ladies, okay?"

After church on Sunday, Mavis stopped Sarah on the way out to ask whether the town officials had voted to have the window restored.

"Yes, they did," Sarah said. "They would like the Friends of the Library to make up the extra funds, however."

Mavis waved a hand. "Not a problem. We'll have that money raised in no time."

"I hope you're right." Sarah zipped up her coat and joined the line to shake hands with Pastor John at the door.

"I read about the library window in the paper," the pastor said. "And you were on hand when the damage was discovered."

"That's right," Sarah said.

"Sounds like you're in the thick of another adventure."

"One I hope will soon be happily concluded," Sarah told him.

"Martha said there'll be a fund-raiser. Let me know if there's anything I can do to help."

"I will. Thank you so much."

She followed Jason and Maggie home for dinner. Maggie's pot roast had cooked to perfection, and they all enjoyed Sarah's salad and the shortbread cookies the girls had made.

"You know that china we unpacked Wednesday, when the power was out?" Maggie asked.

Sarah nodded. "Beautiful pattern."

"Well, Jordan had to help me pack it up again yesterday."

"Oh? Did someone buy it already?"

Maggie smiled. "Yup. Peg Girard. Can you believe it? I only had it in the store three days."

"That's got to be a record," Jason said.

When the meal was over, the girls helped Sarah clear the table.

"So you got two extra days off from school this week," Sarah said, gathering the silverware.

"Yes, but I was glad we went back on Friday," Audrey said.

"Not me." Amy scrunched up her face.

"It was getting boring," Audrey insisted.

"Any day off is better than a day at school."

Sarah laughed. "You two. I guess you didn't get behind on homework, with all that time off."

"No," Amy said. "In fact, we had a big history paper due last week, but because of the storm and all the confusion, Mrs. Hiland said we don't have to turn it in until Monday."

"I turned mine in on Friday anyway," Audrey said with a smug smile.

"Yeah, me too. I mean, I had it done, so what was the point?" Amy said.

"Sounds reasonable to me." Sarah opened the dishwasher and placed the silverware inside and then reached for Amy's stack of plates.

"Well, *some* people were glad to have the extra time," Audrey said archly.

"Yeah." Amy frowned but said no more.

Sarah studied the girls for a moment. "Is everything all right at school?"

"Fine," Audrey said.

"Yeah, fine."

Sarah didn't press the issue, but she wondered if there was more they hadn't told her. The family settled down to watch a basketball game, and later Sarah went home and cut out the pieces for the shamrock pillow she had decided to make for Liam.

Afterward she got out her folder of window pictures and some graph paper. She sat before her fireplace to work on her quilt pattern. She would need to make an actual-size pattern for every piece in the quilt.

She wondered if the police department had found any more clues to the identity of the vandal who had broken the window. Chief Webber would probably tell Spencer if they had, since he was the closest thing they had to a victim in this case. She decided to drop by the library in the morning. It didn't hurt to stay in touch with the principals in an investigation.

The sun sparkled on the snow in the morning. As Sarah filled her bird feeder, she found it hard to believe the chaos last week's storm had caused. Everything was peaceful now. In fact, today would be a good day to run a few errands in town and check in with Spencer, of course. She gathered her investigation notebook, her quilt design folder, and the folder with the window drawings and photographs in it. A plastic bag of frozen caramel brownies also made its way into her tote bag.

Madeline Crosby again manned the circulation desk at the library. She must be getting more hours lately.

"Good morning, Madeline," Sarah said, pulling out the brownies. "I thought you and Spencer might like something to go with your coffee this morning."

"Oh, thank you, Sarah. Those look delicious."

"Is Spencer here?"

"Yes, he's helping someone with the computers."

"Thank you." Sarah stepped away, allowing two other people to walk up with the books they wanted to borrow. She made her way to the area where the library's computers sat. Sure enough, Spencer was helping a gray-haired woman do an online search.

"Just type in the word 'recipe' and the name of the dish there, and when you push 'enter,' the computer will search for Web sites that contain those words. It will give you a list, and then you can click on the one that looks most promising."

A few keystrokes later, the woman exclaimed, "Well, look at that! Who needs a cookbook anymore?"

"Nicely done! You can browse through them and pick the one you like best." Spencer pointed to an icon on the screen. "Then you click on this, and your recipe will print out, over there at the printer."

He straightened and smiled at Sarah. "Good morning." He and Sarah stepped out into the main room.

"Anything new from Chief Webber?" Sarah asked.

Spencer laughed. "I was going to ask you the same thing."

"Nobody's told me anything since I saw you at the selectmen's meeting."

"Sounds like we're equally ignorant," Spencer said.

Madeline placed several books on the top shelf of a loaded cart and pushed it toward them. "Spencer, would you and Sarah have a minute? I'd like to speak to you both."

"Sure." Spencer glanced at Sarah.

"Is anything wrong?" Sarah asked.

"I don't think so, but—well..." Madeline looked around. "Perhaps this isn't the best time, but since you're both here..."

Spencer held out a hand to usher them toward the corner where newspapers were placed on racks for the patrons. They stepped into the quiet nook, and Madeline faced them.

"I'm not sure this is important, but with all the talk about vandals and someone maybe being in here at night ... well, this morning I remembered an incident I'd sort of brushed aside, but you know, sometimes little things you don't pay attention to are important."

Sarah nodded in encouragement. "You're absolutely right. Tell us about it."

"Well, I was driving past the library on a Sunday evening. Of course the library was closed. I turned down Park Street, and I saw someone near the side door."

Sarah caught her breath. Park was the side street she and Maggie had driven up the morning they spotted the broken window.

"Who was it?" Spencer asked.

"It was one of our card holders—Carol Stites."

Spencer nodded. "I know her. She and her kids have a family library card. They take out a lot of books."

Sarah didn't know the family—she assumed they had moved into town within the last few years.

"Yes," Madeline said. "When I first caught a glimpse, I wasn't sure who it was, but I thought she'd just come out the side door."

"That's odd," Spencer said.

Madeline nodded. "I pulled over to the curb and got out. I saw that it was Carol, and I asked if I could help her. She said she was just walking by and thought she'd drop in and ask you if the book she'd ordered on interlibrary loan had come in yet."

Spencer rubbed his chin. "*Hmm*, I do remember she ordered a book a couple of weeks ago."

"Well, at the time she said that when she got up to the door, she realized that of course the library was closed. She said she felt a little silly about it, and she claimed she's always been a bit absentminded."

Sarah said, "But your impression was that she'd come out of the building?"

"Yes." Madeline frowned and shook her head slowly. "To be honest, my very first impression was of someone in a puffy parka shutting the door. But that door couldn't have been unlocked, so I guess it was a trick of the shadows. She was probably trying the door to see if it would open. I'd forgotten all about it until this morning."

"Maybe you didn't imagine the door closing," Sarah said.

"Well ... after Spencer told me that there might have been someone in here after hours ..." She shrugged. "I guess I'd better get back to work. Just thought it might be something you should know—for what it's worth."

"Thank you," Spencer said. He and Sarah watched her go and then looked at each other. "Are you thinking what I'm thinking?" Spencer asked.

"If you're thinking that Carol Stites's last initial is *S*." Sarah saw confirmation in his eyes and nodded.

"Let me grab the phone book," Spencer said. He went for it and returned a minute later.

"*Hmm*, she's widowed, I'm pretty sure. Moved here after her husband died. But I don't see her listed in the white pages."

"Well, if she's widowed, that may be for security. Or maybe she doesn't have a home phone—just a cell."

"Oh, wait a sec. There's a Jerome Stites listed."

"Think that's her?"

"I don't know. I guess she could be listed under her late husband's name."

"You could find out, if you don't think it would be too sneaky."

"How?" Spencer asked.

"Check this phone number and address with the ones on her library card."

"Oh, I like that. Not too sneaky, either." They went over to the desk. Madeline was pushing her cart full of books toward the stacks. "I'll be working the counter for a while," Spencer said. "Take your time."

He went to his computer and clicked a few keys. "*Hmm*, Carol Stites, same address and phone."

"So neither she nor her late husband had the W.D.S. initials." Sarah frowned. "What about her children?"

Spencer studied the screen. "The kids aren't listed by name on the card. But it was a good thought."

Sarah leaned on the counter. "You know, one thing that may be important—Madeline definitely said the night she saw Mrs. Stites was a Sunday."

"Yes, she did."

"But that wasn't the night you got the call about the light in here."

"True. That happened a week ago last Friday."

"Yes. If the two incidents had occurred on the same evening, we might have something."

Spencer nodded. "We may still have something, but we need a link between the two events." Spencer came back in front of the desk, where she stood. "Do you think we ought to tell the police about what Madeline said? I'd hate to get Carol in trouble if it was an innocent mistake, but..."

"But if she's been coming into the library after hours, you want to know why."

"Absolutely. And how she managed it."

Sarah nodded. "Can you go now? I'll go with you."

"Let me check with Madeline. She could probably wait and shelve those books later."

Ten minutes later, Sarah and Spencer were shown into Police Chief Nate Webber's office.

"Hello, Mrs. Hart. Mr. Hewitt." He shook their hands and indicated chairs for them to sit in. "How may I help you today?"

"We've come up with a couple of interesting things that may or may not be related to the library case," Spencer said. He told the chief about Madeline's encounter with Carol Stites. "As I said, it may have nothing to do with the broken window—and it may be just as Carol represented it. But it seemed odd to Madeline, and it did to us too, when she told us."

Chief Webber nodded. "Stites, you say?"

"Yes. She's been a patron for about three years." Spencer gave him the address on the library card, and the chief wrote it on a pad.

"Spencer also had a strange phone call about a week ago," Sarah said.

"Oh?" the chief asked.

Spencer nodded. "Yes, a woman called me about eleven o'clock one night and said she'd seen a light moving about in the library. I went down to check on it, but I didn't find anything suspicious at the time."

"I spoke to the woman who called," Sarah said. "Mrs. Reed was adamant that what she saw was not a reflection in the window, and it wasn't an overhead light. She thought it was a flashlight beam."

"*Hmm*." The chief made another note. "Would that be Bessie Reed?"

"Yes," Spencer said. "She's elderly, but perfectly reliable, I'd say."

"In light of the vandalism, these two incidents seemed important enough that we thought you should know," Sarah added.

"I agree. There seems to be a lot of evening activity at the library."

Spencer sighed. "I hate to think someone might be breaking into the building right under my nose, but I'm starting to believe it. I guess it's time to think about changing the locks."

"Probably wise," Chief Webber said. "I appreciate both of you bringing me this information. I have officers working on the case, and I'll pass this along to them. In fact, I'll probably send one of them over to interview Mrs. Crosby. Is she at the library now?"

"Yes, until two o'clock today," Spencer said.

"Good. And if they feel it's warranted, they can speak to Mrs. Reed and this Mrs. Stites as well."

"I don't want to cause trouble for people," Spencer said.

"I understand. But we need to get to the bottom of this." Chief Webber stood.

Sarah gathered her gloves and purse. "Chief, could I ask you a question before we go?"

He smiled. "Of course. If it's about the stain on the piece of glass, we haven't heard anything yet."

"Oh, not that." Sarah expected it to take weeks to hear back on that.

"Ask anything you like," Chief Webber said. "That doesn't mean you'll get an answer."

Sarah nodded. It was the reply she had expected. "I've been thinking about that partial brick that smashed the stained glass window. Was that a special type of brick?"

"I'm not sure, but my people will look into it. That could be a significant clue. Of course, these things take time."

"Of course. I noticed when I found it that there was a tiny bit of green paint on one side of the piece."

"That's very observant of you. I noticed the same thing when I looked at it."

Sarah smiled at him. "I was sure you would. I've been wondering if your officers found anything when they examined the walkway at the library."

"You mean, like a place where someone had taken a brick or a piece of a brick out of the walkway?"

"Well, yes."

He shook his head. "They didn't find anything like that. They even went back again early this morning, since the snow has receded a lot since the window was broken. And they checked the walkway over near the side door too. But please don't let that out. The truth is, at this point we think it's the same type of brick as those in the walkway, but we couldn't see any that were missing, so I don't really think it came from there. That's just between us."

Spencer nodded. "I won't tell anyone, but it's comforting in a way to know it's not part of our walkway."

"Yes," Sarah mused. "On the other hand, if it's not from there, where *did* it come from?"

CHAPTER SEVEN

On the short walk back to the library, Sarah turned the conversation to a lighter topic.

"So, Spencer, do you have special plans for Valentine's Day?"

He glanced over at her, then at the sidewalk ahead. "Well, uh...not yet. I'm thinking about it."

"That's good. Just don't wait too long—it's coming right up."

"Yeah. Next Tuesday." He kicked a clump of snow from the path. "How about you?"

Sarah smiled. "Actually I do. Liam Connolly asked me to go to a dinner theater show with him."

Spencer eyed her keenly. "Wow. Nice."

"I think so. I expect to have a wonderful time."

After a few more steps, Spencer said, "I'm thinking about asking Karen Bancroft out."

It was all Sarah could do not to jump up and down. She tried to contain her enthusiasm so she wouldn't unnerve Spencer. She had thought for ages that Spencer and the pretty part-time waitress at the café would make a wonderful couple.

"I think that's a lovely idea. Karen is such a sweet person. And Valentine's Day would be the perfect time for a date."

"Think so?"

"Definitely."

"She had me order a couple of architecture books for her through our connection with the university library. Maybe when she comes to pick them up, I'll ask her." He smiled, then sobered as they came to the walkway leading to the library. "Do you think the police can really find out who broke the window?"

Sarah paused at the end of the walk. She couldn't help scanning the partial bricks that edged it. "I'm sure they'll be thorough. But what Chief Webber said is true—sometimes it takes them a while to sift through all the evidence. You know, conduct interviews and follow up on clues. Especially if they get busy with other cases that seem more urgent."

"Yeah, that's one thing I'm afraid of," Spencer admitted. "That they'll be distracted and think the window isn't really that important. I mean—well, you know what I mean, don't you?"

"Yes, I do. If there were something serious, of course we'd want them to give it all their attention. But solving this crime is important, and it involves public property. I don't think they'll set it aside without investigating every angle."

"Hey, there's Jim Brooks." Spencer nodded toward the corner, where the selectman was coming up the sidewalk on Park Street.

"Good morning, Mr. Brooks," Spencer called.

Brooks glanced toward them, and Sarah waved and smiled. He frowned and stared down at the sidewalk as he kept going toward the town office.

"Well," she said.

Spencer grimaced. "He wasn't happy about the board's decision on the window."

"No, but he shouldn't take it out on us." As they turned onto the library walkway, Sarah looked down again at the brick edging. She didn't want to interfere with what the police were doing, but Chief Webber hadn't seemed at all displeased with what she and Spencer had done. The brick that broke the window was a tangible piece of evidence that might lead to more clues. If she could find out where it came from, that might give the police a giant step forward.

"You don't know anything about these bricks, do you? What company made them, for instance?"

Spencer considered that. "I doubt it, but we've got records of who did the work."

"Well, that's something."

"Want to see the file?"

"If it's not too much trouble. I've already taken up a lot of your time today."

He smiled grimly. "I'd like to think we made some progress."

They walked into the main room to find half a dozen people lined up before the circulation desk with their arms full of books.

"Oops," Spencer whispered to Sarah, "looks like I'd better help Madeline. She's swamped."

"It's all right," Sarah said. "I'll come back tomorrow."

"Wow, what a terrific group." Sarah looked around at the dozen women who had gathered at Vanessa's shop for the first session on making the window pattern quilt. Martha had come with her, though she wasn't sure she could attend all the sessions, and the two of them gave Vanessa their coats, which she whisked away to a chair behind the counter.

"It's just like an old-fashioned quilting bee," said Mavis Hoyt. "And it's a charitable project that combines art and fellowship. When I heard about it, I couldn't resist."

"I thought of the old quilting bees too," Janet Stevens said. "We're lucky to be part of this. Sarah, you'll have to tell us all what to do."

"She will," Vanessa said. "I think we've got enough talent here to make a fabulous quilt. And after we've worked for a while, we'll have some refreshments—but not until you're done handling fabrics, please."

"That's right," Sarah said with a smile. She was glad to see Janet, along with Hannah and several other women she knew who did fine quilting work. Most of them usually did their stitching alone, and it warmed her heart that they had come out on a cold winter night to help with this special quilt. She turned to their hostess. "Vanessa, thank you so much for letting us meet here."

"You know I love anything to do with quilts, and this design is going to be a lot of fun," Vanessa said.

Sarah took out the enlarged drawing she had made that afternoon of the quilt pattern. She had colored in the pieces with artist's pencils she had borrowed from Audrey. "This is the design I've come up with for the quilt, based on the stained glass window itself."

"What a wonderful idea," said Martha.

"Whoever buys it will have a permanent reminder of the window and the cause that they helped," Janet said.

"Yes, that was my thinking," Sarah replied. "Though I'm sure the quilt will be much more beautiful than this drawing. I have some color photos here of the original window. I'm going to pass them around so that you can remember it better and get a vision for what we'll be doing. Then I'll ask Vanessa to bring out the fabrics she helped me find for the project."

"Do you have templates for individual pieces yet?" asked Alison Vanter, who owned the Copy Shop and had participated in Vanessa's fabric swap.

"I've drawn some of them out actual size," Sarah said. "I didn't have time to cut them out though. You all can help with that. Alison, I was hoping you could help me get the rest copied tomorrow."

"Absolutely. Bring your drawings by the shop," Alison said. "We'll enlarge and print them."

"Great." Sarah looked at the other women. "I've coded the templates I have ready for the fabric they go with. Each of you can take one fabric and cut out all the pieces for that particular color."

"Are you looking into who broke that gorgeous window?" Mavis asked.

Sarah smiled. "Well, the police are."

Mavis swept a hand through the air. "Haven't they asked for your help? Seems like they never solve a crime in this town if you're not on the job."

Sarah tried to join in with the chuckles from the others, but she had to wonder—was this the way her community saw her? She picked up her template for one of the quilt pieces. She would throw herself into this project, and maybe these ladies would see her as a public-spirited volunteer instead of as a nosy would-be detective.

Sarah's first stop in the morning was the Copy Shop, where Alison Vanter was watching for her. In less than half an hour, Sarah had all of the templates prepared to hand out at the next meeting. She left those for one of the fabrics with Alison and went on to the library to get the information about the brick walkways.

"Here's the name of the contractor who built them." Spencer laid a sheet of paper on the counter for Sarah.

"I looked it up before I went home last night. Don Iverson."

"Thank you," Sarah said. "I'm not sure it will do us any good, but I'll add his name to my file."

"Good." Spencer stacked the papers he had brought out into a neat pile and put them in a folder. "You know, thinking about the bricks and everything reminded me—there is another person out there who might hold a grudge against the library—well, against me, that is."

Sarah eyed him in surprise. "Spencer, I'm sorry to hear you have another...shall we say, less-than-friend?"

"Ha. Yeah, that about says it. See, I had to fire an employee last fall. And he knows about bricks."

"Oh?" Getting fired might make a person angry, all right.

"His name is Lance Beacham," Spencer said. "He's in his early twenties, and I think he lives in a duplex over on Oak Street."

"What does he have to do with bricks?"

"I heard he'd been hired by a brick mason after he left the library. I remember how glad I was that he'd found another job. Lance isn't a bad person, he's just...well, to be honest, he's quite careless. Always dropping things."

"That's not too good for someone working in a library."

"No. But it wasn't just the noise when he'd drop a load of books or knock over a chair. Sometimes he was curt with the patrons. I spoke to him a couple of times. He only worked here a few months, but I had several complaints about his attitude."

"That's a shame," Sarah said.

"Yes. Our budget was tight, and I had three part-timers then. The board said I'd better cut it to two. It wasn't hard to decide which one would go. I gave Madeline and Tristan a few more hours, but not as many total as the three of them had when we had Lance working too." His expression drooped. "I suppose I should tell Chief Webber about it. In a way, I hate to do it, but he did say to tell him if I thought of anything else that would help, and Officer Hopkins asked me that first day if anyone else might have been angry or resentful toward the library."

"Yes, they have to look into every possible lead."

"Lance never blew up at me or anything like that, but I suppose he might still be upset that I let him go." Spencer sighed. "Maybe I can call the station. I'd hate to leave during business hours again so soon. Madeline doesn't work today, and Tristan doesn't come in until after school to help out."

"I could go over there and tell Chief Webber or one of the officers," Sarah said.

"Would you? Just explain to them that I'm happy to talk to them, but I can't keep leaving work." He hesitated, then said, "By the way, I asked Karen."

Sarah smiled. "What did she say?"

"Yes. We're having dinner together."

"I'm delighted for you. I hope you have a wonderful evening."

"Thanks." Spencer looked very pleased.

Sarah decided not to make too big a deal of it, and wished him a cheerful good-bye.

Officer Pratt met her in the lobby of the police station with a smile. "Hello, Mrs. Hart. It's great to see you again."

"Thank you."

"The sergeant said you have more information pertaining to the library case."

"Yes, it's just a small thing, but Spencer Hewitt asked me to tell you, and he can speak to you in more detail if you want, when he's not at work." As they talked, Sarah walked with Officer Pratt into the duty room, where the officers completed their reports and other tasks.

"Have a seat. Your timing is perfect. I was just examining the brick that probably broke the window."

"Probably? Oh, I see," Sarah said. "No one actually observed the vandalism, but it's the only thing we found inside that could have done it."

"Exactly. Seems very likely this was the object that broke the window, but we don't have absolute proof. Especially since there's some question as to people gaining unauthorized access to the library after hours."

"Right." Sarah frowned as she took the chair the officer indicated. "I think that aspect is bothering Spencer more than he'll admit. He'd really like to know if someone is going in there and how they're doing it."

"Not to mention why?"

"Well, yes, that too."

Officer Pratt chuckled. "We'll have to find out who and how before we learn why, I'm guessing. I hope we can put Spencer's mind to rest soon on that question."

Sarah gazed at the piece of brick resting on the desktop. "Has that thing whispered any secrets to you?"

"Not really, but I haven't given up yet." Officer Pratt pulled on latex gloves and picked up the partial brick. "I took pictures of this from every angle. We weren't able to get any fingerprints off it, which is unfortunate, but with porous material like this, it's not unusual."

"Interesting," Sarah said. "And the person who threw it probably had winter gloves on, anyway."

"That's logical."

Sarah pointed to some letters impressed on one side of the brick. "I noticed this before. Is it a word?"

"Part of one. I was able to trace it on the computer. There are hundreds of companies that make bricks, and even more that used to make bricks but no longer exist. Nowadays, most of them mark the bricks they make with their logo or some other identifying marks. This one has the company's name on it. You can see the P clearly." She used a pen to point to the letter. "And right next to it—what do you suppose the next letter was? It's only a partial, because the brick broke, but I think you can guess."

"It looks like the start of an A to me," Sarah said.

Officer Pratt smiled. "Bingo. That made my search a lot easier. This brick came from the Paget Brick Works in Maryland."

"Maryland," Sarah said, studying the fragment.

"That's right."

"And it *is* the same company that made the bricks in the library's walkway?"

"Yes, it is. But—" Officer Pratt stopped and winced. "I'm not sure..."

"Oh, Chief Webber told me and Spencer yesterday that you couldn't find any place along the walk where a brick, or part of one, was missing."

Officer Pratt nodded. "All right then, if the chief told you, I guess it's okay to discuss it with you."

"Spencer and I won't tell anyone else about this," Sarah said. "You know, I was thinking of asking around at local building supply stores, to see if the bricks in the walkway were a common type, but you're way ahead of me. I guess I should stick to my quilting."

Officer Pratt sat back and toyed with her pen for a moment. "I was going to put in a couple more hours on this today. How would you like to tag along, if Chief Webber doesn't mind?"

Sarah stared at her in delight. "Do you mean it? I'd love to watch you work on this."

"Sure. We do civilian ride-alongs occasionally. For reporters or criminal justice students, mostly. But I wouldn't mind having you along while I talk to the building supply store managers. I'd have to do the talking, of course."

"Oh, of course."

"Okay. I'll ask the chief." Officer Pratt rose and left the duty room.

Sarah tried not to get her hopes too high. It was possible the chief would say no, but the officer had seemed reasonably confident in asking. This wasn't the way Sarah had planned to spend the rest of her morning, but the errands she had scheduled could wait.

A moment later, the policewoman returned smiling. "The chief says it's okay. He has respect for your work and your intuition, Mrs. Hart. And I agree."

"Oh, thank you. Won't you call me Sarah?"

"If you'll call me Lisa, when we're not on business."

"Thank you, I will."

Using the local phone book, they made a list of building supply stores in the area.

"According to Spencer's records over at the library, the contractor got the bricks for the walkways at the Build-It store," Sarah said.

"Good to know. We'll put them at the top of the list." Lisa wrote it in her pocket notebook and added the address and phone number. "There are three or four others listed. Some of them aren't actually in Maple Hill though."

"A lot of people go over to Pittsfield to bigger stores, I'm sure." Sarah snapped her fingers. "I almost forgot my original reason for coming by here. Spencer thought of another person of interest, so to speak."

Lisa arched her eyebrows. "You did say you had something for me. I shouldn't have sidetracked you with the bricks."

"But it has to do with bricks. Oh, not these bricks." Quickly Sarah told her about Lance Beacham and his short stint at the library. "After Spencer fired him, he went to work with a brick mason."

Lisa picked up her notebook and looked over the list. "Was it one of these contractors?"

"I'm not sure. Spencer may not have known the name. He said a mason, not a contractor, but those could overlap, couldn't they?"

"Definitely." Lisa made a note. "Well, let's check out what we have. Maybe we can get a line on the person who threw that brick through the window."

Sarah waited while Lisa gathered her gear, and they left the police station together. Outside, Lisa led her to a patrol car with the town's official seal on the side. The emblem included a maple tree, with a mountain in the background, with the words "Town of Maple Hill" encircling them. Lisa unlocked the doors, and Sarah slid in on the passenger side.

"I feel privileged to be riding with you in this car."

"Thanks," Lisa said. "Oh, by the way, I put in a little time on the flashlight. It's sold in a couple of large chain stores. I'm afraid it's not going to give us any help. Anyone who went shopping in Pittsfield could find it easily."

"No prints?" Sarah asked.

"Some smudges. The person who used it may have been wearing winter gloves, or—I don't know, but I didn't find anything usable."

"What about the batteries?"

Lisa pressed her lips together and nodded. "I haven't checked them yet, but I will."

At the supply store, they went inside and Lisa asked at the counter for the manager. Sarah stood by, feeling very official. Soon a man about forty years old came from among the shelves and displays. He walked straight to Lisa.

"Hello, Officer. May I help you?"

"Yes, thank you." Lisa explained what she wanted, and he invited them into his office at the back of the store. They followed him along between displays of sample kitchen and bathroom cabinets.

"Have a seat, ladies." He plunked down in his swivel chair and clicked a few keys on his computer. "We don't normally order from Paget. We usually use another manufacturer's bricks. They're closer. But two years ago, midway through the construction season, we ran short on bricks. We had a lot of orders that summer, for some reason, and our usual supplier had a lot of back orders. So we looked around and found this supplier." He squinted at the screen and nodded. "There it is. I'll print a copy of the order for you."

He hit a few more keys and walked over to a printer in the corner. "Here we go."

"Thank you." Lisa took the paper and looked at it. "Now, did you continue ordering from Paget after this?"

"No. Their bricks are fine as far as the quality goes, but the shipping distance made them slightly more expensive for us, and of course we had to pass that on to the customer. So when the regular supplier was able to provide more, we went back to them."

Lisa nodded. "One more question. I don't suppose you have records of who bought the Paget bricks."

The manager smiled. "As a matter of fact, we do–*if* they used credit cards. And nearly all our customers do. Hold on."

"Don't you love computers?" Sarah murmured.

"I sure do, when they work," Lisa said.

In less than five minutes, he had the information.

"I'm pretty confident in saying that all of the bricks you're interested in were bought by five local people. Three are contractors, and the other two were homeowners."

"Only five?" Lisa asked.

"Well, not that many people use bricks," he said. "The contractors on the list bought the bulk of our supply. Home-owners might buy a small lot of bricks for a patio or some other do-it-yourself project, but most of that shipment went to the contractors." He handed Lisa another sheet of paper. "Of course, a contractor might use those bricks in several different projects."

"Thank you," Lisa said. "This is very helpful."

They left the store and got in the car.

"One of the contractors is Iverson—he won the bid on the library walkways," Lisa said.

Sarah nodded and got out her own notebook. "That makes sense."

Lisa drove back to the police station. As she pulled into the parking lot, Sarah saw a familiar figure mounting the steps to the station. Apparently Selectman Jim Brooks had business with the police department today.

When they got inside the lobby, Brooks was standing in front of the counter, talking to the civilian receptionist.

"No, I can't wait," Brooks said, his voice rising. "I'm on my lunch hour. I need to see him now."

"I'm sorry, sir, but the chief is in a meeting. He ought to be able to see you within fifteen or twenty minutes."

"I told you, I can't wait around that long. This will only take a minute." Brooks's tone and the way he glared at the receptionist made Sarah feel uncomfortable and sympathetic to the woman.

Lisa stepped forward. "Excuse me, Mr. Brooks. Is there anything I can help you with? If this is an urgent matter ..."

Brooks shook his head in disgust. "No, you can't help me. I wanted to see Chief Webber. I just want to have a word with him."

"Well, maybe you could make an appointment for another time. Could you come back on your lunch hour tomorrow?"

"Oh, forget it!" Brooks whirled and strode toward the door. Sarah jumped quickly out of his way.

When the door had slammed behind him, the receptionist said to Lisa, "Thanks. Some people are just used to having their own way, I guess."

"What was that all about, anyway?" Lisa asked.

"Nothing much. At least, I don't think so. He said something about the library."

Lisa shook her head. "He'd get a lot further around here if he'd learn some courtesy. I could have updated him on the spot."

Sarah managed a thin smile. "Well, I should be going. Thank you so much for letting me come along this morning."

"I enjoyed it." Lisa extended her hand. "Call me if you have anything more to share."

"I know one of the homeowners on that list of people who used the Paget bricks. Would it be all right if I called them?"

Lisa considered that for a moment. "Are they friends of yours?"

"I know the woman through some quilting-related activity. I've only met her husband once or twice, but they seem like nice people."

"All right, go ahead. And I'll check with the contractors. I also plan to contact the other building suppliers to see if we can find out who bought Paget bricks from them. Thanks, Sarah, and keep in touch."

No question about that, Sarah thought. She left the old building eager to start her official assignment.

CHAPTER EIGHT

Sarah drove home through the snowy streets. Maple Hill on a sunny winter day was the perfect New England village, with church steeples pointing skyward and smoke curling from chimneys atop snow-draped roofs.

Along the way she waved at several acquaintances taking advantage of the cleared sidewalks. A young mother pushed her toddler along in a sled stroller, and diners were headed into the café for lunch. The lawn in front of the historical society was now home to a snowman wearing a long purple stocking hat and a purple and red striped scarf. The hardware store had toboggans, snow shovels, and scoops leaning against the wall outside the front door.

She would have to work hard this afternoon on the quilting project to make up for the time she had spent investigating this morning. As she went around to the back door and unlocked it, she couldn't think of anything she would rather be doing today—sleuthing and quilting. And she had official permission to ask someone about the bricks. That felt good.

She couldn't resist making her phone call right away. After she had hung up her parka and put away her tote bag and purse, she took out the telephone book. Shelly Andrews was a quilting enthusiast Sarah had met through Vanessa's store. Her husband was listed among those who had bought the Paget bricks from the local Build-It store.

Shelly answered on the second ring, and Sarah told her who was calling.

"I have a quick question for you. I understand you and Mike did some work at your house a couple of summers ago, and it involved bricks."

"Yes, we built a brick patio out back, and a walkway around to the garage," Shelly said. "Mike did all the work himself. Well, I helped some."

"Sounds like a lot of work, but a fun project."

"It was. We love the results."

Sarah smiled. "Glad to hear it. You didn't have any bricks left over, did you?"

"*Hmm*, I don't think so. I'd have to ask Mike. Do you need some?"

"No, but thanks. I'm asking because I was told your bricks were the same type as the ones they used to make the new walkways at the library that year."

"Oh." Shelly sounded baffled, but then her tone changed. "Oh! Does this have something to do with the broken window?"

Sarah had to smile. Shelly was a smart gal. "Just between you and me, it does, but I don't want it broadcasted."

"Sure, I'll keep it quiet. But Mike is out of town right now. I'll ask him and let you know, but I think we used them all up."

"Well, it's not urgent, but I would appreciate it if you'll call me when you find out."

Sarah got out her templates for the quilt pattern pieces. She had distributed less than half the templates at the first meeting, and Vanessa had helped all the quilters identify the material she and Sarah had chosen for their pieces. Each of the women took her templates and fabric home, and would bring the pieces to the next meeting.

Sarah would make several dozen of the more difficult pieces herself. She wanted to be certain the curved pieces of the rose in the center fit together just right. And at the next meeting, she would hand out the templates she and Alison had made to newcomers and to those who had completed their first pieces. She took out some colored markers so she could attach a note to each template with the color and a code for the fabric she and Vanessa had chosen.

She started when her phone rang twenty minutes later. She glanced at the caller ID and saw that Shelly was calling back.

"Hi. I admit you got my curiosity going. I called Mike at work and asked him about the bricks."

"Oh, you didn't have to do that, but thank you!"

Shelly chuckled. "I think he thought I was nuts. I didn't tell him why I wanted to know, but he came through for me. He reminded me that we did run out, and when we went back to Build-It, they didn't have any more exactly like the ones we had used. So the last half row at the far edge of the patio is a fraction of a shade different in color. Nobody notices it at all, but at first I was upset. You know how it is—you want something to be perfect."

"Oh yes, I do," Sarah said.

"The funny part is, I doubt after the time that's passed, even I could tell which ones are different."

"Thanks a lot, Shelly." Sarah hung up and went back to her cutting table, mulling over the puzzle of the bricks.

The next morning Sarah decided to make a double batch of cookies and freeze them. She could take them out next week and frost them for her Valentine's Day deliveries. She took out her recipe box and selected her mother's old sugar cookie recipe. The ones she had at the café had tasted delicious, but nothing could quite match her mother's recipe.

She tied on an apron and sorted through her cookie cutters. As she had thought, she had a heart-shaped one, and she set to work preparing the dough. As she stirred and rolled it out, she thought over the clues that might lead her closer to solving the vandalism at the library. Did the mysterious intruder have anything to do with it? She had just put the last tray of cookies in the oven when her phone rang.

"Hey! It's Martha. Okay if I come over for a few minutes?"

"Sure. I can use a break," Sarah said. "Shall I put the kettle on?"

"Absolutely."

Ten minutes later, Martha was at the back door, and Sarah let her in.

"Nice weather we're having for a change."

"Isn't it?" Sarah took her jacket and hung it on a rack near the door. "What's going on at your house?"

"Well..." Martha's face sobered. "I needed someone to talk to that I don't have to pretend with."

"Oh?" Sarah put a hand on her friend's shoulder. "That sounds serious."

"I hope it's not."

"Let's fix our tea, and then you tell me all about it."

When they had settled before the fireplace in the living room with their mugs of tea, Martha let out a big sigh.

"This is what I needed—comfort. Thank you, Sarah."

"I'm here for you anytime."

Martha smiled. "That means so much. The police questioned Ian yesterday."

"Oh, I'm sorry."

"The officer said they were talking to all of the people charged with vandalism in the last couple of years, and Ian does fit that category. I understand they had to, but..."

"How did it go?" Sarah asked.

"I'm happy to say that Ruth and Tim were able to vouch for him. He stopped for gas on his way home that afternoon.

Then the whole family was at home together the evening of the storm, and Ian didn't go out until he and Tim cleared the driveway the next morning."

"Oh, good. What a relief that must have been."

"Yes, for all of us. And as Ruthie said, they need to realize that Ian's record isn't going away. The police will keep on looking hard at him whenever something like this happens."

"Unfortunately that's probably true—although Ian's vandalism was of a truly artistic sort."

"Exactly. I mean, can you imagine an artist like him destroying that beautiful window? If they'd just given it a moment's thought, those officers would have known the idea was ridiculous."

Sarah smiled. "Ian is becoming quite the young man—as well as quite the artist. You said he had another commission coming up?"

Martha beamed. "Yes, he's going to Rhode Island in April to paint a mural on a bank wall. I'm so proud of him!"

"You should be."

"Well, Ruth and Tim are still a little worried, I think, but Officer Hopkins promised to call them when they've checked out everything."

"And how's Ernie doing?" Sarah asked.

"Pretty well. He gets tired so easily."

Sarah nodded. Ernie's Parkinson's disease had slowed the couple down somewhat over the last couple of years, but Ernie usually kept his spirits up and enjoyed puttering in his workshop and spending time with the children and grandchildren.

Martha sipped her tea, then looked up with new resolve. "You know what?"

"What?"

"I'm going to leave this thing about Ian with the Lord. There's no sense worrying about it. The officer practically said he was in the clear. And if Ian has to go through this again in the future... well, I hope it makes him a stronger, more responsible man. But it won't do any good for me to worry about him."

"You're right. I'm told worrying never does a bit of good."

"I'll keep praying for him but no more worrying, as of now." Martha reached for her bag of yarn and crochet hooks. "Let me show you the afghan I've started for the auction. Vanessa got me some of the most beautiful yarn I've ever seen."

Sarah could see her breath as she strode along the sidewalk Thursday afternoon. She had spent an hour with Maggie at the store and then gone into the Galleria, where she had bought cards for half a dozen friends at Bradford Manor. Now she headed toward the library to touch base with Spencer. She hadn't heard anything new from Officer Pratt or Chief Webber, and she suspected Spencer had no word on the case either, but it wouldn't hurt to check in with him.

As she walked along the edge of the snow-covered green, Jim Brooks rolled past in his car. He must have decided to drive to the town office today instead of walking, since it was so cold out. Sarah waved, but Jim didn't respond.

He put on his turn signal and was about to pull into a parking spot in front of the town hall when a motorcycle roared up the street from the opposite direction.

Sarah gasped as the motorcycle dodged in front of Jim's car and into the empty parking space. Jim hit the brakes. His car skidded a little before it came to a stop inches from the back bumper of a parked pickup truck.

Jim leaped out of his car.

"You stupid idiot! I had my blinker on. I was turning in there."

The motorcyclist ignored him and climbed off the bike. Sarah stopped walking. She had no desire to get closer to the altercation.

"You! Beacham, isn't it? You never did have any sense of fairness or responsibility, did you?" Jim yelled.

Beacham? That got Sarah's attention. Was the motorcyclist the young man Spencer had fired from his job at the library?

The motorcyclist pulled off his helmet and hung it on the bike's handlebar, but the strap slipped off and the helmet fell to the ground. He picked it up and hung it again, then took a knit cap from his pocket. He looked familiar, and Sarah wondered if she had seen him working in the library last fall.

As he put the cap on, he turned halfway toward Jim. "What are you so bent out of shape for, Brooks?"

Sarah got a good look at him. Though his current expression was unpleasant, he wasn't a bad-looking young man—tall, lean, and dark-haired, with a day's growth of beard on his square jaw. She didn't appreciate his disrespectful attitude toward the older man though.

"You cut in front of me, that's what," Jim Brooks said. "I was turning into that spot."

Beacham shrugged. "Get over it."

He walked off in the opposite direction.

Jim huffed out a breath. A car was coming down the street behind his. He hurriedly got back in the driver's seat and drove off. Sarah stared after Lance Beacham. No wonder Spencer had fired him, if that was how he talked to library patrons. She couldn't imagine how she would react if she asked him to help her find a book and got that kind of response.

When he was out of sight, she walked to the corner and checked for traffic. Jim Brooks had found a parking space down the block. He would have to walk back this way to get to his office. Sarah scooted across the street to the library so she would be out of his way.

Sarah spent most of Friday working on the quilt project. The morning passed quickly as she prepared the pieces for the center of the quilt top, cutting, fitting, and pressing. She and five other avid quilters met at Wild Goose Chase and worked all afternoon to put together the center part of the design. Sarah had fitted each piece meticulously, but they still had to make a few adjustments.

By five o'clock, when they packed up their sewing boxes, the middle floral design was mostly stitched together. Sarah would do some decorative hand stitching on the top over the weekend, while the completed portion was still small enough not to be too unwieldy. She had also passed out the rest of the templates to other quilters.

She got home tired but satisfied with the work accomplished. Maybe tomorrow she would have time to think about Tuesday. Valentine's Day. Every time she starting thinking about it, she got a little nervous. What would she wear? She would have to take a good look in her closet and decide whether she had something appropriate. She was sure she and Liam would have a good time together— she always enjoyed his company. But she was still nervous. It had been a while since they had actually gone out together.

She was just as glad the relationship had moved slowly. At first she could hardly believe Liam was really interested in her. He treated her specially, yes, but he made all of his customers feel special. Martha had insisted he liked her in a different way. At last Sarah had admitted it was true, and they had gone on a couple of dates. But over the last few months there had been so much going on—his daughter's wedding, the holidays, not to mention business and mysteries that kept them busy in their own realms—that they hadn't spent much time together. But now she was ready for another outing with him. She was glad Liam was ready too.

"I need to finish making his valentine," she said out loud. She had put a great deal of care into selecting cards and making treats for family and friends, but the pillow top for Liam required more time and effort. She decided to put an hour in on it after supper. And next time she went to Vanessa's, she would pick up a pillow form to stuff it with. Would he give her something special? She decided her gift was small enough not to make him feel guilty if he didn't, but personal enough to make a good exchange for anything he might give her on the occasion.

Spencer called her that evening and reported that Jacob Hull had been cleared of any involvement in the window breaking incident.

"That's great," Sarah said. "I'm glad it wasn't him."

"Me too," Spencer said, "although he did confess to slashing that tire. He's going to make restitution for that and apologize to Mr. Danvers."

"Good. I hope he's never involved in anything like that again."

"So do I. Officer Hopkins told me that all of the young people they've investigated—you know, the past vandals—were found innocent of this."

"Well, the police department is certainly on the job, following up on every possibility. Martha Maplethorpe told me her grandson was exonerated. That was a big relief for his family."

"Yes," Spencer replied, "I'm sure it was. But in a way it's discouraging. I mean, *somebody* did the deed."

"Don't worry," Sarah said. "The police are going to solve this case."

She wished she felt as confident as she sounded.

CHAPTER NINE

On Saturday, Sarah made sandwiches and took them to Magpie's Antiques to eat lunch with Maggie. While they ate, they caught up on their activities and the family news.

"I'm going to Bradford Manor tomorrow afternoon," Sarah said. "Do you and Jason and the kids want to go with me? I thought maybe after dinner we could take some cookies to Leland and some of the other residents."

"I'd love to," Maggie said. "I have a card for Leland, but maybe we could pick up some candy too."

"That would be nice," Sarah said. "I know some of the folks there can't have sweets, though, and I considered making something other than cookies. I'm wondering about blood sugar."

"How about some fruit, or some pretzels?" Maggie said.

"That sounds great. I want to take a little something to Olive Cavanaugh and Chuck Blodgett and a few of the others. I'll bet Chuck would like a large-print crossword book too." Sarah jotted a list.

"I'll get candy and fruit," Maggie offered. "You get whatever else you want to take."

"Great." Sarah glanced up at her. "Listen, I'm making a throw pillow for Liam, but now I'm wondering if it was a good choice. A shamrock, only red for Valentine's Day. Do you think that's too girly?"

"No. He'll love it. It sounds great."

Sarah shrugged. "I don't know. I'm almost finished, but I'm having second thoughts. Maybe I should put something else with it. Something masculine."

Maggie laughed. "How about a monkey wrench? No, seriously, I don't think you need to worry. It's very *you*, but tailored to Liam."

Sarah sighed. "I hope you're right."

"Well...cookies are good," Maggie said.

"Yes, but he sells them in his store."

"True. Ditto for books. I think the pillow is good. And it's not like there was time for you to make him a manly quilt."

Sarah laughed. "You're right. The pillow and a card are enough. Oh, Jenna called me last night." Her daughter lived in Texas, but they kept in frequent contact.

"Great. How are they doing?" Maggie asked.

"Good. The boys are getting into Little League this spring."

"That sounds like fun, but she and David are in for a lot of running around. Or is David getting into the coaching end?"

"Not yet. I think they want to see how the boys like it first. And Jenna doesn't want David to be too distracted when the new baby arrives."

"Yeah, that's coming right up, isn't it?" Maggie said.

"The end of April. Jenna sounds eager to meet her new daughter or son."

"Are you planning to go down there?"

"I'd like to." Sarah was about to elaborate on her plans when the bell over the door in the store rang.

"Oops, customer." Maggie slid out of her chair and hurried out onto the sales floor.

Sarah ate her sandwich and leafed through an *Antiques* magazine lying on Maggie's desk.

A few minutes later, Maggie returned. "Carol Stites. I left her browsing while I came to get my coffee."

"You know her?" Sarah asked.

"She's been in here a few times. Not a big spender, but I think she would like to be. She buys something now and then."

"I'd like to meet her."

"Sure," Maggie said. "I'll introduce you."

Carol was examining a display of old toys and children's books. Maggie led Sarah down the aisle and paused near her.

"Carol, this is my mother-in-law, Sarah Hart."

Mrs. Stites looked up and smiled. "Hello. Aren't you the quilt lady I've heard so much about?"

Sarah felt her face flush. "Well, I don't know what you've heard. I do like quilting."

"Carol has a daughter just one grade behind the twins," Maggie said. "She was in field hockey with Amy last fall."

"Oh, what fun," Sarah said. "What's her name? I was at a few of the games, and I probably saw her."

"Tammy—number twenty-two." Carol grinned. "She looks up to Amy."

"Amy's very good at sports," Sarah said.

Maggie grinned. "That's nice for a mom to hear. You two can just go on all day if you want."

Sarah laughed. "Well, I may be prejudiced, but she is good. So how many children do you have, Mrs. Stites?"

"Oh, it's Carol. And I have three. Tammy's the oldest. Wiley is ten, and Jeremy is seven."

"That's a nice family." Sarah exercised all her self-control. Another "W.S.," and this one was connected to a person seen hanging around the library at odd hours. "Does Wiley like sports, too, or is he more the studious type?"

"Oh, he likes to play ball, but he loves to read too. I take all three of the kids to the library every Saturday."

"Oh, you spend a lot of time at the library." Sarah immediately wished she hadn't let that slip out. Carol's expression changed to a frown and her eyes narrowed.

"Speaking of books," Maggie said, "you had asked me about a couple of nineteenth-century children's authors, Carol. I've had a few books come in since you were last here that may interest you."

They moved away down the aisle. Sarah scolded herself mentally. She wouldn't consider herself a blabbermouth, but there were definitely times when she needed to keep quiet. How would she ever find out if the initials on the blanket stood for Wiley Stites?

Sarah loved taking small gifts to the elderly people at Bradford Manor. Many of the residents were old friends of hers, who had lived in Maple Hill for decades and most of them were delighted to have someone sit down and talk to them for a few minutes. A small treat added an extra dollop of love to the visit.

When Sarah walked into the front entry on Sunday afternoon, she saw Olive Cavanaugh sitting near the aviary with Laura Miller and Claire Whitney. She walked over and smiled at them.

"Hello, ladies. May I join you?"

"We'd love it," Olive said.

"Good to see you, Sarah," Laura said. "How have you been?"

"I'm fine," Sarah replied.

"We miss your father," Claire put in, turning her wheelchair slightly toward Sarah.

"Thanks. We all miss him a lot. I brought something for all of you." Sarah was glad she had given in to an impulse and prepared several extra small gift bags. She pulled three from her tote. "Here you go. A couple of Valentine's Day cookies and some tea for you."

"Oh, how thoughtful. Thank you," Laura said.

"You always were a sweet one," Olive told her, reaching out for a hug.

"And you were always a flatterer." Sarah kissed her cheek.

"Isn't that your handsome son coming through the door?" Claire asked.

Sarah turned and grinned. "It sure is. Jason and Maggie brought their girls in to see Leland Mercer, but I know they'll want to say hello to you too."

The twins walked over smiling, and their parents followed at a more leisurely pace.

"Hello, twins," Olive said, eyeing them closely. "How is school going, Audrey?"

Audrey laughed. "How do you always know which is which, Mrs. Cavanaugh?" When Olive gave an impish shrug, Audrey answered, "School is going fine."

"How about you, Amy?"

"Fine for me too. We brought something for you." Amy turned to her parents. "Mom, can we give some of the candy to these ladies?"

"You sure can." Maggie paused and opened the shopping bag she had brought.

Jason came over to greet the older ladies. He had a hug for Olive, who had been his Sunday school teacher thirty years earlier. "You're looking pretty as always."

Sarah introduced him to Claire and Laura, and he greeted them too. "I'm going to head down to Leland's room," he said after a few minutes. "Nice to meet you ladies."

"We'll go with you, Dad," Audrey said. She and Amy went off with Jason.

"Good-bye, girls," Olive called after them.

Sarah and Maggie lingered to talk to the older ladies for a few more minutes, then headed for the wing where Leland's room was located.

"Go ahead," Sarah said to Maggie. "I'm going to stop in and see Chuck Blodgett, but I won't stay long."

She found Chuck's room and knocked on the door.

"Come in if you dare," a gravelly voice shouted.

Sarah smiled and opened the door. The retired reporter sat at a card table near the window, with a half-finished jigsaw puzzle spread out before him. "Hello, Chuck. How are you doing?"

"*Hmm?* Oh, I'm fine. How are you?"

"Not bad. I brought you something for Valentine's Day."

"What?" He frowned at her.

Sarah held up one of the small gift bags. "Goodies for you."

He smiled. "Well, now. Thanks a lot."

"I had a feeling you wouldn't turn down cookies."

"What?"

She placed the bag in his hand and patted his shoulder. "It's good to see you." She nodded down toward the puzzle. "That's a pretty view of Mount Greylock."

Chuck didn't respond, but he wasn't fooling Sarah. Sometimes he pretended to be hard of hearing so people would tell him more than they might if they knew he was listening. Must be the old reporter in him.

Sarah reached out for a piece of the puzzle that sat outside the border. It held a snippet of the mountain's snowcap, and she thought she could fit it in if she took a minute to study the part he had already done.

"Uh-uh," Chuck said testily.

Sarah drew back her hand. "Sorry." Some people—and Chuck was one of them—liked to do things *their* way. She should have known better than to mess with his jigsaw puzzle.

He pulled the crossword book she had bought him out of the bag and examined it critically. Sarah decided not to ask him if he liked it. She was pleased when he flipped through it and paused to scan one of the puzzles.

"Think we'll get any more big snowstorms this year?"

"How's that?"

Sarah repeated her question.

"Bound to. We're not even half done with February yet, and we usually get at least one good one in March too."

"Yes, that's true. Well, I'm going to go over to Leland's for a bit. Good-bye, Chuck."

"See ya. And thanks."

Sarah made her way down the hallway and paused outside Leland's room. The cheerful voices inside contrasted with her memories from last fall. Her first few meetings with Leland had been anything but cordial.

"If you don't like the dried fruit, just give it to someone else," Maggie said.

"No, give it to me," came Audrey's playful voice.

"I'm not giving it to anybody," Leland said with exaggerated offense. "I'm keeping it, so just keep your paws off it, missy."

The twins laughed, and Sarah smiled as she walked in. "Hello, Leland."

"Hi, Sarah. I suppose you want to grab my treats too."

"As a matter of fact, I brought you some more."

She placed his gift bag and card on his lap. Leland's bag was extra full, because she had given him a few more cookies than the others, and she had added an outdoor magazine, a notepad, and a bright purple pen.

"Huh. Don't know what I'll do with all this stuff."

Sarah was used to his grumpiness. She could tell by Leland's expression that he was pleased.

"Did you watch the game today?" Jason asked.

"Yup. Did you?" The two men and Amy were soon off on a conversation about the upcoming basketball tournaments.

A few minutes later, Leland looked over at Sarah. "What have you been up to?"

"Mostly quilting," she said.

"Oh. I thought maybe you were chasing whoever broke that window at the library."

"Why do you say that?" Sarah asked.

Leland shrugged. "I read about it in the paper, and I thought it sounded like the kind of mischief that you're attracted to."

Jason laughed. "There you go, Mom."

"You're a famous detective, Grandma," Amy said.

Sarah smiled. "Well, I admit I've spoken to the police about it a few times, but only because Maggie and I happened to be the ones to discover the broken window. But if you hear anything that might be useful, let me know, okay?"

"Oh, I will." Leland folded his hands across his stomach. "Windows are funny, you know."

"How do you mean?" Audrey asked.

"You can see through 'em, but you can see in 'em too."

Audrey frowned at him. "You mean, like a reflection?"

"That's right," Leland said. "Take birds, now. You know how birds fly into windows sometimes?"

Sarah said, "A chickadee hit my kitchen window this morning. It was stunned for a minute, but then it got up and flew away."

He nodded. "They do that sometimes. And why did it fly into the window? I'm thinking it wasn't because of what it saw inside your kitchen."

"You mean he saw his reflection?" Amy asked.

"Probably not *his* reflection, but *a* reflection."

"I think you're right, Leland," Maggie said. "Sometimes birds see the sky reflected in a window and think they can fly right through it."

Sarah pondered that. "Yes, but the person who broke the library window wasn't looking at a reflection."

"What *was* he looking at?" Leland arched his eyebrows.

Now Sarah wondered the exact same thing.

Sarah called the police station on Monday morning. Officer Pratt answered her phone promptly, and Sarah told her what she had learned from Shelly Andrews.

"I'm satisfied that the brick didn't come from their house," Sarah said. "I guess it's not solid proof, but it's likely as much as we'll get."

"Thanks, Sarah. I'll check them off. I talked to all the other building suppliers we had on our list. Two of them didn't stock Paget's bricks at all. The last one isn't sure, and I'm waiting for the manager to check their records. He's supposed to get back to me today."

"So it seems likely that the brick that broke the library window came from the Build-It store, but not from the Andrews home or the library walk."

"I'd say that's likely," Lisa said.

"I came across something else," Sarah said.

"Something that may help in the investigation?"

"Possibly. I've been on the lookout for people with the initials W.D.S. since we found that blanket in the library's storage room."

"And have you turned up a possibility?"

"There are a lot of people in town with the initials W.S., and it's harder to determine the middle names. But do you remember Carol Stites, the person Spencer and I told Chief Webber about last Monday?"

"Yes. She's the one the library assistant saw near the library's side door one Sunday evening, when the library was closed?"

"Correct," Sarah said. "And she has a son named Wiley."

"*Hmm.* I'll look into it. I also checked those flashlight batteries. Again, they were a common brand. There are at least six stores here in Maple Hill that sell them. However, I did get a couple of fingerprints off them."

Finally, Sarah thought. Something concrete.

"Unfortunately," Lisa went on, "when I checked them in the computerized database, I didn't find a match."

"Oh. What does that mean?"

"It means the person who handled those batteries isn't in the system."

"Is that a local system?" Sarah asked.

"I checked them on the national one too."

"I see. Well, I guess that's good—in a way."

Sarah thought about the clues as she sat down to finish the edging on Liam's pillow. The flashlight seemed to be a dead end. But the bricks were more distinctive. Where did the brick used to break the window come from? And was the damage at all related to the things in the storeroom?

Leland's words dogged her too. What had drawn the person with the brick to the window? Was it the window itself, or something he saw in the window?

She had almost finished the stitching on the pillow when her front doorbell rang. She hurried into the hallway and out to the front door.

Liam stood on the porch grinning and holding a box of top quality chocolates with a wide pink ribbon tied around it.

"Good mornin', Sarah. I thought I'd deliver this a day early, to put you in the mood for Valentine's Day."

Sarah smiled and stepped back. "Oh, how lovely. Thanks so much. Won't you come in?"

He crossed the threshold and handed her the box. "I can only stay a minute. Lunchtime rush coming up at the store, you know."

"Of course." Sarah looked at the beautiful box. The manufacturer's name was discreetly printed in gold on the creamy cover. "I must say, this is a delightful surprise."

Liam chuckled. "Won't spoil your dinner now, will it?"

"I don't think so, but to be sure, I'll let you help me sample them and keep an eye on me."

He helped her open it. Sarah lifted the lid and stood staring in dismay at the contents of the box. The chocolates had melted and run together, then firmed up again in a landscape of errant milk chocolate rivers and dark and white chocolate creeks and valleys.

"Oh, Sarah." Liam frowned. "I'm so sorry. I left that on the counter in the bookstore, and someone moved it over to a chair when I wasn't looking. It must have been too close to the heater. Let me get rid of this mess and get another box."

"No, don't do that." Sarah smiled at him. "It's not as pretty and precise as it should be, but I'm sure it's still edible. Come on into the kitchen, and I'll cut it into pieces."

Liam followed, and a minute later she handed him a saucer bearing a square of formless decadence. She cut another for herself and bit into it.

"Oh, that's good. I have to say, you have excellent taste in gifts, even if it did have a little mishap before getting here."

Liam smiled sheepishly. "Thanks. I think I ended up with chocolate-mint-caramel-raspberry in my piece."

"Oh, my favorite."

That brought a guffaw. "Sarah, you're the best."

She felt her cheeks go pink. "Well, thanks."

He popped the last of his candy into his mouth. When he had swallowed it, he said, "I've eaten worse. Well, I'd better run. I'm—"

"Don't you dare apologize again." She walked through to the front door with him. "Thank you so much, Liam. I'm looking forward to tomorrow night."

"So am I." The laugh lines at the corners of his eyes crinkled. "I'll see you tomorrow, m'dear."

She watched him go out to his pickup and closed the door with a little sigh. Liam was so much fun. Too bad about the chocolates—she hated to see him embarrassed. She shouldn't have insisted on opening them while he was here. On the other hand, he liked sweets too. It would have felt odd to hoard them all for later—as if she needed that much chocolate.

She went back to the kitchen and covered the box. Amy and Audrey would help her eat the odd confection.

She wished she had had his gift ready to give him when he came. But she could present it tomorrow in a gift bag, with the card she had found for him at the Galleria.

Instead of going back to her sewing room, she picked up the phone and called Spencer.

"Hi, it's Sarah. Just checking to see if you have anything new."

"Not really."

"Me either," Sarah said. "But I've been thinking about Lance Beacham."

"Is he your prime suspect?"

"Well, I haven't eliminated him. I wondered if you know the name of the mason who hired him after his employment with the library ended."

"*Hmm*," Spencer said. "I think it was Rolfe or something like that."

"Okay, thanks. I should be able to find him."

Sarah took out her notebook and turned to the list of brick buyers she and Lisa had made. Alan Rolfe's name was in the list of three contractors. She searched online for brick-layers and masons in the Maple Hill area, and sure enough she found a Web page for Alan Rolfe, Masonry Contractor. The address wasn't far away, and she decided to drive over there.

Apparently Rolfe worked out of his home. She was pleased to note that it was a neat brick house with a sign on the lawn. The house had arched windows and was prob-ably older than the owner, but it fit in with his business and was likely a good advertisement. The pleasing lines and shrubbery drew her eye. In summer this place would be very attractive. A black pickup with a large toolbox in the back sat in the driveway.

She rang the bell on the front entrance, and a woman came to the door. "You caught Alan at home, which is rare," she said when Sarah asked to speak to Mr. Rolfe. "He's taking a late lunch hour today."

She took Sarah into the kitchen. It was fitted with pine cabinets that were definitely modern but fit right in with the Early American furnishings and accessories. The contractor was seated at the pine trestle table eating his lunch.

"I'm sorry to disturb your meal, Mr. Rolfe," Sarah said.

He took a swig from a glass of milk. "Think nothing of it. How can I help you?"

"I understand you hired Lance Beacham on as a helper for a short time last fall."

"True enough. It was near the end of the season, but I needed a short-term hire. Lance seemed happy to get work."

"How long did he work with you?"

"Only a few weeks." He rolled his eyes upward. "October and most of November, I think. I was finishing up a couple of jobs."

Sarah nodded. "And you let him go because of the time of year."

"Yes, I can't do brickwork when it gets too cold." Mr. Rolfe held his plate out to his wife and she took it. "He did all right, if that's what you're wondering. For a green helper. He's a little rough around the edges, but we got along. If he wants to come back in the spring and I have enough jobs lined up to pay him, I'll hire him again."

"That's good to know," Sarah said. "Oh, and I wondered, do you always use the same type of bricks on your projects?"

He shrugged. "Usually. I use what I can get for small jobs. But the suppliers around here have certain brickworks they buy stock from. Are you interested in having some brick-work done?"

"Oh no. Well, not right now." Sarah forged ahead with her questions. "I understand you bought some Paget bricks two years ago when Build-It ran out of their regular brand."

"*Hmm*…yeah, I remember that. We got one load, I think."

"Well, I wondered if you had any of those particular bricks left over, and if you did, what happened to them."

"I don't think so. If I did, they'd be out back. I have an area where I keep extra supplies on hand." He shook his head. "I can look, but it's under snow now."

"That's all right," Sarah said. "I guess you'd know if any-one had disturbed your supplies."

He got up and opened a door that gave onto a rear deck. "I'd say nobody's been in our backyard since the last snow. Is that what you want to know?"

"Yes, partly. I'm sorry to be so nosy, Mr. Rolfe. I assure you, it's for a good reason."

"Okay." He eyed her speculatively. "What's Lance got to do with it? Because I don't think he's ever been here to the house. He usually met me and my other employees at the job site."

"I see. And would it be possible for some bricks or pieces of bricks to be left—oh, I don't know—in the back of your truck?"

He frowned. "I clean it out every weekend. Those old bricks you mentioned—they wouldn't be kicking around. It's been two years."

"I see." Sarah decided there was just no way to prove that a piece of one of the bricks hadn't wound up in Lance's possession. Even if no one had disturbed Rolfe's supply, an odd brick or two from the Paget load might have been tossed in with another batch of bricks later. It was all so imprecise. "Lance Beacham probably has nothing to do with the matter I'm concerned about."

"And might I ask what that is?"

She sighed. "It's the library."

"Lance used to work there."

"Yes."

Rolfe's eyebrows shot up. "That window that got broken last week—is that it?"

"I'm not trying to cast suspicion on anyone. On the contrary, I'm trying to rule out certain possibilities."

"The bricks, then—that's how it happened? And you think Lance might have done it?"

"No, I don't, but I wanted to make sure. I guess it's impossible to prove one way or the other." She smiled. "I'm glad he worked out for you as a helper."

"Yeah. He's a little clumsy, but he was getting the hang of it. And he's willing to work hard. That's important in my business. A lazy man will never make it as a bricklayer."

"I'd appreciate it if you didn't mention this to him. There's no reason to think he was involved, and there were a lot of other people who had opportunity."

"But they think it was one of my bricks that broke the window?" Mr. Rolfe asked.

"No, Alan," his wife said. "I think Mrs. Hart is just trying to find out where it came from."

"Oh. Well, I can assure you it didn't come from me. And Lance…well, he hasn't worked for me for three months. I don't see how it could be him."

At last Sarah left, still not certain that Rolfe would keep quiet about the investigation, though she had tried to impress the importance of his discretion on him and his wife. She hoped the news wouldn't get around town that a brick was used to smash the window, or that the police were looking for people with access to the Paget bricks.

She sighed as she headed home. "Well, Lord, it's up to you to give him sense about it, I guess. It gives me a new appreciation for police work."

CHAPTER TEN

The snow began as a light, pretty flurry on Tuesday morning. Sarah spent several hours working on the center rose of the window quilt. It wasn't until noon, when she left off her sewing and started to fix lunch, that she wondered if the weather would interfere with the plans she and Liam had made. By then the snow was falling steadily, in more compact flakes that seemed businesslike. By midafternoon the snow had changed over to freezing rain. The roads were icing over, and television and radio stations broadcast warnings and travel advisories.

Maggie called her first. "It looks like we're not going out tonight. How about you?"

"I was just looking out the window and wondering," Sarah said.

"Bummer, isn't it?" Maggie sighed. "And I bought that new dress."

"You'll have to reschedule."

"Yes, I suppose that's what everyone is doing. The problem is getting Jason to put it on his calendar. Oh well. The girls were released from school early, so we're going to bake this afternoon and watch *Cinderella*...again."

"Sounds like fun," Sarah said. "Be glad the girls don't think they've outgrown it yet."

Twenty minutes later, the phone rang again. Sarah glanced at the caller ID.

"Hello, Liam."

"Hello, darlin'. I was hoping to avoid making this call, but I think if we try to go out, we'll regret it. I just called the theater, and they've canceled tonight's performance anyway."

"Probably for the best," Sarah said. The tinge of regret in Liam's voice consoled her. "We can do something another time."

"Yes, let's, but I'm so sorry to have to cancel."

"Me too. But the roads are treacherous."

"How about Saturday?" Liam asked. "Are you free?"

She glanced at the wall calendar, disappointed when she read the block letters she had written in. "I'm afraid I've got to spend Saturday evening working on the quilt project. We're having a bee to get the layers put together. I really need to be there. We have to get the quilt done in time for the auction."

"Well, when you come into the store again, maybe we can compare schedules and set up something."

"Sounds good."

"All right, m'dear. Now, don't you eat too many of those melted chocolates and get a tummyache."

Sarah laughed. "I won't, though I must say I sampled a mint-coffee-cherry one last night, and it was very interesting."

At four o'clock she heard a vehicle drive in and went to the window. Jason was climbing cautiously out of Maggie's Tahoe. She opened the door, and he waved.

"Thought I'd sand your driveway and steps."

"Thank you! Maggie said you had to cancel your date."

"Yeah," he replied, "it was bad enough just getting over here. We're staying in tonight."

"So am I. Tell Maggie that Liam called me, and we've cancelled too. Oh, and listen."

He arched his eyebrows in question.

"I have something special for the girls. Can you come to the door for a sec before you leave, and I'll give you their valentines?"

Jason grinned. "Will do."

She bustled about, bagging the special, tissue-lined boxes of heart cookies she had prepared for the twins. Then she popped into each of the girls' bags a package of fine-tipped markers and a red, heart-shaped lollipop. She added a plastic bag of frosted hearts for Jason and Maggie from the freezer.

Last of all, she slid the cute cards for the girls and a romantic floral one for Jason and Maggie into the bags. It wasn't much, but at least they would know she was thinking of them.

She felt a little cheerier when she surveyed her handiwork. The twins, at least, would consider this a good day—early release from school and treats on top of that. Too bad sweethearts all over New England had to cancel their dates tonight. Karen and Spencer had probably called off their outing too. Sarah had hoped those two were finally going to get together, and now the storm had interfered.

She went to the corner of the counter and opened the box of melted chocolates. Looking down at the mess, she smiled. Despite not being together on this special day, there was no doubt about it—Liam was thinking of her.

According to the local news station, the roads were safe again Wednesday morning. Sarah cast aside her low spirits from the noncelebration with Liam the night before and set out for Vanessa's shop. The sun made all the tree limbs glitter as it hit the ice they still held. Temperatures were rising, and by afternoon, the icy coating would melt.

She entered the store to the ringing of the bell on the door. Several other shoppers had come out too, taking advantage of the better weather. One woman browsing the book section caught Sarah's notice—Carol Stites.

Vanessa came toward her smiling. "Good morning, Sarah. What can I do for you?"

"Hi, Vanessa. I was hoping to finalize the backing for the window quilt."

"I hope everyone has their pieces of the top finished by Saturday," Vanessa said.

"Me too. We need to put it together this weekend so we can start the hand-quilting."

"It's going to be gorgeous." Vanessa looked beyond Sarah and grinned. "Find something you like, Mrs. Stites?"

Sarah turned with a smile. Carol Stites had come up behind her. She was wearing a striking blue gauze top with tonal embroidery under her unzipped parka.

"Yes, thank you, and I wondered if you have any patterns with trains in them. But please, you were busy. I can wait."

"That's all right," Sarah said. "I'm in no hurry."

"Is this for a child?" Vanessa asked. "I have some baby quilt patterns with choo-choos."

"Oh, something a little more sophisticated. It's for my seven-year-old."

"I saw one in one of the monthly magazines. Hold on." As she moved away, Vanessa smiled at Sarah over her shoulder. "I've invited Mrs. Stites to our bee on Saturday."

"Lovely," Sarah said. "We can use all the volunteers we can get."

"I . . . thought I might be able to help with the easier parts of the quilting," Carol said. "I've only done two quilts. But it's for such a good cause."

"I'm sure you'd be an asset to the project." Sarah nodded toward Carol's top. "That's a beautiful blouse you're wearing."

"Thank you." Carol hesitated and then smiled wanly. "Listen, I'm sorry I brushed you off the other day at the antique shop."

"Oh, please," Sarah said. "I'm sorry if I made you uncomfortable. I felt afterward that I had been a bit nosier than I ought to be."

"Well, a police officer called me Monday afternoon and asked if she could come by the house to talk to me. She came over and explained everything."

Sarah was glad that Lisa had followed up on her tip so promptly, but she hoped her involvement hadn't caused problems for Mrs. Stites.

"I suppose I might as well tell you," Carol said. "If the police haven't told you already, that is."

"No," Sarah said. Her curiosity burned. "I didn't even know they had spoken to you."

Carol seemed a bit nonplussed by that. Maybe she regretted bringing up the matter. If she hadn't mentioned it, Sarah certainly wouldn't have. But now the topic hung in the air, waiting for an explanation.

"Oh. Well, I know you're famous for solving crimes or something like that."

Sarah felt her cheeks flush but wasn't sure how to respond.

Carol said, "Officer Pratt told me about some things that were found in the library after the window was broken. I put two and two together. I mean, I'd seen you at your daughter-in-law's store that day, and you'd asked about the children."

"I've been wondering how those things got there."

Carol took a deep breath and gazed down the aisle toward where Vanessa was pulling craft magazines from the rack.

"That blanket they found in the library was one my son Wiley took to camp last summer. That's why his initials were on it."

Sarah remained silent, waiting to see if Carol would explain how her son's blanket had ended up in a locked room at the library.

"See, I was just trying to help a friend, so I gave him my son's blanket." Carol's face reddened. "I wouldn't want anyone to think Wiley put it there."

"And do you know how it got in the library? I've been helping Spencer try to find out."

Carol looked away. "I don't think I can say any more without betraying my friend's trust. But I certainly didn't want the police—or anyone else—thinking my son broke into the library."

"Of course not." Sarah almost said, "I understand," but she didn't really. Who was this "friend" of Carol's? Was it someone in the community? And was that friend the person who left the things in the library?

"Here's that pattern," Vanessa said cheerfully, returning with the magazine in her hand. "See, here's the article. Isn't that a cute train?"

"Yes," Carol said, barely glancing at it. "I'll take it. Thank you."

She walked to the counter with Vanessa.

Sarah watched her, marshaling her thoughts. Why had Carol told her as much as she had? Perhaps she felt guilty. But then, why not reveal to whom she had given the blanket? And when she gave it away, did she know that the person she had helped was sneaking into the library? She must have, Sarah thought. That was why she was near the library when Madeline saw her. Maybe she had just delivered the blankets, and perhaps some other provisions, when Madeline caught sight of her and started asking questions. It all seemed very odd, and a hundred more questions popped into Sarah's mind. She hoped Carol had revealed the person's name to the police, but maybe she hadn't.

Half an hour later, Sarah put her large bag containing her purchase in the trunk of her car and drove down the street to the Spotted Dog. Martha was to meet her there, and when Sarah walked into the bookstore and scanned the tables in the café, she saw her friend sitting at a table in the far corner. She was about to walk toward Martha when she noticed Carol Stites sitting at a closer table, with her back to the entrance. The blue gauze blouse and short haircut were unmistakable.

Sarah stepped back behind a swivel rack of paperback books and peered around it. The man across from Carol looked slightly familiar, but she couldn't place him. He had graying brown hair, blue eyes with the beginnings of crow's feet at the corners, and several days' growth of beard. She tried to imagine him without the stubble and younger, but that didn't work.

She realized Martha had spotted her, and Sarah gave a little wave and beckoned to her. Martha's eyebrows shot up. Sarah repeated her gesture, and Martha rose and walked out into the bookstore.

"Are you hiding?" she asked in a stage whisper.

"Sort of."

"Why are you lurking out here?"

Sarah ducked back behind the book rack as the man set his cup down and glanced her way. "There's something you may be able to help me with right away. It's urgent, in fact."

"Does it have to do with your latest mystery?"

"Yes."

"Thought so. That's the only time you act all hush-hush."

Sarah let that go by. "Did you see Carol Stites in there? The woman with the blue embroidered blouse."

"Yeah. I don't know her well, but I met her when I was running for school board last fall."

"Do you know the man sitting with her?"

Martha looked over her shoulder then back at Sarah. "I'm not sure. If you want, I'll try to find out who he is. Are you coming in?"

Sarah hesitated. "I really don't want Carol to see me. She was over at Vanessa's store a little while ago when I was there. We talked a little, but if I go into the café now, she might think I'm deliberately following her."

Martha shrugged. "Okay, I'll do it instead. Go sit down in the history corner, and I'll see if I can find out who the good-looker is."

Sarah smiled at that. "He's quite handsome, but not my type. You won't speak to Carol, will you?"

"Just go read a quilting book or something. I'll get out my crocheting and pretend you're late."

Sarah stifled a laugh and strolled to the periodicals rack. She picked out a book review magazine and carried it to the back corner, where Liam had placed a comfortable settee among the history books. As she browsed through the mystery novel reviews, she kept an eye on the people going in and out of the café.

Ten minutes later, Carol Stites went out the street door, and soon afterward the mysterious man left. Martha hurried over to the bookstore side and beckoned to Sarah.

Sarah picked up her purse and started to return the magazine to the rack. On second thought, she tucked it under her arm. She had read about half the reviews; she might as well pay for it and enjoy the rest at home. When she joined Martha at her corner table, Karen had already cleared the one where Carol and her companion had sat, and two women had claimed the space. Before Sarah could speak, the waitress came over.

"Hello, Mrs. Hart. What'll it be today?" Karen looked the tiniest bit frazzled, with an extra pen stuck behind her ear and a coffee stain on her apron, but she maintained her usual cheerful manner.

"Hi, Karen. I think I'll have a chai latté."

Karen smiled. "All right. Mrs. Maplethorpe, can I get you a refill?"

"Yes, please," Martha said, "and maybe we could split a bear claw?" She looked hopefully at Sarah.

"Well, we can't make a regular habit of it, but you've twisted my arm," Sarah said. As soon as Karen left to get their refreshments, Sarah leaned across the table. "Okay, Martha, spill it. I'm dying of curiosity."

"All right, his name is 'Steve.' I heard her call him that as she was leaving. I almost despaired of learning anything useful at first, because they kept their voices so low. But they loosened up a little after a while, and I caught a few snatches. When she got up, he thanked her for the sandwich and coffee, and she said, 'You're welcome. I'll see you tomorrow, Steve.'"

"Good work. I knew he looked familiar."

"Who is he?"

"Do you remember Steve Furbush?"

Martha's jaw dropped. "Of course! You mean that was him?"

"I think so."

"You may be right." Martha's eyes took on a faraway look. "His family moved away years ago. I haven't seen him since."

"Same here," Sarah said.

"Well, Carol was talking to him about the police, I think. I didn't catch much, but she said something like, 'You know you didn't do anything wrong, so it shouldn't be a problem.'" He said maybe he should just leave town."

"What did she say to that?"

"I'm not sure, but it looked like she was trying to persuade him not to. She bent toward him and held onto his wrist, like she didn't want to let him go."

"Interesting. Did you hear anything else?"

Martha frowned. "Something about blankets and 'suspicious.' Oh, and she said, 'They'll probably question me again.' I heard that quite distinctly. But that was about all I heard. Some other folks came in and—"

A woman at the next table burst out laughing, and her friends joined her. Martha leaned toward Sarah again and said in a conspiratorial tone, "Those three over there were a bit loud."

Sarah smiled. "You did great."

Karen arrived at that moment and set their beverages and a plate on the table. The pastry on the plate was cut in half. "I brought you two forks. They're pretty gooey today."

"Oh, thanks," Sarah said. "It looks positively decadent."

"Hey, Karen," Martha said, "you should show Sarah the—you know." She winked at Karen.

"What, the flowers?" Karen grinned. "I'll be right back." She hurried away.

"What's this all about?" Sarah asked Martha. "Did Spencer send her flowers?"

"No, but wait until you hear." Martha threw a cautious glance toward the counter area. "Karen was having a really bad day. She told me her mom called her and said her father's in the hospital. And Spencer had to cancel their date last night because of the ice, and the café was overrun with people this morning. She had spills to clean up and impatient customers. Well, just as I arrived, a deliveryman brought in a lovely bouquet."

Karen approached them carrying a small arrangement of orchids and white roses.

"Oh, here she comes! Wait until you see it."

"Those are absolutely beautiful," Sarah exclaimed as Karen brought the flowers to their table, grinning from ear to ear.

"Aren't they?" Karen said. "Liam had them sent. Guess he knew I was hitting bottom today."

"That was very thoughtful of him."

"I know. He's the greatest boss." Karen glanced around. "I admit, I was pretty depressed because my dad's ill, and because—well, I had a date scheduled with someone I've liked for a long time, and we had to call it off."

"I'm sorry," Sarah said, holding back her glee with difficulty. Maybe her "dream couple" would get together after all. "I'm sure he'll ask you out again."

"I hope so. Well, I'd better get back to work. Today is really crazy."

Karen took the flowers away, and Sarah looked at Martha, who smiled enigmatically. "What am I missing?"

Martha leaned in close again. "When those flowers arrived, Karen didn't know who they were for, so she checked the card. It was signed by Liam. She was the only female employee here at the time, and I'm afraid she leaped to a conclusion she shouldn't have."

"You mean . . . Liam *didn't* send them to cheer her up?"

Martha shook her head. "As soon as he finished whatever he was doing, Karen started gushing about the flowers and thanking him. Liam looked a bit stunned. When Karen went to get my tea, I remarked to him on how pretty they are. He gave me the funniest look and then glanced over to where Karen was. He whispered, 'Don't you dare say anything to Karen, but those were supposed to go to Sarah.'"

Sarah choked on a sip of her tea. "Me?" She looked quickly toward Karen, but the waitress was taking another order. "How awful. And how wonderful, at the same time." She faced Martha. "We can't let her know."

Martha nodded grimly. "He shouldn't have told me, but I think he was extremely frustrated at the moment. He said he'd ordered them Tuesday and was planning to take them to your house when he picked you up for your date. But you know how that went."

"Right. No delivery people were on the roads then."

"Exactly. Liam said they called him early this morning to see if he still wanted the order, and he said to bring it here, thinking he'd take it to you later."

"Well, it's an understandable mix-up," Sarah said.

Martha lifted her cup. "He was really good about it. I think once he saw how much happier Karen was, he was glad he had brightened her day."

"I won't say anything to him about it. Where is he, anyway?" Sarah looked toward the bookstore, but her limited view showed her no signs of the owner.

Martha chuckled. "I think he's hiding from Karen."

A few minutes later, when Karen had delivered lattés to the people at the next table, Sarah looked up and saw Liam, near the bookstore cash register, watching her and Martha. She smiled and waved. Liam returned the gesture with a smile and turned to his next customer.

When she checked out and paid for her refreshments and the book review magazine, Sarah smiled warmly at Liam.

"You're so busy today, this doesn't seem like a good time to compare calendars."

Liam nodded, glancing at the people lined up behind her. "We'll have to talk soon."

CHAPTER ELEVEN

One thought niggled at Sarah's mind as she drove toward Hillside Avenue and home. Steve Furbush had been away for a long time, and now he was back in Maple Hill. Where was he staying? Could he possibly have slept at the library before the window was broken? If so, where was he staying now? Not at the Stites home, or he wouldn't have had to meet Carol at the café to get the news from her. That left a number of possibilities.

Unless he was staying in a private home, Sarah thought she had a good chance of locating him. Not long ago, she had made the rounds of hotels in the area looking for someone, and she had learned a few things about getting results on such a quest.

On a hunch, she turned at the next corner and, instead of heading home, drove out toward the highway. A motel sat just off the ramp, with its sign poking up where passing motorists could see it. She drove in and parked her car as close to the door as she could.

The desk clerk smiled and asked if he could help her. He didn't seem to remember Sarah, but he probably saw dozens of new faces each day.

"Hello, I'm looking for a friend who I believe is staying here. His name is Steve Furbush."

"Furbush…" The clerk typed the name on his keyboard and frowned at the monitor for several seconds. "I'm sorry, I'm not finding that name. Could you spell it, please?"

Sarah obliged, but still Steve's name didn't show up in the registry.

"Maybe I got the hotel wrong," she said. "I'm sorry I bothered you."

"No problem," the clerk said.

Sarah drove next to the Mountain View Inn. The desk clerk, Bonnie, had given Sarah a hard time on her last visit. She looked every bit as professional as she had then, and Sarah couldn't help recalling her insistence upon keeping customers' privacy. Under ordinary circumstances, Sarah would agree, but she had been a little eager that time. Bonnie's cool smile as she gave a customer his room key was almost enough to send Sarah back out the door. Instead she marched up to the desk.

"Hello. I'd like to see a friend who's staying here. His name is Steve Furbush, but I don't know his room number."

Bonnie eyed her keenly. Sarah wondered if Bonnie remembered her, but if she did, she didn't mention it. She checked the computer and shook her head.

"I'm sorry. No one by that name is registered here today."

"Thank you very much." Sarah knew better than to press the issue with Bonnie.

Lunchtime had come and gone, and Sarah headed home. There were a couple of other places she could check, but they could wait.

Back in her own kitchen, Sarah made a sandwich and heated up a bowl of soup. She ate her lunch while she brought her case notebook up-to-date, including her conversation with Carol at the quilt shop and Martha's report from the café. She added the names of the motel and the inn she had visited. She mulled over Steve Furbush's appearance in town as she finished her lunch, wondering whether or not it was significant.

When she had put her dishes in the dishwasher, she called the police department and asked for Lisa Pratt. The officer wasn't at the station, but she called back a few minutes later. Sarah relayed what she had learned about Carol Stites and her meeting with Steve Furbush.

"Of course, it may not mean anything, but my thought is that Mr. Furbush has something to do with the blankets in the library storeroom. I didn't approach him. I figured I should talk to you first."

"Thank you, Sarah," Lisa said. "I assure you, I'll look into this. It may be totally unconnected to the window case, but it's the best lead we've had so far. Oh, and another thing that will interest you—we've heard back from the lab about the stain on that colored glass. That's definitely human blood.

It's only on that one piece though. They said you can have the rest back."

"Thanks," Sarah said. "I can swing by and pick up the box."

"I can just leave it at the library if you want."

"Oh, that would be great."

"It'll be a while before we know more," Lisa said. "It's a very small sample, but they're running DNA on it. I'll let you know if we get a match."

Sarah had just hung up when the doorbell rang. She walked briskly to the front entrance and looked out. A uniformed deliveryman stood on the porch. She opened the door wondering if Jenna had sent something from Texas.

Instead, the man held out a long box from the local florist. "Delivery for Sarah Hart."

"Oh, thank you!" She tipped him and carried the box to the kitchen. When she opened the lid, she caught her breath. A dozen perfect yellow roses lay nestled in the tissue paper. She opened the little envelope on top and read the card.

"I'm so sorry about last night. Do let's get together soon. Liam."

She hummed as she got out a vase and arranged the roses. What a dear, sweet man. A box of pricey chocolates and two beautiful floral bouquets. On impulse she picked up the phone and called his store.

Karen answered, a little breathless.

"Oh, I'm sorry, Mrs. Hart. He went out back to sign for a delivery. I'll tell him you called."

"Thank you." Sarah went to work on the quilt top again, now and then gazing at the roses. Their fragrance filled the house, but Liam didn't call back.

Sarah couldn't stay away from the library the next day. On her way to run an errand, she stopped in to confer with Spencer. He looked up from his work at the circulation desk and broke into a smile.

"Sarah! I have good news." He set aside a stack of books and leaned across the counter. "You'll be delighted to hear that the police know who left the things in the storage room."

"Oh, let me guess," she said.

Spencer raised his eyebrows. "Did they tell you?"

"No, but I think I know."

"Who?"

"Steve Furbush."

Spencer's jaw dropped. "How on earth?"

Sarah chuckled. "I saw him with Carol Stites yesterday. You know Madeline saw her outside the library one night when it was closed. And I found out that she had given her son's blanket to someone. So when I saw them together and learned they mentioned the blankets in their conversation . . . well, I put two and two together."

"I have to hand it to you, Sarah, you've got a great knack for solving mysteries."

"Thanks, but we still don't know who broke the window."

"True. We can't be sure Steve Furbush had anything to do with it," Spencer said. "But Officer Pratt called this morning and told me that Carol admitted to helping Mr. Furbush. He didn't have a place to stay or anything, and she bought him some meals and gave him the blankets. She knew he was sleeping here in the library, but she claims she didn't help him get in."

"So what happens now?" Sarah asked.

"The police are looking for Mr. Furbush so they can question him. Apparently Carol didn't know where he went after the window was broken—or if she does, she isn't talking. I really want to know how he got in and out of the library."

"We all do. And even if he didn't break the window, he might be able to tell the police something that will help them solve the crime."

"I'm starting to think he did it," Spencer said. "I mean, if he didn't, why is he hiding? Why doesn't he just come forward and talk to the police?"

"You know, he was hiding before the window was broken," Sarah said. "And because it was broken, we discovered his things and he had to stay away. So I don't think he broke it."

"Well…yeah, you're probably right. Oh, and Officer Pratt brought back the box of glass, minus that one piece. Did she tell you that it's definitely blood?"

"Yes, she did. Now if we can just learn who the blood came from…."

Sarah decided to check out a new mystery novel she had read about in her review magazine, though she wasn't sure she would have time to read it with all the quilting bees she had coming up and the time she was putting in on the mystery. She went to the grocery store next and then stopped at the bank. Finally she drove out to Mavis Hoyt's house to drop off a piece of fabric she had chosen specifically for the part of the quilt pattern Mavis was working on.

"Oh, Sarah, that's just beautiful," Mavis said as she spread out the quarter yard of material on her kitchen table. "It's much better than the one you gave me last week, and it's almost a perfect match for the color of the glass that was in the window."

"I'm glad you think so. It was among some pieces I got at a shop in Lexington last summer, and I never found just the right project to use it in. I should have thought of it earlier."

Sarah headed home through the pretty residential neighborhood. The old houses held New England charm at its best, many of them with lacy caps of snow.

One of her favorite houses on this route was the bed and breakfast operated by Lorna Tate and her daughter. Their establishment catered to the foliage season tourists, and winter was the slow season for the business. Even so, two cars sat in the driveway, and a woman wearing a red and black jacket climbed out of a car. Sarah was surprised when she recognized the woman. Carol Stites headed for the steps that led to the Victorian house's front porch.

Sarah drove on by but slowed down and pulled over to the side of the street. She looked back, but couldn't see the driveway or any part of the house except the roofline from her position. She drove down the block, turned around, and crept back until she could see Carol's car. She parked at the curb and took out her cell phone. Martha picked up on the third ring.

"Hey, it's me. Are you interested in a stakeout?"

"Oh, now that's intriguing. Where are you?"

Less than fifteen minutes later, Martha drove up and parked down the block. She slid into the passenger seat of Sarah's car carrying a thermos bottle and her crocheting bag.

"Hi. Did I miss anything?"

"Nope. Carol is still inside."

"Great." Martha rummaged in her bag and pulled out a mug. "I brought coffee and snickerdoodles."

Sarah grinned. "Bless you." She filled Martha in while they ate cookies and kept an eye on the driveway of the bed and breakfast.

"So you think Carol Stites going in there has something to do with the library case?" Martha asked. "What if she's just a good friend of the owner?"

"That could be," Sarah said. "But I know she's been helping Steve Furbush, and since Spencer and I found his things in the library he hasn't been back there. So where's he staying now?"

"Good point." Martha popped the last bite of her cookie into her mouth and wiped her hands on a paper towel. She reached for her crocheting project.

"Is that the afghan you're making for the silent auction?" Sarah asked.

"*Mm-hmm*. It's a new pattern."

"Very pretty, and I love the colors." Sarah could picture the afghan in the sitting area on her stairway landing. "I just might have to bid on it." She looked toward the Victorian house again. The door had opened and someone came out. Though they were stationed too far away to see the woman's face, Sarah recognized the red and black jacket. "There she is."

"Oh!" Martha shoved her crochet hook and yarn into her bag. "What is it they say now? We've got action?"

Sarah laughed and set her mug in the cup holder.

"Are we going to follow her?" Martha asked.

"No, I don't think so. She'll probably just go home. I'm more interested in who she came here to see."

"Right."

Carol Stites drove out and turned down the street, away from them. She didn't seem to notice Sarah's car.

"Now what?" Martha asked.

"I'm trying to decide whether or not to go up to the door."

"Have another cookie while you're thinking." Martha passed her the bag.

Sarah ate another snickerdoodle. "I think I'll give it ten more minutes. If nothing happens by then, I'll go knock on the door and ask Lorna if Steve is staying here."

Martha nodded. "That might work."

Sarah grimaced. "I'm not really doing anything horrible, am I?"

"No. You're trying to find out who broke the window at the library. And you know the police are looking for Steve."

"That's right. And so far as we know, they haven't located him yet. So if we can find out where he's staying, we're helping the police in their investigation."

She was nearly ready to drive up to the house when the door opened once more and a man came out.

"Look! Isn't that him?" Sarah said.

Martha peered toward the man walking out the driveway. "Sure looks like him."

Sarah opened her car door. "Come on. He's walking this way. We can bump into him, so to speak."

Martha scrambled out on her side, and they met on the sidewalk. Sarah walked toward Steve with Martha right beside her.

Steve looked up and met Sarah's gaze.

"Well, hello," Sarah said. "Aren't you Steve Furbush?"

He eyed her in surprise. "Do I know you?"

"Sarah Hart." She held out her hand. "I was Sarah Drayton, and I married Gerry Hart. I was ahead of you in school, but maybe you remember my father, William Drayton."

"Oh, sure. He used to be the postmaster."

"That's right," Sarah said.

He clasped her hand briefly and glanced at Martha. "I think I know you too."

"I'm Martha Maplethorpe." She shook Steve's hand.

"Ernie's wife?"

Martha beamed at him. "That's right. I'm surprised you remembered. You've been out of town for a while, haven't you?"

"Yes, I have. I thought I'd come back to my old hometown and see if I wanted to move here again. Haven't had much luck finding a job in the area though."

"That's too bad," Martha said. "This economy has hit a lot of people hard."

"Mr. Furbush," Sarah said, "I'm a friend of Carol Stites."

His eyebrows rose. "Oh?"

"Yes. I'd heard you were back in town—in fact, I saw you at The Spotted Dog yesterday."

His eyes narrowed, and she could feel him pulling back from his friendly attitude. "I don't understand—did you come here to see me on purpose?"

"Yes, I did. You see, I'm the one who found the things you left in the library. I don't want to cause you any problems, but I know you were staying there."

He sighed heavily but said nothing, studying her and obviously waiting for her to go on.

"The police would like to talk to you about that," Sarah said gently.

He chuckled. "Well, I'm not sure I want to talk to them."

"Please—they only want to find out who broke the stained glass window. If you were around when that happened, you might be able to help them out. I don't think anyone's going to worry about you having been in there, so long as you weren't connected to the vandalism."

Steve looked away for a moment. "I guess I could do that. It's just... I didn't steal so much as a paper clip, and I didn't break that window. I sure don't want to get arrested."

"I understand your concern."

Martha laid her gloved hand on Sarah's sleeve. "Do you think Jason might advise you on this?"

"That's not a bad idea." Sarah turned to Steve. "Mr. Furbush, my son is an attorney. Would you mind if I called and asked him what he thinks about this? I don't want to pressure you, but I think you might be able to help solve this crime. Jason could tell you what your rights are."

"Well... okay, I guess."

Sarah was surprised that he gave in so easily, though his expression was still guarded.

"I really hoped to stay here in Maple Hill," he said. "Now I'm not so sure. But I don't want to leave with people thinking badly of me."

She nodded. "I'll call my son."

Sarah left Martha chatting with Steve on the sidewalk and strolled a little way back toward her car. She called Jason's office, and he answered.

"Jason, I need your advice on something, if you don't mind."

"Sure, Mom. Is this legal advice or family stuff?"

"Legal advice, for an acquaintance. I found out who left the stuff at the library."

"You mean the things Maggie told me about? The blanket and crackers and things?"

"Yes. Turns out it wasn't kids. It was an adult, and I'm pretty sure he was sleeping there, though he hasn't said so. But I've found him, and I told him the police would like to talk to him, to see if he knows anything that will help them solve the vandalism to the window."

Jason was quiet for a moment. "Are you sure he didn't do it?"

"No. But I can't think why he would. I know that's not evidence though. It's just a feeling. But Steve Furbush's family was always very civic minded. I can't imagine him deliberately doing something like that, and he says very adamantly that he didn't."

"So what do you want me to do?"

Sarah looked toward where Martha and Steve were standing. Steve looked at her, anxiety lining his face, though Martha continued her valiant effort to carry on a conversation.

"I guess I hoped you could talk to him about going to the police. He's afraid they won't listen to him and he needs someone on his side to advise him of his rights."

"Where are you?" Jason asked.

"Over near the Maple Leaf Bed-and-Breakfast. Do you know—"

"Yeah, I do. I don't have any appointments this afternoon. What if I come over there and meet this gentleman and get a better handle on his situation?"

"You'd do that? He might not be able to pay you. I mean, he's been sleeping in a public building."

"I understand," Jason said. "But you've got me curious now, and I'd like to meet him, if he's willing."

"Sure. Let me check with him. Hold on."

Sarah went back to Steve and Martha. "Jason has offered to come over here and talk to you about this if you would like. He could listen to your story and help you decide what to do."

"That's really nice of him," Martha said.

"Well, I'm kinda…broke." Steve waited as though expecting her to withdraw the offer.

"That's all right. He's interested in the library case, and he's willing to come talk to you without billing you."

Steve inhaled deeply and after a moment let the breath go. "All right."

"Are you staying at the Maple Leaf?" Sarah asked.

"I am now. Some friends said I could sleep on their couch, but I thought that might cause problems, so here I am. But if I don't get a lead on a job within a few days, I'll have to leave town. I won't stay here and let friends foot the bill."

"I'll tell Jason to come, and he'll be right over."

"Well…won't you ladies come inside?" Steve asked.

Sarah told Jason to come ahead and meet with Steve. Then she and Martha walked with him down the driveway and up to the front porch.

"I love this house," Sarah said.

"It's beautiful." Martha looked around at the porch. "I'll bet it's cozy sitting out here in the summertime."

"Guess I don't need to knock," Steve said. "Seems funny though."

"Just think of it as a small hotel," Martha said.

Steve grunted and opened the door. The scent of baking bread wafted toward them. As they walked into the entry, Lorna Tate came from another room wearing an apron.

"Oh, hello, Sarah. May I help you?"

"We're here to see Mr. Furbush," Sarah said. "Do you know Martha Maplethorpe?"

"I think we've met," Lorna said, and she took Martha's hand for a moment. "Welcome. Why don't you take your friends into the living room, Mr. Furbush? May I bring you some tea?"

"We're fine," Sarah said, "but thank you. And my son Jason is coming over to see Steve as well. He'll be along in a few minutes. I hope you don't mind."

"Of course not," Lorna said.

Sarah went with Martha and Steve into the sunny front room. The decorations gave it an updated Victorian feel with period art and floral wallpaper, but not the clutter of ornaments so typical of Victorian days. Sarah walked slowly around the room, examining the framed prints, the lacy curtains, and a colorful embroidered wall hanging designed to look like an old fashioned bell pull.

"Oh, the crocheted doilies are lovely," Martha exclaimed.

Sarah smiled and walked over to look at the one her friend was studying.

"It's beautiful. It reminds me of the one you made me last Christmas." She noticed Steve was still standing near the door, probably waiting for her and Martha to sit down. She went to the sofa. "Won't you have a seat, Mr. Furbush?"

When she sat, he plunked into an armchair nearby. Martha came over, carrying her tote bag, and sat on the other end of the sofa. She took out her crochet hook and yarn. "It won't take Jason long to get here."

Steve kept looking toward the door as though he might bolt at any second. Sarah wondered if they shouldn't have accepted the offer of tea, in spite of the thermos of coffee she and Martha had drunk in the car. It might be a distraction for Steve. She hoped he wasn't getting nervous and regretting his decision to talk.

CHAPTER TWELVE

"S o, what have you been doing since you left Maple Hill?" Sarah asked Steve.

"We moved to Worcester, and I had a good job for a while. But it didn't work out."

"I'm sorry," Sarah said.

Steve clasped his hands loosely between his knees and looked down at the rug. "It gets to the point where you wonder why you keep on. What's the use, anyway?"

His face had taken on a hopeless look that frightened Sarah.

"You have a couple of children, don't you?" Martha asked, glancing up from her crocheting.

"Yeah. My daughter lives with her mother. My son...Conrad was killed in Iraq."

Sarah's heart sank. No wonder Steve was so melancholy. It sounded like he had a heavy burden to bear.

She was about to suggest she go to the kitchen and ask for the tea after all when the crunch of tires on the driveway outside announced Jason's arrival. They heard the bell ring, and Lorna's warm greeting. Sarah exhaled in relief.

After a moment the hostess brought Jason to the living room. He came in without his coat, wearing a gray sweater that made him look, in Sarah's opinion, very handsome.

"Hi, Mom. Mrs. Maplethorpe." He smiled at them.

Sarah jumped up. "Hi, Jason. Thank you for coming. This is Steve Furbush. His family lived in Maple Hill for many years, but he's been living elsewhere for the past—what? Ten years?"

"Closer to twelve." Steve stepped forward and shook Jason's hand, eyeing him warily. "I'm not sure what I should be doing, Mr. Hart. I do appreciate your offer to give me some advice."

"You're welcome."

"I ... hope this is confidential," Steve said.

"Absolutely. Would you rather it was just the two of us?"

Steve glanced at Sarah and Martha. "No, it's okay. I guess."

Jason sat down in the unoccupied armchair, and the others resumed their seats. He studied Steve for a moment, sitting back in a relaxed, open posture. Sarah hoped Jason's appearance and manner inspired the trust Steve needed to feel.

"Now, Mr. Furbush, I'm not familiar with your story," Jason said. "Mom called and said you may need a legal opinion on whether or not you should step forward concerning your part in the recent events at the library, so why don't you tell me about that? Just take your time and give me the story."

Steve sighed and ran a hand through his hair. "I've always loved Maple Hill. My family lived here for four generations. We Furbushes put a lot of time and energy into making it a *nice* town—a good place for people to live. It's my hometown, and I didn't want to leave it."

"Why did you?" Jason asked.

"I got fed up. I wish now I'd had more patience and stuck around to work things out, but ... " He was silent for a moment, then he stirred and gave Jason a wry smile. "It was Jim Brooks. My old enemy, you know."

"No, I don't know about that," Jason said. "I do know who Mr. Brooks is, but I'm not sure what you mean by being enemies. Can you explain it to me?"

"Well, it started with our fathers. My dad and Jim's were both involved in town politics. We're talking thirty or more years ago. They served on every board in town between them, and they had a three-year term on the school board at the same time. Some issues came up, and Dad and Edgar Brooks took opposite sides on every one of them. Whatever my father supported, Edgar opposed. And I have to admit, Dad was just as bad. There were some things that maybe he should have voted the other way on, but he was stubborn. If Edgar was voting for it, Dad was against it."

Jason smiled. "I've known a few people like that."

"Then Dad ran for selectman. Edgar was still on the school board, but he would go to the selectmen's meetings and heckle my dad and argue against him in front of people."

"That had to be annoying," Jason said.

"You bet. It drove my dad nuts, but he carried on. Well, after Dad died, I decided to run for his spot. I was in my late twenties and idealistic. So I got my signatures and started campaigning. And guess who decided to run against me."

"Edgar Brooks?" Jason asked.

"Nope. His son, Jim. Now, you have to understand that all through school Jim and I had been rivals. Of course we followed our fathers' positions on political issues, and it carried over into things like sports competition and academics. We were archrivals at everything."

"Wow." Jason spread his hands and shook his head. "Didn't that cause a lot of stress?"

"Oh yeah. Whenever we were in the same room, you could have cut the tension with a buzz saw. We went to different colleges, which was probably a good thing. But we both came back here afterward and started our families. We avoided each other as much as possible. But when Jim took out papers against me for the selectmen's race, well, the fight was on."

"Oh, I can sympathize with you there," Martha said. She clapped a hand to her mouth. "Sorry. Didn't mean to interrupt."

Jason smiled. "It's all right." To Steve he said, "Mrs. Maplethorpe ran for school board last fall."

"Ah. Did you win?"

Martha shook her head. "No, but it was probably for the best. I enjoyed the campaign, though, and I got to know a lot of people because of it."

Steve nodded. "Well, I won that one, but Jim ran again the next year, and he won. Our terms overlapped. I'm afraid the town office never saw so many heated arguments. The newspaper reporters loved it. Every week the *Monitor* ran a story about our disagreement over whatever issue had come up."

"I remember that," Sarah said. "I wasn't heavily into politics at the time, but I did care about the town."

"So did I," Steve said. "I couldn't stand to see Jim pushing some of his harebrained ideas. And he accused me of being a spendthrift. I favored recreational programs and things like that. He kept saying that you can't tax everyone to death to pay for extra programs for special groups."

"Well, that's not a bad attitude, to a point," Martha said.

"Oh, I know, but I tried to put my support behind worthwhile projects. Programs that would help our kids, our senior citizens, and low-income folks. Nothing wasteful. But he voted against every one of my ideas. It was just like when our dads were on the board."

Sarah recalled Jim Brooks's insistence that replacing the stained glass window would be too expensive and would cost the town extra money in fuel too. It seemed he still had his thrifty tendencies. But Steve made it sound as though he didn't object to spending the public's money if he thought of it first. Did he simply not support the window restoration because it wasn't his idea?

"Sounds like an ongoing difference of opinions," Jason said.

Steve nodded. "I won't go into all the details. Suffice it to say that we fought and bickered for years. Neither of us would give in on anything. I admit I caused the town some embarrassment, and I'm sorry about that now. There were times I probably should have just backed off. But he made me *so* angry." He shrugged. "If it had been anyone but Jim … But it *was* Jim."

"So you just couldn't work together?" Jason asked.

"Not at all. And then we had a big blowup, and I quit. I couldn't take it anymore. I not only quit the board, I quit the town. Moved away." Steve was silent for a moment. "That was fine for a while. I found a new job in Worcester, and Mary and I moved over there. But I missed Maple Hill. And three years ago, I lost my job. Downsized." He gave a bitter chuckle. "I know the economy has hit everyone hard, but for me it came early." He looked up and met Jason's gaze. "I couldn't find work. Mary got a temporary job. I had just found a part-time one when hers ended. We lost the house after a year. My wife left me six months later and filed for divorce. It's been …"

"I'm sorry," Jason said.

"You've been through some very difficult times," Sarah added. Her heart was heavy after hearing Steve's tale and knowing his son had been killed in action during that time too.

"What brought you back to Maple Hill, Mr. Furbush?" Jason asked.

"I thought maybe my old town would help me. Call it nostalgia or wishful thinking—anyway, I thought somehow if I came back here things would be different. My family did so much to build up this town. The schools, businesses, the library, the police department—we've left our mark everywhere in Maple Hill. I was desperate, and I thought I would go to the selectmen and ask for some assistance."

"What did they say?" Jason asked.

Steve shook his head. "I never went in to the board meeting. I planned to, but I got to the town office as they were starting, and I heard Jim Brooks yakking away. I looked in the doorway and I saw him sitting at the table with Jack Handelman and the others, and I couldn't go in. No way was I going to walk in there and ask for help from Jim Brooks."

They all sat in silence for a moment. Martha paused in her crocheting and studied Steve's face. "If I may ask, how did that lead you to the library?"

"The library." Steve glanced at Jason. "First of all, I didn't break in. I want you to know that."

"Fair enough," Jason said.

"I went to the library the day I got to town and read the local paper. I hoped I could find some job ads. There weren't any that I could qualify for, but I went back every day. It was a comfortable place to visit, you know? Peaceful."

"I've always loved the library," Sarah said.

"My family had a lot to do with that library," said Steve. "Fund-raisers and so on. My mother was a lifelong member of the Friends of the Library. And I always voted for any measure that would support it. That was one of my favorite causes, you might say. And when I came back to town, I naturally went to visit it." He let out a long sigh. "When I left the selectmen's meeting, I didn't know what to do. I had no place to go, and I couldn't afford a hotel." He looked around at the cozy room where they sat. "I couldn't afford this. I wouldn't be here now if not for the generosity of friends—which I accepted with great reluctance."

"Because after the window was broken at the library, you couldn't stay there anymore," Sarah said.

He nodded, avoiding her gaze. "Yeah, I admit it. I slept at the library for a couple of weeks. I wasn't doing any harm."

Sarah wished she could have offered him a room at her house, but even if she had known of his plight, she had an unbreakable rule—female boarders only.

"How did you get in after hours?" Jason asked.

"Easy. I went in during the regular hours and hid when the librarian locked up. It wasn't hard—there are tons of nooks and niches in there, especially in the stacks. The first time I did it, I was petrified he would catch me, but he didn't. After he had gone, I took the key to the storage room from the front desk. I had seen him put it in there, with the restroom keys. I thought about sleeping on the rug in the children's room, but I figured that if I slept in the storeroom, there would be less of a chance that someone would come in while I was asleep and discover me." He shook his head. "I felt so guilty—like a kid breaking into the school on a weekend. But it was a safe place for me, and I needed that, so I told myself it was okay."

"If you went out while the library was closed, how did you get back in?" Sarah asked.

"I would just leave the side door unlocked."

"You had a friend helping you, I understand," Jason said.

"Well, yes. After a couple of days I ran into Carol. Once the library was open and it got a little busy, I would slip out to the reading room and go through the newspapers, looking for a job in the classifieds. Spencer would see me and figure I came in the front door, like everyone else. And then I would go out around town and check out the job openings if there were any and just wander around most of the day. One day Carol spotted me in The Galleria and invited me to lunch. By that time I was flat broke and happy to get a hot meal. She was an old friend from school."

"I thought she was new in town," Sarah said. "Didn't she move here after her husband died?"

"Yeah, that's right," Steve said. "She actually grew up in Pittsfield. We met at a basketball tournament. We dated some my last two years in high school, and I always liked her. When we ran into each other a couple of weeks ago, I was shocked. Hadn't seen her in ages. I didn't know she had been widowed, and we had a lot to catch up on. Before I knew it, I had told her the whole story. She said I could sleep on her couch, but that didn't seem right."

"Why not?" Jason asked.

"I didn't want anyone thinking there was anything going on. You know what gossip can do. I'm divorced. She's a widow, and she's got three kids. And I didn't want to do anything that would hurt the kids. They're really good kids. Right now they like me, but if I was sleeping on their couch every night ... well, I don't know."

"So she gave you a couple of blankets," Sarah said.

Steve nodded. "That's what gave me away, isn't it? She told me the police found my stuff, and one of the blankets had her son Wiley's initials on it. Too bad. I didn't want to get her mixed up in this."

"But the stained glass window," Jason began.

"No! I didn't have anything to do with that."

Sarah, Martha, and Jason all stared at Steve.

"I was there when it happened," he conceded, "but I was in the storage room. It was that really stormy night, and the wind was blowing. I went in and settled down early. Then I heard the crash. I went out to the stairway and saw the glass. I knew I had to get out of there before someone came to look over the damage, so I left. That's the last time I was in the library."

Sarah watched him thoughtfully. His jaw was set almost defiantly. Was he denying his involvement too quickly? Or was he telling the truth?

Jason sat forward and met Steve's gaze. "This Mrs. Stites—did she do anything else to help you?"

"She bought me a few meals and gave me some snacks. She was watching out for job opportunities for me. She met me in town for lunch several times."

"She paid?" Jason asked.

Steve winced. "Always. The only income I've had since I got here was ten bucks for shoveling the walk at the church over on Bridge Street."

That's just like Pastor John to pay Steve to shovel the walk, Sarah thought. She supposed she would have done the same thing if she had known Steve was in town and hungry.

"We've renewed our friendship," Steve went on, "and I think Carol would like to see me get back on my feet and stay in town. I went over to her house once last week and had supper with her and the kids. I really appreciated that—having an evening with the family." He sighed heavily. "There are just so many things to consider."

"Where did you go after you stopped sleeping at the library?" Sarah asked.

"When I refused to stay at her house, Carol offered to help me look for a place to live. Some friends of hers were going out of town for two weeks, and they let me stay at their apartment. I fed the cat and watered the plants. Before they came back, she found this place."

"She's paying for your room?" Jason asked.

Steve hesitated then looked away. "Yeah, she is. She and another friend of mine—one of my old basketball teammates. I didn't get in touch with him until last week. He didn't have a place for me to stay—his mother-in-law lives with him and his wife. But he offered to chip in on a room for me. I protested, but I absolutely couldn't stay at the library anymore, and it was either here or on Carol's couch. I intend to pay Carol back once I find work."

"Okay." Jason studied him for a moment. "You say you had nothing to do with the window incident."

"I . . . no. Like I said, I was there, but I sure didn't do it. I mean, why would I? It ruined my hideaway."

Sarah couldn't argue with that. The fact that Steve had lost his free lodging seemed to destroy any motive he might have for damaging the window.

"Well, if you want my advice," Jason said, "I think you should go to the police. Tell them the whole story. Don't hold anything back."

"What if they don't believe me? The police might not be as understanding as you folks. Could they charge me with trespassing?"

"I don't think they'll arrest you," Jason said. "But if you want, I can go with you as your attorney."

"See, here's the problem. I don't have any money for a lawyer," Steve said.

"Don't worry about that. And if you can get Mrs. Stites and your school friend to corroborate your story, it will help. And can the couple who let you use their apartment confirm that you took good care of their place?"

"Well, yeah, I guess so. I mean, I didn't break anything or steal any of their stuff. The cat likes me." Steve hesitated, then raised both hands in surrender. "Okay, I'll do it."

As they walked out to their cars a moment later, Martha nudged Sarah. "Good work, detective."

Sarah smiled. "Thanks. I wasn't sure Steve would agree to talk. But I'm glad he did, and that Jason could help him."

"That was terrific of Jason."

"Yes." Sarah took out her keys. "I'd say we did a good day's work, but it's not over. See you at the quilting bee later?"

"I'll be there," Martha said.

Sarah wondered if her role in the investigation had ended. The police would hear Steve's story and follow up on any leads it gave them. She supposed she should just concentrate on the quilt project and let them handle the mystery. But the question of who had thrown the brick through the window still nagged at her. Did Steve know more than he was letting on? Maybe her work *wasn't* done. She had a feeling that if she could find out where the brick came from, she would learn who broke the window.

"Is there any news about the mystery at the library?" Mavis Hoyt asked Sarah that evening. The volunteer quilters had gathered at Vanessa's store to put together the layers of the quilt. They laid out the backing, batting, and top on two tables pushed together.

"I'm sure the police are doing their job and looking into it," Sarah said.

"Aren't you involved?" Mavis asked.

Hannah Grace, an old friend of Sarah's, said, "Of course she is. But she's discreet."

Several of the women smiled at the remark.

"I'm confident they'll find out who broke the window," Sarah said. "It may take a while, but they're being thorough." She was glad Steve's part in the story hadn't been made public. She could see no purpose in broadcasting his story, so she said no more. Soon the eight women who had gathered were busy tacking together the layers of fabric.

"Think we'll be able to start quilting next time?" Vanessa asked. "If you do, I'll have the quilting frame set up and ready to go."

"I'm not sure," Sarah said. "It depends on whether we get the layers sewn together tonight. If it's ready, maybe I can come over early and the two of us can mount the quilt."

"Just let me know when." Vanessa turned away to help some of the women find the right needles for the project.

"Sarah, tell us more about this library thing," Hannah said. "I'm really curious about it. How do you help the police?"

"In this case, I was there when the broken window was discovered, but believe me, the police are the ones doing the legwork. Maggie and I helped Spencer pick up the glass, and I located a stained glass artist to work on the restoration, as part of my role with the Friends of the Library. But I'm afraid I get too much credit when it comes to detective work."

That seemed to put the questions to rest for a while, and Martha kept her own counsel. Sarah drew the ladies' attention to the task before them, and they put in nearly three hours' work. But when she drove home to her dark house that night, Sarah wondered how things had gone for Jason and Steve at the police station.

She let herself in via the back door. The scent of the yellow roses greeted her, and she smiled as she flipped the light switch. They were so beautiful. She walked into the dining room, where she had positioned them in a vase on the table. She had expected Liam to call her back, but she hadn't heard from him. She wished she weren't so busy with the quilting project right now, but that would all be over soon. And when that was done, she and Liam would have some catching up to do.

CHAPTER THIRTEEN

After a quiet morning in her sewing room on Friday, Sarah called Jason.

"Hi, Mom," he said. "I can't tell you anything specific, but I can assure you Steve was cooperative."

"Glad to hear it. He sounded so worn out yesterday."

"Yes," Jason said. "I think he's glad he doesn't have to hide anymore. Chief Webber and the officers treated him respectfully. Steve gave a full statement."

"And they let him go back to Lorna Tate's?"

"Yes, I drove him to the B and B when we finished."

Sarah let out a sigh. "I hope things turn around for him. He really was a hard worker for the town. I can understand his bitterness in a way, though I think he and Jim Brooks carried it to an extreme."

"Anyway," Jason said, "for the time being I think he's all right, and he seemed more determined than ever to find work in this area. I think he and this Carol woman might have a chance at a permanent relationship, but he needs to find a job."

They signed off, and Sarah made herself a sandwich and then went on with her work on the quilt. She was determined to get the basting done on the last long edge so tonight they could begin the quilting. For the hundredth time, she questioned her decision not to machine quilt it. The hand-quilting would take a lot longer, but it would also raise the value of the piece, and the camaraderie among the women working on it was priceless. She knew the memories of these bees would be treasured by many, and whoever bought the quilt would know a huge amount of love was stitched into the finished product.

With hard work, she finished her task, and that night she and Vanessa, with Martha's and Hannah's help, got the quilt mounted on the frame. The other women arrived and began quilting each piece of the design. Sarah could see that it would take all the time they had left, but the volunteers seemed committed to completing the job.

When Martha dropped her off that night, she gave Sarah's arm a pat.

"I don't mean to insult you, but you look exhausted. You'd better get some rest tonight."

"That's my plan." Sarah gave her a big hug. "Thanks for being there all the way through this with me."

On Saturday morning, she slept in a little later than usual. After a leisurely breakfast, she felt ready to face another full day.

First she drove to the grocery store. Nancy Loren, her friend behind the bakery counter, greeted her with a smile. Sarah inquired about Nancy's family and gave a quick rundown on her own.

"I'd like a loaf of fresh cheese bread if you have some," Sarah said. That would go perfectly with the spaghetti dinner she planned to serve Jason's family on Sunday.

"You'll never guess who came in here this morning," Nancy said as she slipped on latex gloves.

"I can't imagine."

"Steve Furbush. Do you remember him? I hadn't seen him since he moved away."

"I remember," Sarah said. "I did hear he's back in town."

"Yes, he came in and bought one doughnut." Nancy laughed. "He said that was all the money he had. What a card he is!"

Sarah didn't comment on Steve's alleged penury. "His family was prominent in Maple Hill back then."

"Oh yes, they did a lot for this town. He says he's staying over at Lorna Tate's."

Sarah just smiled.

"Then he told me he came into the store to fill out a job application. I asked him if he was looking for a management position, and he said no—he'd take anything. Even bagging."

"I heard he was looking for a job," Sarah said. "I'm sure he'd give it his best effort."

Nancy frowned. "It was kind of funny. Jim Brooks had come around a week or two ago asking if anyone had seen Steve. I told him I hadn't seen hide nor hair of him for years and years. And then he turned up, just like that."

"Strange," Sarah said. Nancy handed her a bag with her loaf of bread inside. "Thanks, Nancy. I'll see you soon."

On impulse, Sarah stopped in at Maggie's store. Amy was there, helping her mother dust the displays of antique china, utensils, and tools.

"Where's Audrey this morning?" Sarah asked.

"She's over at Pru's house working on a school project," Amy said.

Maggie cashed out a customer, and when the shopper left, Sarah went to the counter.

"Hi, Sarah," Maggie said with a bright smile. "You know, February was a slow month last year, but this year people keep coming in and buying things."

"I'm sure they're as glad as I am that you stay open all winter. Say, did Jason tell you about Steve Furbush, the man I connected him with on Thursday?"

"A little," Maggie said. "Why do you ask?"

"It's the strangest thing. Nancy Loren at the market just told me Jim Brooks had been asking around about Steve before most people knew he was back in town."

Maggie snapped her fingers. "I *knew* that name sounded familiar when Jason mentioned it. Mr. Brooks was in here ... oh, it must be close to two weeks ago. Asked if I knew this person, and at the time I didn't. I had never heard of him. I reminded Mr. Brooks that I'm fairly new in town, and he left. Didn't buy anything either."

Sarah smiled, but she wondered why Brooks had been asking around the downtown area about his old rival. "Well, Steve is looking for a job," Sarah said. "Don't be surprised if he comes in and asks if you're hiring."

Back at home, she decided to do some experimenting with her all-in-one printer. She took Gerry's pictures of the library window and scanned them into her computer. They looked so good, she thought they would be a good advertisement for the auction. She called Cate Goodman.

"Hello, Sarah," Cate said.

"Hi. I scanned some of those photos I showed you of the library window. I was looking at them, and I thought they'd make a nice poster for the auction."

"That's a great idea. We could make some fliers and hang them around town."

Sarah spent a good two hours fiddling with the pictures and lettering, and the results were worthwhile. Eye-catching and to the point. She e-mailed the file to Cate and Irene with a note—"What do you think?"

Ten minutes later, Cate replied: "Fantastic! Maybe Alison will make copies for us."

Sarah e-mailed back that she would take a sample to the quilting bee that evening. The auction committee could distribute them throughout the town.

That evening the women worked industriously. Everyone was excited when they realized how much progress they had made on the quilting.

"You're definitely going to have that done before Saturday," Vanessa said as she prepared tea for the quilters.

"Think so?" Sarah asked. "I actually hoped we could finish by Thursday, but I was afraid we were cutting it close. If we finish a couple of days early, Spencer said we can display it at the library."

"That would bring a lot of people in to the auction," Hannah said.

Alison Vanter, owner of the Copy Shop, said, "This was a great idea, Sarah. I haven't had so much fun with quilting since Vanessa held the fabric swap."

"We'll have to do that again," Vanessa said with a smile.

Sarah held up one of the fliers she had printed. "I hope to have a stack of these for you to take next time we meet, if Alison is willing to help us out. The auction committee chairmen think it's a good advertisement."

"I love it," Hannah said.

Alison reached for the paper. "I'd be happy to make some. How many do you want?"

A few minutes later, Vanessa announced, "Ladies, tea and sugar cookies are ready for anyone who wants them."

Several of the women left their places around the quilting frame to get refreshments. They had been working for an hour and a half, but Sarah wanted to finish the section she was working on, so she kept stitching.

Mavis, who sat a short distance down from her said, "Sarah, is it true that Steve Furbush was arrested for breaking the library window?"

Sarah raised her head, startled. "I'm pretty sure that it's not."

"Well, I heard he was back in town, and someone saw him going into the police station the other day."

"That doesn't mean he was arrested," Sarah said.

Mavis cocked her head to one side as she stitched one side of a triangular piece. "True. Maybe he was a witness."

"Why do you think he's connected to the library case?" Sarah asked.

Mavis shrugged. "I just couldn't think of another reason he'd be there."

"I could think of plenty of reasons," Hannah said from across the frame. "Maybe he's good friends with Chief Webber or one of the other officers."

"Well … I heard your son was with him, Sarah."

"*Hmm.*" Sarah kept her eyes on her work. "Jason often goes to the police station. It's part of his work."

"Were you talking about Steve Furbush?" Alison asked, coming over with her tea. She stood back away from the quilting frame, so there would be no chance of spilling on the quilt.

"Yes," Mavis said. "He's back in Maple Hill."

"I wondered about that," Alison said. "I was shopping at the Galleria a week or so ago, and Jim Brooks was in there asking C. J. Wyatt if he'd seen Steve."

"I'd love to see Steve, if he's really around," Hannah said.

"Well, Jim didn't sound like he was very happy about the prospect," Alison told her. "He said he hoped Steve wouldn't come back and stir up trouble."

"What sort of trouble would he cause?" Mavis asked.

"I don't know. But when Steve lived here, they never agreed on anything."

"That's true," Mavis said.

Sarah pushed her chair back and got up. She didn't like to hear all the gossip, and yet she couldn't defend Steve too strongly or the others would guess that she knew more than she was telling them. Vanessa walked around the frame, examining their handiwork and commenting on several of the women's stitching artistry. Soon the conversation turned back to quilting, much to Sarah's relief.

By the time she reached home that evening, she felt very fatigued. She wanted to take a hot bath and climb into bed. She dragged herself inside and set down her tote bag and purse, checked on the items she had planned for dinner the next day, and then checked the house phone for messages.

The one message got her attention. "Hello, Sarah? This is Mavis Hoyt. I guess you're not home yet. I have something interesting to show you. I wanted to speak to you alone after the meeting tonight, but I didn't get a chance. I'll show it to you at church tomorrow. Bye."

Sarah hung up the phone with a sigh and went upstairs to start her bath water.

As Sarah drove to church Sunday morning, she wasn't sure whether to try to avoid Mavis or to seek her out. In the end, she didn't have to make the decision. Mavis spotted her in the narthex between Sunday school and morning worship and immediately buttonholed her.

"Sarah! Did you get my message?" Mavis peered intently at her through her glasses.

"Yes, I did."

"Step over here and I'll show you."

Mavis drew her toward the coatrack. Sarah looked around a little self-consciously, but no one seemed to be paying them any attention.

Mavis took out her phone. "Here. Look at this." She pushed a button and handed Sarah the phone.

A picture filled the small screen. Sarah squinted at it. Two men were standing near each other in a parking lot. The one standing with his side to the camera looked like Jim Brooks, with one hand raised in a clenched fist. The man he was talking to was turned with a three-quarter profile toward the camera, his face distorted in anger. Steve.

The photo had been taken in broad daylight. Sarah inhaled deeply. "You didn't mention last night that you'd seen Mr. Furbush."

Mavis smiled in satisfaction. "I didn't want to show that to you at Vanessa's because so many people were around. Didn't want to cause a sensation, you know."

"That was probably wise," Sarah managed.

"Yes, but I knew you'd find it interesting."

"Oh?"

"Yes. I spotted those two in the parking lot at the market last week, and I recognized Steve then. I always did like him when he was younger. He was so intense about everything, but I'm sure he had good intentions. He got a lot done when he served on the town committees. My husband was on the planning board with him once, and he liked Steve too. Anyway, I was going to speak to him, but Jim Brooks was yelling at him right there in front of the store. It seemed suspicious, so I just clicked the picture and went on with my shopping. I forgot all about it until I heard Steve had been arrested."

Sarah cleared her throat. "Mavis, I told you Steve was *not* arrested." She had checked with Jason before Sunday school, just to make certain, and he had assured her that Steve had left the police station a free man.

"Right. I have no idea what Jim was so mad about," Mavis said, "but then, those two never needed a reason to fight, did they?"

"I'm sure I don't know." Sarah looked around, hoping to find an excuse to cut the conversation short. If she wasn't careful, Mavis would ferret out some information better kept private for the time being. "I liked the way your part of the quilt top came out," she said.

"Thank you! I put in a lot of effort to make it look nice. You know, those curved pieces were hard to put together. They don't like to lie flat."

"Oh, I know," Sarah said, grateful that Mavis had followed her off onto the new topic. Martha peeked out between the double doors to the sanctuary, and Sarah waved. "Would you excuse me, Mavis? I think someone is looking for me."

She ducked through the doors.

"Did you want me?" Martha asked.

"Desperately. Were you looking for me?"

"No, I wondered where Ernie went."

"Oh. Well, I needed to be rescued, and you're my pick of rescuers. Thanks for coming along at the right moment."

"Mavis, huh?" Martha asked.

Sarah gave her a tight smile and put her hand through the crook of Martha's elbow. "I'm sure Ernie will be along in a minute. Shall we sit down?" They walked to the row where the Maplethorpes usually sat and settled in.

After dinner at Sarah's house that afternoon, Audrey and Amy helped Sarah clear the table and load the dishwasher while Maggie put away the leftover food. Sarah went back and forth between the kitchen and dining room several times, instructing the girls on where to put things in between trips.

"Grandma," Amy said as Sarah removed the tablecloth, "have the police found out who broke that window yet?"

"Not yet, honey. But they're working on it."

"Do they still think it might have been a kid?" Amy asked.

Sarah bundled the tablecloth up so that any crumbs on it wouldn't fall on the floor. She turned to look at Amy and saw lines of worry etched across her granddaughter's forehead.

"I don't know as they've narrowed it down that far. The brick could have been thrown by someone of any age. But I do know they've questioned several young people who've been in trouble in the past, and as far as I know, they've ruled them out."

Audrey came in from the kitchen and looked from her sister to Sarah. "What's up?"

"We were just talking about the vandalism at the library," Sarah said.

"Oh." Audrey shot a glance at Amy. "Anything new?"

"Not really," Sarah said. "Why do you ask?"

"We wondered—" Amy stopped and looked at Audrey.

"No reason," Audrey said.

Maggie breezed in from the kitchen. "I started the dishwasher. Is there anything else we need to do before the game comes on?"

Sarah looked around, gathering her thoughts. "No, I'll just put this in the laundry room. I think Jason already has the TV on. Go ahead in." She took the tablecloth to the hamper, wondering about the girls' concern over the vandal. Were they afraid their mother's store or even their home would be targeted? Or was there something else—something they knew but weren't talking about?

CHAPTER FOURTEEN

The yellow roses were beginning to droop and lose their petals. Sarah removed the two that had wilted beyond reviving and added two aspirin to the water the rest sat in. Enough was enough. She was going to see Liam, if she had to follow him all over Maple Hill to talk to him.

She busied herself with housework until she was certain the café was open, then drove downtown. When she pushed open the door to the shop, Murphy bounced toward her with a little woof and sniffed her boots.

"Hello, you handsome little canine, you." Sarah bent down to pat him as she glanced about the store. Liam was over in the café, carrying coffee to customers. He saw her and grinned. Sarah waved with a smile and turned to examine the rack of new books. His face had lit up when he saw her, so their relationship mustn't be too far off track.

She picked up a new historical romance by Marjory Middlefield, an author she had helped out with a mystery. The woman was in her eighties but continued to write the stories that kept her fans fascinated. Sarah turned to the back and studied the photo. Marjory never used to allow her publishers to put her picture on her books. The fact that she did so now pleased Sarah.

"Have you heard from Ms. Middlefield lately?" Liam asked in a low voice, so close his breath tickled her ear.

She turned toward him, unable to ignore the way his nearness made her heart flutter. "No, but her friend Joan e-mailed me recently and said Marjory is doing fine. They had been to the museum together."

"That's nice. And I'm glad you came in today. Seems like I hardly get a glimpse of my favorite customer these days."

She looked into his emerald green eyes. "I've missed seeing you too. Liam, the roses were gorgeous. I called here after they were delivered, but I wasn't sure you got my message."

"No, I guess I didn't."

"Well, they're lovely. Thank you."

"I'm glad you liked them. I did think it a bit odd that you didn't comment on them. Karen must have forgotten to tell me." He reached for her hand and gave it a quick squeeze. "We've both been too busy."

"Yes. This quilt thing has me tied up almost every night."

"I drove over to Concord to see Caitlin and Travis for the weekend."

"Wonderful," Sarah said. "How are they?"

"Doing well." His smile went deep, and the lines at the corners of his eyes crinkled. "Those kids are so idealistic it hurts. But they'll be fine."

"Of course, they will."

Liam cocked his head to one side, his expression more serious than she usually saw from him. "Have you got any idea when we can get together for dinner? We ought to just pick a day and make it happen."

Sarah felt her face flush. She longed to do just that. "Well, the auction is Saturday. After that's over …"

He nodded. "Plan on it."

That afternoon, Sarah dropped in at the library to tell Spencer the quilt was nearly finished.

"That's terrific, Sarah."

"I hope we'll have it done by Thursday," Sarah said. "A lot of people have gone into Wild Goose Chase to see it, and Vanessa's left the frame in the middle of the store, so folks can't miss it when they walk in. But once the quilting is done and it's off the frame, I thought maybe it would be appropriate to display it here."

"Great idea." Spencer nodded toward a glass case where he exhibited new books and occasional themed displays. "We can show it off the final few days before the auction. Abby McCormick might even run a picture of it in the *Monitor*."

"Do you want to call her?" Sarah asked.

"Sure. I'll talk to her today. Just let me know when you have it ready. I'll get the display case ready on Wednesday." Sarah looked toward the stairway and the covered gap in the wall over the landing. "It'll be good to have that frame filled again."

"Irene Stuart tells me the committee's had great success in getting merchandise donated," Spencer said. "She mentioned a porcelain doll and a microwave oven. They've got several gift certificates too. Build-It is giving a hundred dollar certificate, and the Old Mill and the Galleria both donated certificates. And the Berkshire Furniture factory is giving a quilt rack."

"Wonderful," Sarah said.

Spencer threw up his hands. "I can't remember everything, but Irene has a list. And she said they've put it on community bulletin boards on the radio and TV stations."

"I'm getting excited about it." Sarah pulled on her gloves. "Right now I have a date with my granddaughters. I'm picking them up from school."

"Have fun," Spencer said.

She drove to the middle school and waited in the parking lot until the bell rang and the students came out. All the kids seemed eager to leave the grounds and head for home. Amy and Audrey spotted her car and ran over. Audrey claimed the front seat, and Amy jumped in the back with her backpack. They launched into excited accounts of their school day, and Sarah let them chatter on the way home, glad to hear their eagerness.

Over cookies and milk at the dining room table, Sarah told them about the auction prizes, hoping to gently steer the conversation to the library window again.

"That's cool," Amy said. "But won't people try to get the gift certificates for less than they're worth?"

"They might," Sarah said, "but sometimes when it's for charity, folks are willing to pay full price or even more. For instance, if your dad was going to go and buy some supplies at Build-It, he might figure it's money he'd have spent there anyway, and he might add a little more to his bid because it's for such a good cause."

"Makes sense, I guess," Amy said.

"Will the stained glass man be able to put the window back together exactly like it was before?" Audrey asked.

"I don't know if it will be exactly the same, but I'm sure it will be close. He's going to use any of the old pieces of glass that are big enough, and he'll match the original glass as closely as possible. I think they use different materials for the strips between the pieces now, but he knows how his great-grandfather did it, and I know he'll do a great job."

"I'm glad." Audrey picked up her glass and took a drink.

"If they catch the person who did it..." Amy glanced at her sister.

"Yes?" Sarah said.

Amy twisted a lock of her hair. "I just wondered what would happen to them."

Sarah considered that for a moment. "I'm not sure. It might depend on why they did it, and whether or not they were sorry."

"Would they...go to jail?" Audrey asked.

"You'd have to ask your father about that. I'm sure he knows more than I do about what the charges and the punishment would be."

Sarah watched them closely. The girls kept throwing quick glances at each other and then looking away. She got the feeling they wanted to say more but weren't sure they should. Maybe they needed a chance to confer.

She stood. "Would you like some more milk?"

"Yes, please." Audrey held out her glass.

"I have enough," Amy said.

Sarah took Audrey's glass to the kitchen and poured more milk in it. She stood by the window for a moment, looking out at the bird feeder. Again she thought of Leland's words about the birds and windows. Did the vandal throw the brick for a reason other than random destruction?

When she returned to the dining room, the girls were eating their cookies in silence. She handed Audrey her glass and sat down.

"I've noticed that you girls seem a little upset whenever we talk about what happened at the library. If there's anything you'd like to talk about, I'll listen."

Amy bit her lower lip and glanced at Audrey.

"I guess we'll have to tell Dad," Audrey said. "I mean, if someone did it when they were mad, but then they were sorry later, would they go to jail? Or maybe be suspended from school? I just..." She looked down at her hands and fell silent.

"Do you know someone who felt that way?" Sarah asked.

Audrey said nothing.

Sarah looked at Amy. "It would help a lot if we could find out who was responsible. For one thing, Mr. Hewitt wouldn't have to wonder if that person was likely to do more damage to the library. And some folks in town are starting to spread rumors about someone being arrested when it's not true. Everyone wants to see the case solved, but it's not fair when an innocent person is accused."

"Well..." Amy said.

"There's this boy," Audrey looked quickly at her sister.

Amy opened her mouth, then closed it and shrugged.

A boy, Sarah thought with dismay.

Audrey seemed to take Amy's silence as permission to continue. She turned to face Sarah and said, "There's a boy in our class who was mad because he couldn't get into the library."

"Really? On the night of the storm?"

Audrey nodded. "He went there, but the library had closed early because of the snow."

Sarah nodded slowly. "Did this boy tell you what happened?"

Audrey shook her head.

"We saw him at the library," Amy said. "We were walking over to Mom's store, and it was cold and snowy. But we saw C—we saw someone from our class pounding on the door of the library."

"It was Cole Rosenthal," Audrey said.

Amy glared at her.

"She won't tell on him, will you, Grandma?"

"Well, that depends," Sarah said carefully. "Did you see him break the window?"

"No," both girls said.

"But we're afraid he might have," Audrey added.

"Have you asked him about it?"

The twins shook their heads.

"Why do you think Cole did it?"

"He was upset about his history paper," Amy said. "Mrs. Hiland had told him that morning that his sources weren't good enough."

"That's not it," Audrey said. "He'd done the research, but he didn't do his bibliography right. You're supposed to put all the references in a special way, with the name of the publisher and all that stuff."

"I remember," Sarah said with a smile.

"Well, Cole didn't have it right," Amy said, and Audrey nodded. "He had used some books from the public library, so Mrs. Hiland said he needed to go back to the library and get the information or he'd get an F."

"The paper was due the next day," Audrey added. "So when we saw him at the library door, we figured he was pretty upset because it was closed and he couldn't get in to get the sources for his paper."

"I can understand how frustrating that would be," Sarah said.

"Yeah. Well, what if he was so mad that he picked up a rock and threw it at the window?" Amy asked.

"That wouldn't be good." Sarah reached for a cookie. "But I haven't heard anything here that says Cole did it. I seriously doubt that he did."

"You do?" Audrey said. Both girls stared at her hopefully.

"I do. For one thing, you saw him there after school, right?"

They nodded.

"If the window was broken that early, I think someone would have noticed it that night. Someone like the snowplow driver or a police officer."

"Maybe."

"But so far as we know, nobody noticed it until your mom and I drove past the next morning. Besides," Sarah said, "the police are working hard on this case, and they have some evidence they're following up on. I seriously doubt that Cole is the person who broke the window. And I think Chief Webber and his officers will find the real culprit soon."

"Thanks, Grandma," Audrey said.

"Yeah." Amy took the last cookie from the plate. "I sure hope you're right. It seemed so pointless if he did do it, because school was canceled the next day."

"He's probably over it by now. But you girls really should talk to your parents about this. Let them know what you saw."

The twins looked at each other doubtfully.

"I guess we could," Amy said.

Sarah smiled at them. "I think you'd feel better. Now, you never told me what happened at school for Valentine's Day. Did your teacher do anything to celebrate?"

Audrey shook her head. "Not a thing. I was glad."

"But we liked what you did," Amy said. "The cookies were awesome."

"Thanks. I printed out the card you e-mailed me. It's hanging on the fridge."

"They did have decorations in the cafeteria that day, and they gave us cupcakes with red and pink frosting," Amy said.

Sarah smiled. "So, what else is going on at school?"

As the twins chattered about their activities, Sarah couldn't help thinking about what they had said. Their concern for their classmate touched her, but she couldn't cast the boy as the culprit in her mind. He had a motive, if they were right, although not a very strong one in Sarah's mind. His opportunity was also questionable. Could the window really have been broken by four in the afternoon? She doubted that. Of course he could have gone back later, though not many people were out in the storm. And she didn't believe for a minute that Cole had taken a piece of a brick with him when he went to the library. But somebody did.

CHAPTER FIFTEEN

On Tuesday morning, Sarah still couldn't shake the unease that the twins' story had brought. It wouldn't have bothered her so much if it hadn't bothered the girls. They had brooded over Cole's conduct for more than two weeks. She hoped their talk had helped, but she wished she could completely erase their doubts about their classmate.

She got out her notebook and went over all her notes pertaining to the bricks—where they had originated and who had purchased them. There were still too many questions as to who had access to those bricks. At last she called the police station and asked for Lisa Pratt.

"The girls didn't tell me for a long time because they didn't want to get the boy in trouble," she said after briefly recounting the story. "I don't want to do that either, but maybe it's something that needs to be ruled out. Someone else may have seen Cole at the library that night."

"I think I can look into that gently," Lisa said. "But I agree with you—most boys don't leave school with a broken brick in their backpack. And we're pretty sure it wasn't picked up on the spur of the moment at the scene."

"Thanks. It seems unlikely that his parents would have let him go out again later, with the weather the way it was." Sarah fingered her notebook. "I've been looking over what we know about those bricks. Have you talked to the other people who bought them from Build-It?"

"I'm sorry. I haven't had time, though I intended to do it."

Sarah took a deep breath. "Can I help?"

"Well, let's see." There was a moment's pause, then Lisa said, "You were successful in contacting the Andrews family. Would you like to talk to the Burks?"

"Sure."

"Okay. And I'll try to get over to see the other contractor tomorrow if I can manage it."

It was the best Sarah could hope for, and she checked her calendar. She would be tied up tonight with the quilt project, but her day was free. She might as well tackle her new assignment as soon as possible.

She checked the Burks' address and went out to her car, thankful for another cold, clear day. As far as she was concerned, they had had enough snow for one winter.

A man not much older than herself answered the door. He eyed her curiously from behind his bifocals.

"Mr. Burk?"

"Yes."

"I'm Sarah Hart."

"Oh, I know you, don't I? You're Gerry's wife."

"Well, yes."

"Come on in," he said.

Surprised, Sarah walked with him into a neat living room decorated with country-style antiques. A woman with light brown hair came in from another room, and Mr. Burk introduced her as his wife.

"Did you know my husband?" Sarah asked.

"He did some work for me several years back," Mr. Burk said. "Oh, it must be ten years ago now. I was sorry to hear he had passed away."

"Thank you." Sarah cleared her throat. "I'm hoping you can help me learn about some bricks."

"Bricks?" He smiled. "That's an odd request."

"Particular bricks?" his wife asked.

"Yes. Some that you bought two summers ago from the Build-It store."

Mr. Burk nodded. "I remember, but it beats me why you'd care."

"I'm working on a bit of a puzzle. I'm trying to find out where a certain brick came from, and it's from a batch Build-It sold that year. So I'm asking everyone who bought any if they had bricks left over from their construction projects."

"Nope. Used 'em all. Had to go back for more."

"Three more bricks," Mrs. Burk said with a chuckle. "Ed was put out because he thought he had the exact number he needed."

"What were you building?" Sarah asked.

"A kiln for her pottery," Mr. Burk said.

"Oh, how interesting. Do you use it often?"

Mrs. Burk frowned. "Some, but mostly in the summer and fall. It doesn't work quite as well as a commercial one, but we've had some fun with it. Since Ed retired, we've had time to indulge our hobbies."

Sarah nodded. "So you had to get more bricks when you were nearly done?"

"Yes," Mr. Burk said. "I'm not sure how that happened, exactly, but I went back to the store for three more bricks."

"And they didn't match."

His eyes widened. "That's right. But it didn't really matter for the chimney, so that didn't bother me."

"Would you like to see the kiln?" Mrs. Burk asked.

"I'd love to."

The Burks got coats and led Sarah to the back deck, from which she could see the beehive-type kiln resting in a corner of the fenced yard.

"There's still too much snow to get over there without getting your feet wet," Mrs. Burk said.

"That's all right," Sarah assured her.

"It's a bit hard to control the temperature inside the kiln precisely," Mr. Burk said. "If Doreen has something she's fussy about, she takes it to her teacher's studio and they fire it for her. But she's made some nice pots and bowls in this one." He pointed to the kiln. "The three bricks I got last are right at the top. No one would ever know."

"I agree," Sarah said. "It's lovely."

"Would you like a cup of coffee?" Mrs. Burk asked.

"Oh no, thank you. But I appreciate your help." Sarah excused herself and went back to her car. She drove to Hillside Avenue and had just pulled into her drive when a police car pulled in behind her. Her pulse lurched as the inevitable "What did I do?" flashed through her mind, but then she recognized Lisa getting out of the squad car.

"Hello!" Sarah met her on the driveway between the two cars.

"Hi," Lisa said. "Thought I'd swing by and see if you were home."

"Yes, I just got back from the Burks' house. Another dead end on the bricks, so far as I can tell. Of course, someone might have a half brick left over from a project and not remember."

"True," Lisa said, "and if they were guilty, why would they tell you in the first place?"

"Right." Sarah pressed her lips together.

"Well, I had a talk with Mrs. Rosenthal, and she agreed to go over to the middle school with me so I could have a word with Cole."

"That was obliging of her."

"Yes," Lisa said. "Cole told me that it's true he was angry about the library being closed the day of the storm, but he didn't do anything except go home and find another way to get the information he needed."

"Oh?"

Lisa nodded. "He used his computer to get the publishing information for the books in his bibliography. That's all he was lacking. He seems like a good kid. I believed his story, though he was a little nervous at being hauled out of gym class to talk to an officer."

"I'll bet," Sarah said. "Well, I'm glad you went. I don't like to see youngsters get mixed up in vandalism."

"I have a feeling this wasn't done by kids," Lisa said. "It's not the type of thing one lone teenager would do, and a group of rowdy kids would have drawn attention." She looked at her watch. "Well, I'd better get rolling. I have another case I'm working on, so I won't have time to go talk to that last contractor today."

"Let me know if I can help," Sarah said.

She waved as Lisa backed out of the driveway, then went inside and checked her baking ingredients. She wanted to give the twins the good news about Cole that afternoon, and she had a feeling they wouldn't be upset if she arrived with a box of macaroons in her hand.

On Wednesday evening, all of the women stayed late at Wild Goose Chase to finish the quilting. At half past nine, Hannah placed the last stitch in the border at one end while Cate pushed her needle through the layers at the other end for the final time.

"Done!" Cate looked up expectantly.

"Me too," Hannah said.

Everyone clapped.

"Well done," Vanessa said. "Alison brought a special treat tonight—cheesecake, now being served by Alison and Martha."

Janet Stevens moaned. "I think I've gained five pounds this month because of the goodies at these quilting bees."

The women stood around the quilting frame for a minute, admiring their work.

"It's beautiful," Sarah said with satisfaction.

Vanessa gave her a quick hug. "Yes, and I'm sure it will bring in a large donation for the window."

The next afternoon, Sarah returned to Wild Goose Chase so she and Vanessa could take the finished quilt over to the library. They took it out of the quilting frame and spread it out to look it over and make sure every piece of fabric had been quilted.

"It's gorgeous," Vanessa said.

"Isn't it?" Sarah was proud of the volunteers. While some were more skilled than others, the overall result couldn't have been much better. The small differences in the stitching only proved it had been created by many loving hands.

They carefully folded it and wrapped it in a white sheet. Vanessa left her assistant, Kathy Earhart, in charge of the store and rode with Sarah to the library. Spencer had emptied and shined the lighted display case, and they arranged the quilt inside with a few of their quilting tools. On top they placed photos of the stained glass window that Sarah had framed and one of the group of ladies gathered around the quilting frame, hard at work. Last of all, she positioned a small framed poster advertising the auction.

"You ladies did a great job," Spencer said when everything was in place. "I'll make sure all of our patrons see that and I'll tell them to go to the auction Saturday."

Sarah dropped Vanessa off at Wild Goose Chase a few minutes later.

"I'll bet you feel a big weight off your shoulders now that the quilt is done," Vanessa said.

"I do, but I'll be even more relieved Saturday night, if we've raised enough to pay for the window." Sarah smiled. "You must be glad it's done too—now you can get the quilting frame out of the middle of the store. Would you like me to come in and help you?"

"No, that's all right. Kathy and I can do it," Vanessa said.

It was getting dark when Sarah arrived home. Her phone rang as she let herself in.

"Sarah, it's Lisa. I wanted to apologize and tell you that I just haven't been able to get to that contractor. I fully intended to do it today, but it's been hectic."

"No need to apologize," Sarah said, "but thanks for letting me know. Again, if there's anything I can do unofficially..."

Lisa jumped on her offer so fast that Sarah wondered if that had been the initial purpose of her call. "I suppose you could talk to him, if you don't mention the police department. As an interested party, I mean ... I'd really hate to let this drag on much longer."

"Of course," Sarah said. "Let's see, I think I have his name." She rummaged in her purse for her notebook.

"It's Don Iverson," Lisa said. "He lives a few miles out of town, toward Piedmont. If that's too far—"

"No, no," Sarah said quickly. "So long as this weather holds, I don't mind driving a little ways for a good cause."

"Thank you." Lisa gave her the address. "Just ask him what projects he used his bricks on and if he had any left— you know. The same things we've been asking everybody else."

"Got it. I'll let you know what I learn. As an unofficial, interested party."

"Fantastic. Talk to you soon."

Sarah wondered if Chief Webber knew about this. Perhaps it was better if she didn't ask.

One thing was certain—she would be extra scrupulous when she went about her assignment.

Don Iverson kept his office for the contracting business in his home, and Sarah arrived there at eight the next morning, having spoken with him on the phone the evening before.

"Thanks for seeing me," she said as he let her in.

"Thanks for coming so early. I need to meet my crew in North Adams in an hour."

"This shouldn't take long," Sarah said.

He led her into the cramped office. A printer-copier, file cabinets, and boxes lined the walls on both sides of the narrow room. His desktop was covered with papers, with a phone and a half-full mug of coffee poking out from among them.

"You said you're only interested in the Paget bricks," he noted.

"That's right."

"Well, I didn't keep a strict record of how many bricks of which type went into each project, but I can tell you everywhere we used bricks that season. There were five jobs that required bricks, but the first two were completed before we got that shipment of new bricks that you're interested in, so there are only three where they could possibly have been used. I might have had some left from the other brand—I just don't remember."

"That's all right," Sarah said.

"Okay." Don sat down at his desk and waved at a straight chair for her. He reached for his mug. "Oh, sorry. Would you like some coffee?"

"No, thank you."

He took a gulp from the mug and began sifting the papers. "Right here. These three." He held up three invoices. "I can make copies if you need them. One was the library walks, and the other two were at private residences."

"It would be nice to have copies," Sarah said. She could share them with Lisa later.

"Sure."

While Don stood at the copier, she asked, "Do you know if there were any left after the last job?"

He frowned. "I think there might have been a few. Not enough to do anything major with. Hold on." He peered at one of the invoices for a moment. "Let me check my files."

He took the three copies from the machine and handed them to Sarah, tossing the originals on his desk. He considered the file cabinets and pulled open a drawer.

"Here we go." He selected a folder and opened it, leafing through the papers inside. "It looks like there were a few left, and we left them at the last customer's house. He said he could use them for something—a barbecue, maybe, or a path. My next batch from Build-It was the brand we'd used before."

Sarah shuffled the three papers he had given her, comparing the dates. She located the latest of the three and looked at the name and address. "Very interesting. Thank you."

CHAPTER SIXTEEN

T he Brooks house was a neat garrison with brick facing on the lower level. The new double garage to the left—Don Iverson's contracted project—had brick facing as well. Sarah drove in and sat in her car for a moment, studying the garage. It matched the house so well, she wouldn't have guessed it had been added several years after the house was built.

She dreaded talking to crotchety Jim Brooks, but there was no sense in procrastinating. She got out of the car, went up to the front door, and rang the bell.

Mrs. Brooks, whose brunette hair was streaked with gray, opened the door with a smile.

"Hello," Sarah said. "I'm Sarah Hart. I think we've met before at town functions."

"Of course. How may I help you?"

"Is Mr. Brooks in? I'd like to speak to him."

"I think he's on the phone right now with Jack Handelman. Is it about town business?"

"Yes," Sarah said. The library window qualified as town business, she supposed.

"Won't you come in?" Mrs. Brooks said. "I'll see if he's done yet."

"Thank you." Sarah followed her through the entry, into the large, airy living room. At the far end, glass-paneled patio doors overlooked the back yard, with a view of the Berkshires in the distance. On the left wall, a large seascape hung over a brick fireplace. The sofa and easy chairs, upholstered in burgundy tweed, picked up colors in the rug, cushions, and drapes, but Sarah felt the room was a bit impersonal. It held no portraits of grandchildren or overflowing bookshelves; no television was in evidence. Perhaps this was their more formal living room, and they had a family room elsewhere.

"Have a seat," Mrs. Brooks said. She walked down a hallway. Sarah could hear a muffled voice. Probably Jim was still talking to the chairman of the board of selectmen.

Sarah sat down on the sofa. The glass-topped coffee table before it held a potted aloe plant and a cut glass dish of candy—foil-wrapped mints. She leaned in close for a good look, almost certain she had seen a wrapper from the same type of candy in Lisa Pratt's plastic bag as she had picked up trash from the sidewalk at the library the day they had discovered the broken window.

She hauled in a deep breath and sat back. It wasn't proof of anything—lots of people bought that brand of mints. But maybe she could troll for a little information from

Mrs. Brooks. Her husband must have discussed his old enemy's arrival in town with her.

Mrs. Brooks came back with a regretful smile. "I'm sorry. They're still talking. Could I offer you a cup of coffee?"

"Oh no, thank you," Sarah said. "You know, Steve Furbush is back in town. Didn't he used to serve on the board of selectmen with your husband?"

Mrs. Brooks's smile slipped for a moment. "Yes, he did. I heard he's back. In fact, I heard he may be connected somehow to that business at the library."

"Oh?" Sarah asked. "You mean the broken window?"

Mrs. Brooks shrugged. "People talk."

"Yes. But I saw Steve a couple of days ago. He was very cordial." Sarah hoped that would bring out something more specific.

Mrs. Brooks sat down on the edge of a chair, as though she didn't plan to stay there long. "I haven't seen him myself. Jim's spoken to him, I understand."

"Now when did he get back?" Sarah asked. "I thought he had just arrived when I saw him in the café, but someone else told me he's been in town for weeks."

"Yes, Jim first mentioned it to me around the first of the month. I don't really remember what day."

Sarah decided that if she stayed with that line of questioning, Mrs. Brooks would think it odd, so she changed the subject. "I noticed the brickwork on your garage. That's very nicely done. Does Mr. Brooks do that type of work?"

"No, but thanks. Don Iverson built the garage for us a couple of years ago. We're pleased with it."

"It fits with your house perfectly."

"Yes. And his crew is very professional. It was a bit pricey, but I think you get what you pay for."

"Oh, I agree," Sarah said. "I've seen some other examples of Mr. Iverson's work, and was impressed with that too. But I thought your husband did some of his own handyman projects."

"He does, but the garage was bigger than Jim wanted to tackle. The biggest thing he's built from bricks was a barbecue out back."

"Oh, to match the garage?"

Mrs. Brooks frowned slightly. "Yes. Don had some bricks left over."

Sarah decided she had better say something to explain herself or Mrs. Brooks would be suspicious. She had already asked a great many questions. "I'm thinking of having a permanent barbecue built at my house. I have my son and his family over all the time in the summer, and I know we'd use it a lot. Was it a difficult project?"

"Not really." Her face relaxed. "Jim bought a book with plans in it."

"I'll bet my son could use something like that." Sarah made a mental note to at least mention the idea to Jason. She stood up. "Would it be an imposition if I asked to see it while we wait?"

"Not at all," Mrs. Brooks said. "Come on out through the kitchen." If she thought the request odd for a February day, she didn't show it, and Sarah swiftly followed, casting a glance down the hall. Jim was just coming out of a doorway near the far end.

"Oh, hello, Mr. Brooks." Sarah stopped and waited until he reached her.

"Mrs. Hart. Was there something I could help you with?"

His wife had paused in the kitchen doorway. "I was just going to show her the barbecue, but I'll wait until you're finished talking."

"The barbecue?" Jim stared at Sarah with a baffled expression. "Is that what you came for?"

"Well, not exactly," Sarah said. "I also wanted to speak to you about the silent auction tomorrow."

"Auction? Oh, the one to help pay for the library window."

"That's right."

He walked over to the seating area and sat in the nearest recliner. "What about it? Waste of time and money, if you ask me."

"Well, I just thought that, since the board approved the fund-raising end of it, it might be helpful to the Friends of the Library if you came to the auction, even if you only stayed a few minutes."

"Why would I want to do that?" He glared at her.

Sarah decided the slight discomfort he was causing her now was preferable to what could happen if she pressed him about the bricks. The conversation could get really uncomfortable, given his already antagonistic mood.

She managed to smile and glanced toward his wife, hoping for a smidgen of support. "I realize you didn't favor this option—replacing the stained glass window—but since it's going forward, I simply thought you might want to throw your support behind the effort. A lot of people in town look up to you, and they follow your leadership."

Sarah could see his expression changing subtly and decided she was on the right track. Maybe a little more flattery would get her out of here without more unpleasantness.

"Smoothing ruffled feathers can go a long way in small-town politics," she said. "After all, you have to keep on working with the other board members, and if you showed a gracious spirit about this, they might give you their support when another issue comes up and you have to look to them for help."

He was still frowning but not as severely, and she could see that he was considering her words.

Mrs. Brooks stepped closer to Sarah. "Maybe we could go over for a little while tomorrow, Jim. Just make an appearance. And I heard they've got a nice chain saw as one of the auction items. You know you need a new one. You could bid on it."

"That would be a magnanimous gesture," Sarah said. She wondered if she could get Abby McCormick to take a picture of him doing it. Now, that would make Jim's day, if he got a little favorable publicity out of it. She didn't dare suggest it, but she said, "I understand Abby McCormick will be there to take pictures and write a story for the *Monitor*."

"Well…" Jim pushed himself up out of the chair. "I'll think about it. Who's donating the chain saw?"

Sarah opened her mouth to tell him she didn't know, but his wife jumped in.

"Maple Hill Hardware. You could probably call them and ask them which model it is."

"Maybe I will," Jim said. "My old one isn't worth trying to fix."

"Well, thank you so much," Sarah said. "I should be going."

"Do you still want to see the barbecue?" Mrs. Brooks asked.

Sarah wished she had forgotten, but she smiled brightly. Nothing would make Jim suspicious more quickly than if she lost all interest now. "Certainly, if it's not too much trouble."

"Not at all." Mrs. Brooks smiled and gestured toward the kitchen. "Right this way."

The kitchen's country French décor appealed to Sarah, and under other circumstances she would have remarked on its loveliness and stopped to see all the special features. However, she hadn't reached the middle of the room before she realized Jim had followed them, and she didn't want to prolong the visit if he was going to tag along.

Her hostess opened a mullioned patio door onto the back deck. "Oh, it's chilly out here."

"I'm sorry," Sarah said.

"It's all right. You can see the barbecue over there." Mrs. Brooks stepped outside and pointed.

Sarah crossed the deck to the railing and gazed at the brick barbecue. "Oh yes. Your husband did a very nice job." She was sure Jim was right behind her, hearing every word.

Snow covered the back lawn, but the path along the back of the house had been cleared. Without asking permission, she went down the steps and walked all the way to the barbecue and gazed at the bricks. Around the chimney area, she could plainly see the "Paget" designation on several bricks.

"It only took me a weekend."

Turning, she found Jim standing close behind her, eyeing his handiwork with satisfaction.

His wife stood on the deck several yards away, hugging herself and shivering. An expression of mild puzzlement was fixed on her face.

"It looks great," Sarah said. "How is it for cookouts?"

"Terrific," Jim said. "We used it a lot last year. Even had a family reunion here in August. We served about thirty people."

"That must have been quite an event," Sarah said. "I love reunions. Well, thank you for showing me." On impulse, she decided to throw caution to the wind and try one last ploy for information. "You know, Mrs. Brooks was telling me that Steve Furbush has been back in Maple Hill most of this month. I ran into him the other day, and I thought he had just gotten back, but I guess I was one of the last to know."

Jim's face darkened, and Sarah wondered if she had bungled badly asking him directly.

"He's been hanging around. Up to no good, if you ask me. I heard the police had him in for questioning."

"Oh?" Sarah glanced toward the deck. Mrs. Brooks still waited there for them, and she might be able to hear the conversation. "You don't think he had something to do with the broken window, do you?" she asked Jim in a conspiratorial whisper.

"I wouldn't be surprised. I know he was in town when it happened."

As Sarah reached the deck, she looked down at her snowy shoes. "Oh dear. I don't want to track this into the house. Maybe I should just go around."

Mrs. Brooks pointed toward the back of the garage. "You can go out through there."

Jim opened his mouth as if to say something, but then shut it and opened a small door, and Sarah saw that it did indeed lead into the garage. Mrs. Brooks came along the pathway, rubbing the arms of her red sweater and looking puzzled.

Sarah went inside and Jim followed her. A gray Toyota sedan and a black Ford pickup took up most of the space, but where they came in, at the back of the garage, Jim's workshop was set up. It was a lot like Gerry's basement workshop, with a variety of tools hung neatly on the wall over the bench. A jigsaw and a wood lathe told her Jim was serious about his woodworking.

Mrs. Brooks came in behind her husband and closed the door.

"Are you sure you don't want to go back inside, Mrs. Hart?" she asked. "I've got coffee all made, if you two want it."

"I don't think so," Jim replied. "Unless Mrs. Hart has more questions." He sounded rather stern, and Sarah shook her head.

"I think we covered everything, thank you. I appreciate your time."

Mrs. Brooks went to the two steps leading up to the door into the house. Jim followed her and pushed a button on the wall that started the nearest overhead door rising. Sarah headed toward it, continuing to look about.

In the corner near the steps sat a small stack of bricks, only ten or twelve of them. Something caught her eye. She stopped and looked closely at them. A small spray of green paint stained the floor beside them, and a little had landed on the near edge of a couple of the bricks.

She glanced up at Jim. His wife had opened the kitchen door, and he lingered at the bottom of the steps, watching her.

"It looks like you've been doing some painting," Sarah said.

His wife looked back. "Yes, he spray-painted the garden cart, and he got a little on the floor."

"Faye," Jim said.

He had spoken quietly, but with a firm warning in his voice. He definitely didn't want her to say any more.

His gaze raked coldly over Sarah. "What exactly are you looking for, Mrs. Hart?"

She tried to smile, but she couldn't. The look in his eyes was too hard. He knew exactly what she wanted.

"It's not important, really. I'm so glad you're going to the auction tomorrow."

Jim glanced down at the brick pile, then back at her. "I'd like you to leave, please."

His wife's jaw dropped. "Jim, really—"

"This has nothing to do with you, Faye." He glared at Sarah. "Please go."

Sarah stepped toward them, knowing the ruse was over. "Mr. Brooks, don't you think it's time you sat down and talked to Chief Webber?"

"What for? To have him send someone to remove you from my home? What don't you understand?"

Sarah drew in a deep breath. "Oh, I understand, Mr. Brooks."

"Well, I don't." Faye looked bleakly from Sarah to her husband.

"Thank you for your hospitality, Mrs. Brooks." Sarah turned and walked out through the garage door to her car. She made herself keep her steps even and not too quick. When she opened the car door and turned, Jim stood in the garage doorway scowling at her. She got into her car and started it, then backed out of the driveway. She drove down the street, but only until she could no longer see the Brooks house. She pulled over to the curb and took out her phone with shaking hands.

"Hello, this is Sarah Hart. I'd like to speak to Officer Pratt, please. It's important."

She was afraid they would be too late. Jim would have time to remove the evidence before the officers got there. The paint would still be on the floor, but she wasn't sure if that would be conclusive or not. She made herself sit still, though she watched the end of the driveway constantly. At last Lisa came on the phone. Quickly Sarah told her what had happened and her fears that Brooks was destroying clues.

"We'll be right there," Lisa said.

The minutes passed, and Sarah kept checking the time. Nearly ten minutes elapsed before a police car rolled down the street and pulled up in front of the Brooks home. Sarah started her engine and drove to the end of the block. She turned around and crept back along the street until she had a view of Jim's driveway. His truck was now sitting on the pavement, halfway down the drive, and two officers— Hopkins and Pratt—were standing beside it, talking to Jim. He must have been trying to leave when they pulled up.

Sarah was about to move on when Officer Hopkins climbed up into the back of the pickup. He held up a spray paint can for a minute, examined the label, and dropped it into an evidence bag. Then he picked up a brick and looked closely at it.

Sarah let out her pent-up breath and eased the car down the street.

Sarah's doorbell rang a couple of hours later, while she loaded the dishwasher. She hurried to the front entrance and opened the door. Lisa Pratt stood there in her uniform.

"Hi, Sarah. Thanks for the call. I think we may have our vandal, but he's not admitting it yet."

Sarah gulped. "Do you think I'm wrong? I didn't intend things to go that far, but when I saw the green paint ... I'd hate to bring false accusations against anyone."

"No, I think you're right," Lisa said. "I'm sorry you ended up in a tight spot. I could tell Brooks wasn't happy with you. Can you come down to the station and give a statement?"

"Sure," Sarah said.

"You can wait until tomorrow if that's better for you."

Sarah smiled and shook her head. "The auction is tomorrow. I'd better do it today." She got her coat and purse and followed the squad car to the police station. Lisa took her statement in a small interview room.

"Is he still here in the building?" Sarah asked when she had finished answering Lisa's questions and writing out her statement.

"No. He had his wife call his lawyer before we even left their house, and the lawyer met him at the station. He's gone home, but he'll be arraigned Monday."

"He posted bail that fast?"

"Apparently he has a lot of connections."

"Do you think there will be enough evidence to prosecute him?" Sarah asked.

"By the time we're done, I certainly hope so," Lisa said.

CHAPTER SEVENTEEN

Saturday's skies were a clear, crisp blue, and cottony clouds shrouded the mountaintops. Sarah dressed in green slacks, a cream-colored top, and a tapestry jacket. The temperature hovered just above freezing, and she felt a yearning for spring as she refilled her bird feeder.

After breakfast, she drove to the middle school. The auction was scheduled to open at nine o'clock. People could come in and bid throughout the day, and door prizes would be awarded every hour. The bidding would close at four, and between four and five o'clock, Cate and Irene would announce who had won each item. Sarah didn't plan to stay all day, but she wanted to be on hand for at least the opening and closing hours.

Cate, Irene, and the other auction committee members were finishing the last-minute details of the setup when she arrived, straightening tablecloths and checking the tickets for the door prizes. Irene had brought the quilt over from the library, and it was given the most prominent spot in the room.

"Sarah," Neil Lawton called when he saw her. When she walked over to join him, he asked, "I heard Jim Brooks was arrested yesterday for breaking the window. Do you know if it's true?"

Sarah had expected some questions today but not quite so soon. "Well, I know the police took him in for questioning," she said. "It's my understanding that he is being charged."

Neil was an accountant, and he had been a friend of Sarah's since their school days, though he was a few years older. "I can't believe it," he said. "Of all people. I mean, Jim's done so much for the town. Why would he vandalize town property?"

"I don't know," Sarah said. "It surprised me too."

Neil shook his head. "They must have made a mistake. He's the hardest working public official I know."

Sarah changed the subject. "Are you in charge of the bidding sheets?"

"No, Cate is. I'm displaying the door prizes. A few of them haven't arrived yet, so I guess I'll call the donors and see if they're bringing them."

Sarah was glad to see him back on track for the auction. She looked around at the displays. The committee must have spent hours last night getting things in place. Near the cafeteria window, two women were setting up a few small tables and chairs for the refreshments area.

Most of the auction items were laid out on long rows of tables set end to end, down the length of the school's cafeteria. The quilt was draped over a box and an easel on a table at the far end of the room. Next to it stood the colonial-style quilt rack donated by the Berkshire Furniture Company. The women had managed to arrange the quilt so that a maximum amount of the design showed. The vibrant colors drew the eyes of everyone who entered, and the prospective bidders would walk toward it as they made their way between the tables, examining the other merchandise. On the table beside the quilt stood a photo of the stained glass window and the framed list of all the volunteers who had worked on the quilt.

"Irene, everything looks wonderful," Sarah told her friend.

"Oh, thank you," Irene said, sticking her pen behind her ear so she could adjust the arrangement of a set of dishes. "I love this pattern. I may have to bid on the set."

Sarah looked at her watch. Twenty minutes until opening time. "What can I do to help?"

"Well, Cate's gone to make a new bidding sheet for the weekend at the Mountainview Inn. The one I made had a typo. Maybe you could just walk around and make sure each item has its clipboard and bidding sheet and a pen that works."

"I sure can." Sarah set off on her task, admiring the merchandise. She was amazed at the variety of things the committee had brought in, and the value for the buyers. Liam's contribution from the Spotted Dog made her grin. A china Dalmatian sat with his glossy paw on an envelope containing a fifty-dollar gift certificate for either the bookstore or the café.

Sarah tried every one of the pens on a scratch pad to make sure the bidders wouldn't have any excuses not to write down their names. When she had checked all of the sign-up sheets and pens, Cate hurried in from the school's office with the last paper in her hand.

"Hi, Sarah," Cate called. "Irene, we've got four phone bids already."

"Phone bids?" Sarah asked.

"Yes, we advertised that we'd take them, and we've got two ladies in the office taking calls."

"It's time to open." Irene tucked a roll of tape into a box under one of the tables. "Shall we?"

The three of them went to the front doors. Dozens of people waited outside. Irene pushed the double doors open and stood back to welcome the crowd.

Martha was the first one inside. "I'm so glad you opened. It's cold out there!"

"Well, come right in and get warm," Irene said. "The committee is selling coffee, hot chocolate, soft drinks, and snacks at the cafeteria window."

The people spread out over the room, chatting and eyeing the auction items. Aiden McLean and his wife came over to speak to Sarah and Irene.

"You've done a marvelous job," Aiden said, taking Irene's hand.

"Oh, thank you. Tell me that again tonight, when we've added up all the money," Irene said with a laugh. She looked toward the tables. "I'd better circulate, in case people have questions."

After she walked away, Mrs. McLean said to Sarah, "I'm going to bid on the quilt. I saw it yesterday at the library, and I fell in love with it. I can just see it on our living room wall."

"Now, dear, don't get too carried away," Aiden said with a smile.

"Of course not." His wife leaned closer to Sarah. "He wants to bid on the golf clubs, and we've agreed on a maximum amount for each of us."

"That sounds like a good way to do it," Sarah said with a smile.

When the McLeans had walked off toward the exhibits, Sarah ambled that way as well, greeting several friends on the way. She noted a cluster of people around the quilt display. It seemed to be drawing the attention she had hoped it would. She couldn't resist going back to the china Dalmatian. In her mind's eye, she could see that little dog in the sitting area at the top of the stairs back home. Bending over the clipboard, she wrote her name and a bid of twenty-five dollars to start things off.

"You can't resist him, then?" said a deep, lilting voice behind her.

She turned, laughing, to face Liam. "He's adorable. Maybe a smidgen less cute than Murphy, but you're right."

Liam chuckled. "Couldn't find a corgi on short notice, so I had to take a Dalmatian."

"I don't think most people will mind," Sarah said. "You've got a lot of Dalmatians at the store." Liam's décor included several stuffed and ceramic spotted dogs, as well as the white awning with black spots over his front door.

"True." Liam held out a disposable coffee cup. "Brought you something."

Sarah smelled the steaming liquid through the small opening. "Oh, vanilla chai. Thank you!"

"You're very welcome. I hope the auction committee won't care that I brought it in from the store. Didn't realize they were selling concessions."

"I don't think anyone will throw you out. Especially if you bid on something."

Liam gazed toward the quilt. "So that's the main attraction." He walked toward it, and Sarah kept pace. "Seems to be drawing a lot of interest."

"Yes, I'm pleased about that," Sarah said. "The ladies worked very hard on it, and I think it came out well."

"If the brouhaha ever calms down, maybe I can get close enough to put me name down."

Sarah looked up into his dancing green eyes. "Don't feel you have to, just because it was my project."

"Not just because of that. 'Tis a lovely piece of artwork and a worthy cause."

She couldn't argue with that.

"Of course, I want to bid on the tackle box too, and I heard that the filling station donated a card for fifty gallons of gas."

"Yes, that's quite a prize," Sarah said. "With gas as high as it is now, maybe I ought to bid on it too."

They walked around the tables slowly, discussing several of the items up for bids. After Liam had written down his offers on several items, he smiled at her with regret. "Well, I suppose I need to get back to the store. I told Karen I'd only be gone an hour, and then I'd let her take an hour off to come over and have a look-see."

"That sounds like a good exchange."

"Will you still be here later?" Liam asked.

"I'm staying for a while, and then I think I'll go home and catch up on some work I've let go. I'll come back toward the end though. I want to be here when they announce the winners."

He squeezed her hand. "All right. I hope you have a lovely and successful day."

At ten o'clock, Cate turned on the microphone and announced, "Ladies and gentlemen, we're going to draw the winner of our first door prize. In this hour we're giving a coupon for a free large pizza at Floro's."

Everyone paused to listen as Cate held up a jar full of tickets and Irene pulled one out. Cate took it and looked at it.

She grinned and leaned toward the microphone. "And the winner is Colin Maplethorpe."

Sarah looked over the crowd. She hadn't realized Colin and Mandy were present, but she spotted them as Colin broke away to go and claim his prize. Martha and Ernie stood with Mandy, their daughter-in-law. Sarah walked over and greeted them.

"Well, hi, Ernie. I knew Martha was here, but when did you sneak in?"

"I came with the kids," Ernie said.

"After I looked around, I called him and told him to get over here," Martha said. "There are some beautiful things here."

"I'm glad you and Colin brought him," Sarah said to Mandy.

They still stood talking a few minutes later, and Irene rushed over and grabbed Sarah's arm. "The bidding on the quilt is already past two hundred dollars!"

"Wow, that's great," Martha said. "I'd better start writing my name down on some clipboards, or I'll miss out on everything."

"Can't let that happen," Ernie said.

Sarah smiled as she watched them go. "Well, Irene, I think that's a good start for the first hour. I believe I'll go home now and come back this afternoon, if you have enough volunteers to help you."

"I think every one of the committee members is here," Irene said. "You go ahead. Thanks for being here this morning though."

"I wouldn't have missed it. Call me if you need me." Sarah went to the door and looked back. The cafeteria surged with eager bidders. She smiled and went out to her car.

She spent a quiet day, and at quarter to three she went back to the school. The crowd, though not quite as large as it had been that morning, was still plentiful, and growing every minute as bidders anticipated the revelation of the winners. Abby McCormick strolled the perimeter of the room with her camera, ready for a good photo opportunity. Sarah found Martha helping Irene prepare to draw the three o'clock door prizes.

"Oh, Sarah, I'm glad you're back," Martha called. "Did you see the latest bid on the quilt?"

"Not yet. What is it?"

"Don't tell her," Irene said quickly. "Make her go look."

Sarah shook her head in amusement. "Just like a couple of kids."

"You're only as old as you feel," Irene retorted.

"All right, I'll go look." Sarah made her way to the quilt display, easing gently through the crowd. Hannah Grace stood beside the table, talking to Vanessa Sawyer and another woman, who held the clipboard.

"Yeah, we thought about putting the quilt on the quilt rack to display it," Vanessa was saying, "but since the rack is one of the items for bid too, we thought that might be confusing. And people can see it better without the quilt on it."

"Hi, Sarah." Hannah's face lit up. "Did you hear? The bidding on the quilt just went over the thousand mark!"

Sarah's jaw dropped. "I had no idea."

The woman holding the clipboard looked down at it with a rueful expression. "I wanted to bid on it, but it's a little out of my league ow."

"It's a wonderful tribute to all the hard work you gals did," Vanessa said. "Worth every penny, if you ask me."

"May I?" Sarah asked.

The woman handed the clipboard over, and Sarah scanned down the names. Several of her friends had bid early, and Aiden McLean's wife had weighed in at five hundred dollars. After that came two names she didn't recognize, and the final one so far—Bob Hutchins IV.

"Mr. Hutchins bid on the quilt?" she asked, astounded at both his gesture and the amount.

"He sure did," Hannah replied with a grin.

"Is he here?" Sarah looked around, hoping to spot the tall artisan.

"No, he phoned in his bid about twenty minutes ago. Said he wished he could come over, but since he couldn't, he'd bid by phone."

"Wow." Sarah stared at the clipboard again. "Why would he bid so much, when the money is to help us pay him?"

Hannah smiled. "He said he loves the window and the quilt, and he wants it for his wife's birthday."

"Sarah!" Martha hurried over and halted beside her, panting. She grabbed Sarah's arm. "Cate just got another phone bid on the quilt. You'll never guess who."

"Doesn't matter who," Hannah said. "How much?"

Sarah chuckled. "Of course it matters who. Tell us."

Martha looked deep into her eyes and said distinctly, "Marjory Middlefield."

"The author?" Vanessa shrieked.

Sarah smiled. Vanessa loved historical novels, and Marjory Middlefield was her all-time favorite author.

"Ladies and gentlemen," Cate Goodman said via the microphone, "I have a very special announcement. We've just received another bid on the stained glass window quilt, from the well-known author Marjory Middlefield. She phoned us a few minutes ago from her home in Lexington. The top bid is now twelve hundred dollars."

Martha beamed at Sarah. "With all the money from other items, we should have plenty to pay Mr. Hutchins."

"That's right," Hannah said. "The last time I looked, several items had bids as high as the value of the item or higher."

"Well, I guess the Friends of the Library will have to decide what to do with the extra," Vanessa said.

Sarah looked toward the door and saw Spencer Hewitt and Karen Bancroft enter together. She walked over and met them as they reached the first display tables.

"Hi! I hope we're not too late," Spencer said.

"Oh no, you have plenty of time to spend money," Sarah replied with a smile. "It looks as though we'll more than meet our goal, though, so don't feel you have to break your budget."

Karen said, "We've been really busy at the store today. I was going to come over this morning after Liam came back, but we got a big rush that lasted through lunch. I think a lot of people went from here to the café. It was great for us, but I was afraid I wouldn't get a chance to come over and see the displays."

"I went over and kidnapped her," Spencer said with a shy smile.

"A bold move that seems to have paid off," Sarah said. "I'll let you enjoy the auction while there's time."

"Thanks," Spencer said.

Karen glanced at him and grinned. "We're having dinner together afterward. It's our late Valentine's Day date."

"Wonderful," Sarah said. As she turned away, she wondered fleetingly if she and Liam would ever have theirs.

She noticed another couple and halted in her tracks. Standing not six feet away and exclaiming over a basket of children's sports equipment were Carol Stites and Steve Furbush. They stood close together with hands clasped. Sarah walked over to them and touched Carol's sleeve.

"Hello. It's good to see you both again."

Carol smiled at her. "Hello, Mrs. Hart. Steve's told me how kind you and your son have been to him."

"We were glad to help," Sarah said. "Are you still at the Maple Leaf, Steve?"

"Actually, no," he said. "Another of my old classmates heard I was in town and invited me to stay with him and his family. And he helped me get a lead on a job. I had an interview yesterday afternoon."

"I'm glad to hear that."

Carol looked up at him. "Steve hopes to settle in Maple Hill again, if he does get the job. This one or some other job. He applied at the market last week, and they said today they might have an opening for him, so that's two possibilities."

"I'm trying to be optimistic," Steve said sheepishly. "It seems there are quite a few people in this town who are willing to take a chance on me after all."

"Oh, excuse me just a second." Carol stepped away to speak to an acquaintance.

Steve turned to Sarah with a rueful smile. "I guess I owe you an apology."

"What for?" Sarah asked.

"I didn't level with you completely the other day."

She studied his face. "I was pretty sure there was more you weren't telling us. You knew who did it, didn't you?"

He nodded. "I called Jason later and gave him the whole story. Thanks again for connecting me with him."

"You're welcome. I hope everything works out for you."

Carol turned and beckoned to Steve, and he nodded to Sarah and went to join her.

"Well, Lord," Sarah said softly, "once again, you've worked in strange and mysterious ways."

A few minutes later Jason came in with the twins.

"Grandma," Audrey said, bouncing on her toes, "can you show us where Mrs. Maplethorpe's afghan is? Mom wants us to bid on it for her, if it's not too late."

Amy gave her a quick hug and added, "Yeah, Mom saw it while Mrs. Maplethorpe was working on it, and she thinks it would be a good gift for Aunt Jenna."

"That's a great idea," Sarah said. She put an arm around each girl and guided them toward the afghan.

Jason said, "While you girls do that, I'm going to check out the tools."

Amy rolled her eyes. "He wants the chain saw. Mr. Carper and Mr. Maplethorpe were telling him about it out in the parking lot."

"There's been a lot of interest in that," Sarah said.

They found Martha's afghan, which already had eight bids. Audrey carefully wrote in her name and the maximum amount Maggie had authorized.

"Good job," Sarah said. "Now why don't we mosey over to the refreshments window and get some hot chocolate?"

"Sounds good to me," Amy said.

At four o'clock, Irene and Cate stood together at the microphone.

"Folks, it's with great reluctance that we bring our auction to a close," Irene said. "Thank you all so much for coming out and bidding so generously."

Cate leaned into the mic and said, "Our auction committee members are now collecting the bidding sheets. In just a few minutes, we'll start reading off the winners. And while you wait, we're going to draw names for the final two door prizes of the day."

The cafeteria was crowded with people, and more kept coming in, eager to hear the results of the auction. Winners who weren't present for the announcements would be notified afterward by phone, but Sarah couldn't help thinking most of them had returned to get in on the excitement.

While Cate held up the jar of tickets, Irene went to help the other committee members tally the sheets and verify the winners.

Cate said into the microphone, "Our own librarian, Spencer Hewitt, has agreed to draw the names for the final door prizes. Mr. Hewitt, thanks for doing this, and we hope that very soon we'll have some good news for you and all the people who love the library."

"Thanks, Cate," Spencer said as he stepped up beside her. "What am I supposed to do?"

Everyone chuckled.

"Just pull out a couple of names for us," Cate said. "First, we have a handwoven sweet grass basket from the Raven's Wing." Another of the volunteers held the basket up so the crowd could see it.

"All right." Spencer reached into the jar, drew a ticket, and handed it to Cate.

Cate looked at it and smiled. "And the winner is Mavis Hoyt."

A shriek came from across the room, and Mavis made her way through the throng.

"Excuse me. Pardon. Excuse me." She arrived red-faced and grinning at the microphone.

"Here you go," Cate said, handing her the prize.

"Oh, thank you so much," Mavis said, examining her treasure.

Cate said to Spencer, "One more. The final prize is dinner for two at the Old Mill."

Spencer drew out the ticket. Cate looked at it and said, "Our final winner is Steve Furbush."

Sarah joined the others in applause as Steve walked over to accept his prize.

"Thanks," Steve said to Cate and Irene. "This is fantastic." He accepted the envelope and waved to the clapping crowd.

Irene walked over to join Cate, carrying a clipboard.

"It looks like we have our final results," Cate said. "Folks, here's our cochair Irene Stuart to tell you who won the bid on each item."

The crowd quieted. Irene started with the lower-valued merchandise and worked her way higher. Martha's afghan was bought by a woman expecting her first grandchild. She had slipped in behind Audrey and made a last-minute bid.

"Don't be too disappointed," Sarah told the twins. "It brought in a good amount for the window, and I'm pretty sure Mrs. Maplethorpe would make another one for your mom if she asked her."

Jason topped the bids for the chain saw. If Liam had bid on the gasoline card, he had missed out on it—Aiden McLean had outbid all the others. His wife had to be satisfied with the certificate she had bid highest on, for a custom cake from the market's bakery.

Finally Irene said into the microphone, "And now, folks, our last item—the beautiful quilt made by more than a dozen volunteers, led by Sarah Hart."

A hush spread over the crowd.

"The quilt's new owner is giving twelve hundred dollars to our fund. She writes history, and now she's part of our town's history. She's the famous author so many of us love, Marjory Middlefield."

Everyone applauded wildly, but Sarah felt just a little regret that Bob Hutchins hadn't gotten the quilt.

Cate raised her hands and the crowd quieted once more. "And now our grand total." She nodded to Irene.

Smiling, Irene said, "Ladies and gentlemen, we've raised four thousand twelve dollars—"

Anything after that was lost in the raucous cheering.

CHAPTER EIGHTEEN

Sarah drove to the historical society on Monday morning and was surprised to find Jack Handelman inside talking to Irene.

"Hi, Sarah," Irene called with a big smile.

"Mrs. Hart, good to see you," Jack said. "I was just delivering the good news to the auction committee chairmen. In fact, I'm going over to see Cate Goodman next. The selectmen have authorized the expenditure."

"Isn't it great?" Irene asked. "They called Mr. Hutchins, and it's a done deal. He'll start work on the window next week."

"Fantastic," Sarah said.

Jack nodded. "The board was very impressed that you raised so much money."

"And of course, the Friends of the Library can use the extra for whatever we want," Irene added. "We thought maybe one thing would be to buy some authoritative books on stained glass craftsmanship."

"I like that," Sarah said. "We might also want to consider funding extra hours for the part-time library assistants. Spencer had to lay off one worker last fall, and I know he can always use extra help."

"Oh yes," Irene said. "There are so many people looking for work, I know a part-time job would be a real blessing to someone."

Jack nodded. "Whatever you decide, of course, but..."

"What were you thinking?" Sarah asked.

"Some new locks, maybe. I looked over the maintenance budget for the year, and there's not much there."

"*Hmm*," Sarah said, "I suppose we could discuss it."

"It's really the town's responsibility," Irene said.

"Yes, but now that we know how easy it was for someone to go in and out of the building at will, I think we should consider replacing all the locks," Jack said. "And maybe put in some sort of security system."

"Sounds like a major project," Sarah said. "The board might want to suggest it in next year's budget." Meanwhile, she thought, the town really hadn't done such a bad job of keeping watch. She thought of all the people who had noticed oddities and reported them.

"Spencer would probably address the board about the need for it," Irene said. "And I do think the residents would vote for it—at least the locks and a few new dead bolts."

"Well, I'll certainly recommend we do something. I'll get over to Ms. Goodman's and let her know."

When Jack was out the door, Irene turned to Sarah.

"What can I help you with? Are you working on something new?"

"Not yet," she said. "I just came in to see you."

"I'm glad you came while Jack was here. Fantastic news, eh? The window should be finished in a few weeks."

"Yes. I hope you'll get lots of photographs when they put the new one in, for the town archives."

"I will," Irene said, "and I expect Abby McCormick will do another big story on it. Wasn't her piece on the auction great?"

"It was super. I thoroughly enjoyed it with my breakfast yesterday."

"She got a great picture of Hannah."

Sarah smiled. "The one of you and Cate was pretty good too."

When she left a few minutes later, she decided to stop by the library. Now that the quilt was finished, she might have time to do more reading, and she wanted to touch base with Spencer. The parking spaces in front were filled, so she turned the corner and found a spot on Park Street, near the side door.

A man in a black jacket and knit cap was standing on the brick walkway, staring up at the covered window frame.

"Well, Mr. Furbush," Sarah said as she shut her car door. "How are you today?"

He turned, frowning, but smiled after a moment. "Not bad. And it's Steve. I was just thinking about the window and what a pity it is that this happened."

"Now that we know who did it, I hope we can put it behind us," Sarah said.

"I still feel crummy about it."

Sarah studied his face. "I don't know the details—Jason didn't tell me anything you said at the police station."

Steve let out a big sigh. "I didn't do it, but I still feel like it was partly my fault. You were right when you asked if I knew about who did it. And I also knew why. But I don't think it's something that should be told all over town."

"Everyone is amazed that Jim would do something like this," Sarah said gently. She had known about Jim Brooks's temper, but the wanton destruction of the window still baffled her. "I'm sure the people would like to know why he did it."

"It was because of me," Steve said.

Sarah stared at him. "Didn't you tell us that you had nothing to do with breaking the window?"

"That . . . that wasn't strictly true." Steve sighed. "I didn't break that window, Mrs. Hart, but if I hadn't come back to Maple Hill, it probably wouldn't have been broken."

Sarah stepped closer to him. "Does this have to do with the old feud between you and Jim?"

"You could say that. He heard somewhere that I was back in town. I'm talking about a few weeks ago, right after I got here and before all this happened."

"I heard he had gone around asking about you." Sarah remembered the photo Mavis had shown her. "I also heard that he had caught up to you over near the market."

"Yeah. He lit into me the minute he saw me. We had a few choice words, and he basically told me I wasn't welcome here. I don't remember what I said, but it probably wasn't very polite. And I walked away. I probably would have left town then, but it was later that day that I ran into Carol. She helped me believe that not everyone in town felt the way Jim did."

"I'm sure most of us don't," Sarah said.

"Well, maybe so. I'd like to think that. Anyhow, a day or two later—the day of the snowstorm—Jim apparently saw me again and followed me. I didn't realize it. I had been out to Carol's house to eat supper, and when she took me back to the library, I had her drop me off at the corner. I didn't want people to connect her to the library. The only thing is, Jim was out for some reason. Why he was walking in the snow, I don't know."

Sarah shrugged. "Maybe he stayed late at his office that day. He often walks to and from work, and that route takes him right past the library."

"Yeah, you're probably right. Anyway, he saw me. I didn't know it, but he followed me down Park Street. I had just gone in the side door and was heading for the storage room, and someone pounded on the door behind me. Scared me out of my wits."

"I'll bet." Sarah shivered, just imagining the situation. "Did you open the door?"

"No. I was afraid it was a cop. I went up the stairs to the landing and looked out. You couldn't see out through most of the colored glass pieces, but there were a couple of small pieces of clear glass in the border that you could see through."

Sarah nodded. "I hadn't thought about it, but you're right. I noticed them while I was drawing the quilt design. I ended up putting pale blue fabric in those spots." She had wondered about those at the time. Maybe Bob Hutchins could tell her if that was common in stained glass windows—a sort of peephole for those inside.

"Well, the corner street light was on," Steve said. "I couldn't see Jim at first. He knocked again, and then he stepped away from the door. I saw his face, and I got this awful feeling. I knew my time of sleeping at the library was over, and maybe something a lot worse would happen. Because I didn't have a doubt that Jim would turn me in to the police."

"But he didn't," Sarah said.

"No."

"Because then he would have had to tell them what he did next. He saw you looking out at him, didn't he?"

Steve gave her a rueful smile. "That's right. And when he saw me, he threw a brick at the window and broke it. And he certainly didn't want the police—or anyone else—to know he did that, so he didn't tell them. He just … went home, I guess. It must have brought him to his senses when he saw what he'd done."

"You know, there's still one thing that puzzles me," Sarah said. "Why did he have the brick with him? I'm sure he didn't walk around all the time with a broken brick in his pocket."

"That's a good point," Steve said. "I'll have to ask the police if they've gotten an answer to that out of him, because the only explanations I can think of turn my blood cold."

Sarah had to agree. "Well, Steve, it's been nice talking to you. I don't suppose you've heard anything about that interview you had Friday."

He smiled. "As a matter of fact, they called and left me a message with Carol. Said they'd like to have me come in again Wednesday. A second interview is good, right?"

"Very good. I wish you the best."

"Thanks."

Sarah went in through the side door and walked to the circulation desk. Madeline was on duty.

"Well, hi," she said with a big smile. "Spencer's helping someone with the computer catalog."

Sarah lingered near the rack of new books until Spencer was free. He spotted her and walked over smiling.

"Well, hello. How are you today?"

"Great," Sarah said. "Have the selectmen given you the official word?"

"Jack Handelman was just here. We're all set on the window."

Sarah nodded. "I was with Irene when he told her. I'm glad everything's approved and things are moving forward."

"Me too."

Sarah said, "Did you have a nice time Saturday night?"

"Very much so. Karen and I are going out again next weekend. We're going to the play at the university—they're doing *A Midsummer Night's Dream*."

"Sounds like fun." She noted the sparkle in Spencer's eyes.

"Karen's never seen it. She asked me to check out a copy for her, so she can read it between now and then. Isn't that something?"

"Yes, it is. I'm sure she'll enjoy the play—and I hope you have a great time."

By Tuesday, Sarah was feeling the tiniest bit blue. The turmoil of the auction was over, and the yellow roses had wilted beyond reviving. But she hadn't heard from Liam since Saturday. She had deliberately kept busy around the house, hoping he would call her.

They were long since past the early stages of liking and wondering about each other. Or were they?

An hour after she knew the bookstore and café had closed that evening, she looked at her calendar. February was coming to a close. Since it was a leap year, one day remained.

She went to her computer and brought up a search engine. Typing in "Leap Day," she almost felt guilty. Wasn't she too old to play flirtation games? She tossed that aside and read the article at a site she had used before for historical information.

"A tradition was introduced many centuries ago to allow women to propose to men during a leap year, especially on Leap Day."

Out loud, she said, "Well, I wasn't planning to go that far." She read on with interest.

"A man was expected to pay a penalty if he refused a marriage offer from a woman. The tradition's origin stemmed from an old Irish tale referring to Saint Bridget striking a deal with Saint Patrick to allow women to propose to men every four years."

When she read the words "old Irish tale," Sarah burst out laughing. Before allowing time to talk herself out of it, she snatched up her phone.

"Sarah, me darlin', I'm so glad you called," Liam said.

"Really?" The tension fell away at the sound of his voice.

"Most decidedly. I meant to call you all day, but it seemed every time I turned around, I got interrupted. First it was a customer who needed assistance and then it was the inspector showing up without warning..."

"You poor thing," Sarah said. "I hope you can unwind tonight."

"Thank you. I'm beat. What's going on with you?"

She hesitated. Maybe this wasn't the right time to bring up their nondate after all. She didn't want him to feel pressured, especially when he was tired. And yet, she couldn't imagine him not being amused by what she had discovered.

"Sarah?" he asked. "Anything wrong?"

"No, it's just—well, we haven't managed to reschedule our date yet, and I—I miss seeing you, Liam."

"Well, there. We can do something about that, can't we?"

Sarah's anxiety vanished, and she smiled. There was nothing like honesty to bring about a resolution to a problem. "Of course. Liam, have you ever heard of Leap Day?"

"Now you're talking Irish lore. Of course I've heard of it, and I'm thinking that's tomorrow. Am I right?"

"Yes, you are. I just now learned it was an Irish invention."

"Well, we didn't invent the day, of course, but we used to call it Bachelor's Day." He laughed. "Is there something you'd like to ask me, m'love?"

Sarah felt her cheeks warm and was glad he couldn't see her. She mustered her courage and strove for lightness in her tone. "I heard someplace that it's all right for a woman to ask a man for a date on Leap Day."

"Aye, that's allowed, all right. Of course, nowadays a man doesn't think it's odd if a lady invites him out anytime she pleases."

"Well, I'm a bit old school, you might say, but I thought, in view of the holiday, I'd be bold. Do you think you'll be ready to go out this weekend?"

"This weekend? No, I don't think so."

"Oh." Sarah swallowed hard. Things weren't going as well as she had thought.

"We can't wait that long," he said. "What about tomorrow night? There's no dinner theater, but we can get a nice supper together and maybe see a picture afterward. What do you say?"

"Yes! It's perfect. If you don't think you'll be too tired."

"I'm heading for bed early tonight to get my beauty rest," he said.

Sarah laughed. "All right, then. Tomorrow."

"I'll come by for you about six. And who knows? This weekend we might be daring and go out again. What about that?"

"Shocking," she said, "but I like the way you think."

"Sure and Saint Patrick would be proud."

The next morning, Sarah hummed as she bustled about the house. She straightened the living room, where she and the twins had played marathon games the night before. When all was harried back into her usual neatness, she was about to call Martha and ask if she could go to the Maplethorpes' for tea, but her phone rang as she reached for it. To her surprise, Lisa Pratt was calling.

"Hi. I was wondering if I could drop in and see you—unless you're planning to be downtown today."

"I can come there," Sarah said. "Is now a good time?"

"That's perfect."

Sarah stopped only long enough to call Martha. "Meet me at Liam's in half an hour?"

"Sure," Martha said.

Sarah checked the thermometer—only thirty degrees outside. She quickly pulled on her jacket, hat, and gloves and grabbed her purse.

In less than ten minutes, she arrived at the police station. Lisa came out to meet her and take her to the duty room. She offered coffee, but Sarah declined.

"I'm meeting my friend Martha at the café in a few minutes, so I'll wait until then, thanks."

Lisa nodded and seated herself behind her desk. "The chief authorized me to let you in on the latest. It's not for public knowledge yet—he'll decide how much to give the press."

"All right," Sarah said.

"Jim Brooks confessed to breaking the window, but not until another witness told us he'd seen him do it."

Sarah nodded. "I saw Steve Furbush Monday, and he told me that much. I'm assuming the motive was their old rivalry."

"Yes. Mr. Brooks was angry when he learned that Steve was back on his turf and drumming up support. He said he couldn't stand to see Steve come back to Maple Hill and pick up where he had left off. It seems Mr. Brooks has a deep-seated grudge against him. I'm not an expert, but in my opinion it borders on an obsession."

"It's unfortunate," Sarah said. "I think Steve was willing to give up the feud, but he still didn't want to have anything to do with Jim."

"I got that impression too. Things could have turned out a lot differently."

Sarah leaned forward earnestly. "What I really can't understand is why Jim was walking around with half a brick in his pocket. That was so handy. And it wasn't something he picked up on the spur of the moment."

"No, it wasn't. We know now, thanks to you, that it came from his garage."

"Did he have any explanation for that?"

Lisa nodded. "Unfortunately, yes. I didn't think he'd ever tell us, but after Mr. Furbush came in and gave us his side—that he'd seen Jim outside the library and saw him throw the brick—Mr. Brooks came clean."

"Steve's lucky it didn't hit him," Sarah said.

"He did have a couple of small cuts, where pieces of the glass hit him, but they'd healed by the time we started talking to him."

Sarah tried to recall whether he'd had any bandages showing when she and Martha talked to him at the Maple Leaf B and B, but she didn't think so. "I guess the blood on the glass was his."

"Almost certainly," Lisa said, "though we still don't have the DNA testing results back. I asked Mr. Brooks the very question you've raised. Why did he have that brick with him the night of the storm?"

Sarah had mulled the matter for days, but suddenly it all fell into place. She snapped her fingers. "He'd seen Steve go in there before. That's got to be it."

Lisa smiled. "You have a gift, Sarah. That's exactly what happened. The previous night, he had spotted Steve leaving a store and followed him. He shadowed him all the way to

Park Street, and then Steve seemed to disappear near the library's side entrance. But the library was closed—it was after nine o'clock and the building was dark."

"What did Jim do?"

"He waited outside the library. And then he saw a light inside—not an overhead light, but a small, moving light."

"Steve's flashlight," Sarah said. "He saw it, just like Mrs. Reed had before."

"Yes. He went home and thought about it. He says he almost called us, but he didn't. It's too bad. Because the next night he went back."

"Carrying the brick."

"Yes."

Sarah gazed at her across the desk. "But . . . did he go there intending to break the window?"

"We're not clear on that. He says he thought he'd use it to break in if Steve wouldn't open the door, and that way he could force Steve to talk to him. At least, he'd like us to believe that's what he had in mind."

"Not something . . . more sinister."

Lisa nodded. "His version doesn't make a lot of sense to me. The district attorney will probably use that in prosecuting him."

"You mean, he'll say Jim took the brick intending to hit Steve with it?"

"I don't know exactly what they'll argue if this goes to court, but . . . " Lisa shrugged. "Personally, I'm finding it hard to think otherwise."

"Yes, I agree," Sarah said. "You say 'if it goes to court.' Is there some question?"

"There's always a question. There could be a plea bargain, for instance. Mr. Brooks would probably rather settle it out of court to avoid publicity. I expect your son can tell you the ins and outs, but personally, I hope there's a trial. That way people would be able to hear the details. I think the people of Maple Hill deserve that."

Sarah left the police station and walked to the café, thinking about what Lisa had said. Might Jim have put the brick in his pocket planning to ambush Steve? The idea made her shudder.

Martha was already waiting inside. After giving her order at the counter, Sarah joined her at a small table.

"So, what's up with you?" Martha asked as Sarah took off her jacket and settled in.

"Well, let's see...I'm finally having my Valentine's Day date tonight."

"Wonderful!" Martha glanced around, then leaned toward her and whispered, "I wondered if that was ever going to happen."

"You're not the only one." Sarah smiled. "Jason and Maggie had theirs last night. I got to spend the evening with Amy and Audrey."

"Fun! What did you do?"

"First we played Uno, then we watched a silly video and ate too much popcorn. Then we got out the Scrabble."

"Sounds like a good grand-sitting night," Martha said.

"I loved every minute of it."

Liam came in from the bookstore and walked straight to their table.

"Good morning, dear ladies. And a happy Bachelor's Day to you."

Sarah laughed, but Martha eyed him suspiciously.

"Is there something I don't know about?"

"It's Leap Day," Sarah said. "The Irish have their own traditions, it seems."

"That's right." Liam winked at Sarah. "I wish I'd thought about it ahead of time. We could have had a big promotion for the store based on it."

"Next year," Martha said.

"Oh no, not for another *four* years," he said with a grin.

"Well, that gives you plenty of time to plan," Sarah said.

"True." The bell over the door rang, and Liam looked toward the bookstore. "Excuse me, ladies. Enjoy your tea. And Sarah, I'll see you tonight."

"Blarney and all, he really is a treasure," Martha said.

"Oh yes, I know."

Mischief twinkled in Martha's eyes. "*Hmm*...Ernie's not a bachelor, but I'm wondering if I can wangle dinner out of this somehow."

"You just might," Sarah said. "After all, it *is* a holiday."

That evening Sarah felt surprisingly calm as she prepared for her date. She showered early and fixed her hair and makeup.

The temperatures had fallen to below twenty degrees, so she put on a burgundy knit dress that always made her feel toasty warm.

The phone rang, and she approached it warily, afraid something else had happened to sabotage her time with Liam, but to her relief the caller was Bob Hutchins.

"Mrs. Hart, I have a request for you."

"I'd be happy to do anything I can to help with the window restoration," Sarah said.

"Actually, it has nothing to do with that. I missed out on the quilt at the silent auction, and I wondered if you would consider making another one."

"You want to commission a quilt?"

"That's right," Bob said. "I couldn't get over to the auction in person, and I was told some popular author outbid me. I wondered if you would have time to make another quilt similar to that one, using the window design."

"I'd enjoy that very much. Of course, a dozen people helped make the one for the auction. Yours wouldn't be identical, but I can make it very close."

"Sort of like my window compared to Great-grandpa's?"

"You might say that."

They settled the details of the transaction, and Sarah quickly took a new notebook from her sewing room shelf and wrote on the first page "Window Quilt for Bob Hutchins." She placed it on her desk, beside her computer. Tomorrow she would have a wonderful new project to plan.

Liam arrived punctually, carrying a bouquet of blue flowers. He kissed her on the cheek and handed them to her. "They say these are called bachelor's buttons."

Sarah smiled. "Yes. How did you ever get them at this time of year?"

"As soon as we hung up last night, I began to hound the florist. She wasn't sure she could get them so quickly, but she managed. It seemed appropriate for the day."

"Yes, very much so. Thank you." Sarah hurried to put them in a vase. "I'm surprised the cold air didn't shock them. They're beautiful."

Liam eyed them critically as she set the vase on the dining room table. "Not the loveliest flower in God's creation, nor the most fragrant, but they almost match your lovely eyes."

"Thank you. I'm partial to them myself."

"I made a reservation at The Old Mill. Is that agreeable?"

"Very. I've heard they've added some new seafood dishes to the menu. Oh, and don't forget—I initiated this date, so I'm paying."

"In a pig's eye."

Sarah laughed. "I'm so glad we're doing this. You always make me smile, Liam."

Liam touched her cheek. "Every time I'm with you, I'm smiling deep inside." He brushed her lips with his for an instant, then stepped back. "You said you're old school. Well,

I graduated with honors." He stepped to the door and flung it open with a flourish. "If you're ready, madam."

"Oh, thank you, sir. I'm very ready."

Sarah shut off the lights, flipped the lock on the door, and stepped outside with him. Liam closed the door, and she slipped her hand through the crook of his arm.

About the Author

Susan Page Davis has published more than thirty novels in the historical romance, suspense, mystery, and romance genres. She's a past winner of the American Christian Fiction Writers' Book of the Year Contest (Carol Award), and a two-time winner of the Inspirational Readers' Choice Contest. A Maine native, she now resides in Kentucky with her husband, Jim, who is a freelance book editor. The two youngest of their six children also live at home. The Davises have six brilliant and adorable grandchildren and an array of pets: a black Labrador retriever cross, a calico cat, and a Tennessee Walker colt. Susan loves to read and do needlework, logic puzzles, and genealogy research. She's a long time homeschooler and former schoolteacher. Visit Susan at her Web site susanpagedavis.com

THE PRICE OF TRUTH

BY CAMY TANG

 CHAPTER ONE

Sarah Hart exited her Boston hotel with a deep breath of crisp March air and a sense of excitement in her chest. The sun gilded only the tops of the nearby business buildings even though it was already eight o'clock in the morning, but Sarah was anxious to get to Lowther Auction House for their weeklong collectors auction.

Ahead of her, her daughter-in-law, Maggie Hart, chatted with her friend from California, Nicole King, as they walked down the sidewalk toward the auction house. Maggie's auburn hair contrasted with Nicole's dark long locks, and both women moved with easy grace as they walked.

"And do you remember Anita Mabry?" Nicole asked her friend.

"Anita!" Maggie cried. "I haven't thought of her in years. How is she?"

"The same. Her husband is still some type of executive for Paramount Pictures."

"And does she still get a new car every year? It was so much fun to go car shopping with her, even though she was the only one buying anything."

Sarah stifled a small sigh as she walked behind the two women. They weren't deliberately excluding her, but they hadn't seen each other since Maggie left Los Angeles almost two years before to move to Maple Hill with her family. They chatted on the phone regularly, but Sarah knew it wasn't the same as meeting face-to-face, and they were making up for the time lost.

Nicole, a stay-at-home mom who hadn't had a solo vacation since her kids were born, was only on the East Coast for this one week to visit Maggie and have fun at the auction with her. A casual collector, she was determined to bring home some fun pieces as a memento of her trip.

Their hotel, the Ramsgate Arms, was only a couple of blocks from the auction house, so they had opted to walk. Boston in March was cold but sunny, and the clear morning lifted Sarah's spirits even as she hastened toward the auction with quick steps.

The Lowther Auction House rose from the corner of two busy streets like a sentinel, four floors tall with a small row of narrow banners hanging along the second story on the outside of the building. The familiar blue and gold banners had only "Lowther" printed on them in elegant script over the Lowther Auction House logo, which looked like a coat of arms.

The three women walked past taxis parked along the curb unloading passengers arriving for the auction and hurried under the blue and gold awning over the front doors of the auction house. Lowther valets opened doors and directed people down the blue and gold carpet inside the large building.

Once inside the double sets of doors, the women removed their outer coats, scarves, and gloves to hand them to a young woman just inside the doors, dressed in the Lowther blue and gold uniform. She gave them a smile and coat tickets, then directed them through the archway into the entry hall.

The front entry hall was high-ceilinged and magnificent, edged with graceful columns that rose to the ceiling where a beautiful mosaic medallion adorned the center like the star on a Christmas tree. Along the walls of the square room, discreetly placed between columns, were desks for Registration, the Coat Room, and a small archway with "Restrooms" scrolling above it.

In the center of the room sat a gigantic circular marble table with a lovely flower arrangement atop it. Around the table comfortable seats were arranged in groups of three or four, surrounding tiny low tables.

Sarah stepped forward and noticed a subtle softness underfoot. She glanced down to find the massive paisley carpet that spread down the length of the entry hall.

Maggie and Nicole gave each other identical awed looks, then turned back to drink in the sight of the room again. "Sarah, have you been here before?" Maggie asked her.

"No," Sarah said. "Although I wish I'd come sooner. This is amazing."

"Let's get registered," Nicole said. "And then I want to look at the auction items."

They each registered at the desk on their left. They were given bidding paddles in blue and gold, each with a unique number to correspond to their registration information.

"This is a copy of the catalog," the young woman, one of several at the registration desk, said to Sarah, handing her a full-color catalog. "And here are last-minute changes." She handed her some papers stapled together with corrections to the catalog. "Preview of the lots will open in about thirty minutes, and the first auction of the day will start at ten o'clock."

"Where are the preview rooms?" Sarah asked.

The woman pointed to Sarah's right, through a large archway on the other side of the entry hall from where she had come in. A red velvet rope hung between two brass stands, guarding the way into the large area beyond. "The auction foyer beyond the archway has three rooms on the right side and three on the left, each room numbered above the door. The catalog will identify which room each item is in. The double doors at the end of the auction foyer lead to the auction chamber."

"Thank you."

"You're welcome, Mrs. Hart. Enjoy the auction."

Sarah turned to join Maggie and Nicole, who had also completed their registration. "Well, we're early for the preview," Maggie said.

"Let's get some coffee," Nicole suggested, pointing to a coffee bar.

They weren't the earliest arrivals for the auction event. Several other people had bought coffee and pastries from the refreshment bar and were sitting in chairs, chatting as they ate and sipped.

Nicole ordered a large double-shot mocha, then surprised Sarah by turning to her. "What do you want, Sarah? My treat."

"Oh no, you shouldn't do that for me."

"Of course I should." Nicole smiled at her. "You better decide before I order you the same thing I got."

"Gracious, that would make me bounce off the ceiling. I'll take a chai latte with extra whipped cream, please."

"Mmm, that sounds good right now," Maggie said. "I think I'll take one of those instead of coffee."

Nicole ordered their drinks as well as a trio of muffins, and they found three open seats ringed around a squat, glass-topped table. While the table top was a thick glass circle, the table bottom looked like a small barrel standing on its end.

"How cute," Maggie said, peering at the barrel through the glass top. "It looks old."

"I think it's an authentic French brandy casket." Nicole looked closely at it. "It's a bit small, but I think it's from the mid-nineteenth century."

"You would know." Maggie slid into the modern cushioned seat next to the table. "I bow to your great wisdom."

Nicole laughed and explained to Sarah, "Maggie and I always used to argue about European antiques from the nineteenth century. It was so strange, because we could usually come to the same assessment on nineteenth-century collectibles from America, or on early twentieth-century things from all over the world."

"It was always nineteenth-century European furniture," Maggie said with a grin as she sipped her chai.

"So then we decided to take one of those night classes at the local state university, 'Nineteenth-Century European Art and Collectibles.'"

"And Nicole got a better grade than I did!" Maggie admitted. "After that, I stopped arguing with her."

"How did you both get into antiques?" Sarah asked. She sipped the fragrant chai, which had been piled with whipped cream almost as high as when Liam made one for her at his café, the Spotted Dog.

Nicole selected a blueberry muffin and pinched off a bite. "We met during art history classes in college. We were always competing for the top grade in our classes."

"So at first, we hated each other." Maggie smiled. "But then a teacher stuck us together for a class project, and we found we did better when we studied together."

"Plus we both had a crush on a teacher's assistant in our Impressionist Art course, do you remember?" Nicole said to Maggie.

Maggie groaned. "Gibbs Huntington. What a jerk."

"We didn't know that when we first met him. You were floored by his golden curls." Nicole laughed.

"You weren't exactly immune to his baby blue eyes," Maggie retorted.

Sarah listened to them reminisce with each other. It did make her feel a bit like an eavesdropper on their conversation, but she didn't want to interrupt them or change the subject when they were having such a good time.

However, Nicole soon turned back to Sarah. "I'm so jealous that Maggie can use her love of antiques and her college classes to open her store. Antiques are only a hobby for me." She looked at her slim red watch. "It's almost time. Are we ready to view the 'treasure'?"

Maggie and Sarah finished their drinks and muffins. And now Sarah could see that there were several people gathering behind the red velvet rope in the archway that guarded the way into the auction foyer.

The three women lined up, and at eight thirty on the dot, a Lowther employee came to unhook the velvet rope. "Come on in, everyone," she said with a polite smile.

They entered the first lot room on their left. The auction was set to run over five days, and the room they entered was apparently full of items being auctioned off on the fifth day, not today. Sarah didn't mind, because the item she was most interested in was here, the "lost" Stifflemire friendship quilt.

She found it near the back of the room. The quilt looked quite large displayed on the wall, although Sarah knew it was only about seven feet square, which was small compared to other quilts from the early twentieth century. The background was a lovely light blue striped fabric, and marching across it were fifteen bright, colorful multipointed stars, each with a white circle in the center. In the circles were barely detectable names and addresses written in ink— a nineteenth-century address book for the bride, Laura Stifflemire, upon her marriage, from her friends and family.

The beautifully wrought Sunburst pattern took Sarah's breath away. Each sunburst medallion was made with different combinations of colored cotton fabrics. Sarah could almost imagine each woman whose name was on the quilt piecing her own sunburst medallion before inscribing her name and address upon the center. Then an expert quilter had appliquéd each circular medallion to the blue striped background cloth and quilted the whole with tiny stitches in intricate geometric and floral designs.

A table stood in front of the quilt and was deep enough to prevent people from touching it. On the table was a large sign that said, "PLEASE DO NOT TOUCH THE QUILTS."

Sarah frowned at it in frustration. She had brought gloves with her so that she could examine the quilt more closely, but while she leaned against the table, she couldn't touch the quilt or inspect the stitching and construction as closely as she would like.

Maggie saw the sign also. "Can you verify the quilt is authentic without touching it?"

"I don't know," Sarah said. "Perhaps I can ask an auction employee for permission. Irene specifically asked me to verify it before I bid on it for the Maple Hill Historical Society."

"What's this?" Nicole read the information card. "'The Stifflemire Friendship Quilt'?"

"This is a quilt that was supposedly lost," Sarah said. "It belonged to Laura Stifflemire, from one of the founding families of Maple Hill. There are documented records that it existed—letters from friends and family mentioning the quilt—but no one knew where it went because it wasn't in the Stifflemire estate when it was donated to the Maple Hill Historical Society."

"When Irene Stuart, the historian at the historical society, heard that it was being auctioned here, she went nuts," Maggie told Nicole. "But Irene was already scheduled to teach at some major historical convention in New York."

"I would have come to this auction with Irene, just to see the quilt," Sarah said, "but when Irene found out she couldn't come to bid on it, she asked me to authenticate it and then bid on it for the historical society."

"Look at all the names on it," Nicole said in wonder. "From so many different places. Massachusetts, Virginia, New Hampshire, New York."

"Laura was cousin to Ben Draper, the founder of Maple Hill," Sarah said. "She married Agnus Stifflemire and they settled on a beautiful estate just on the outskirts of town. This was the quilt her family and friends gave her when she married so she would remember to write to them." Sarah peered at some of the names. "Most of her family already lived near her when she married. I'm surprised to see so many names from places outside of Massachusetts."

"Did she go to boarding school?" Nicole asked. "Maybe these are friends she made at school."

"Let me check." Sarah pulled from her purse the thick folder of information about the quilt that Irene had given to her before she left for the auction. "Irene's notes don't mention a boarding school. Unfortunately, the historical society has more information about Laura's cousin, Ben Draper, since he founded Maple Hill, and less information on Laura. Irene said there's also very little known about the quilt, only that it existed."

"Did Irene include the Draper or Stifflemire extended family in your folder?" Maggie asked.

Sarah checked. "She included things like Laura and Agnus's immediate family and any friends she knew Laura had. Some of them are on the quilt." Sarah pointed to a few names. "That's Laura's cousin, who was a close friend, and that's Agnus's sister. But most of the other names . . ." She stared intently at them, but then realized looking at them wasn't going to make them reveal anything more. "Perhaps you're right, and these are Draper or Stifflemire extended family too distant to be on the family tree Irene gave to me."

"Or maybe they're friends of Laura's, but Irene didn't know about them," Maggie suggested.

"That's possible," Sarah said. "Irene's husband Chris is holding down the fort in Maple Hill. I'll call and ask him if he can look these names up for me." She took out her digital camera and took several pictures of the quilt, including one of each name. She had her computer back in the hotel room, and she could blow up the photos to cipher out the names and addresses scrawled in fading ink. Then she could e-mail the list of names to Chris Stuart, along with a short note asking him if he would look into this for her.

Maggie sidled closer to ask in a low voice, "How much would this be worth if it's real?"

Sarah considered it. "It has a higher value to the historical society because it's linked to Laura Stifflemire, but to the average quilt collector, I would say it would be appraised at about a thousand dollars."

She looked down at the information card, which included the estimated range of value determined by a professional appraiser. The appraiser had valued the quilt at a range of eight hundred dollars to $1,500. "That's a largish range," Sarah said.

Maggie nodded, also reading the card. "I wonder why?"

A Lowther employee in the familiar blue and gold uniform strolled by. "Anything I can help you with, ladies?" the young woman asked.

"Can you tell me why we're not allowed to touch the quilt?" Sarah asked. "I brought gloves, naturally."

"Oh." The employee gave an apologetic look. "We were open for preview yesterday, and Mr. Bartholomew put up the signs and the tables then because some people were manhandling the quilts, even though there were signs saying they had to use gloves."

"That's too bad," Sarah said, barely able to suppress a shudder at the way some people disregarded instructions on handling antiques. The oils and dirt on unwashed fingertips could make the fragile fabric and thread degrade faster.

"Let's go to room one," Nicole said. "I want to see the items up for auction this morning."

Room one was, predictably, full of people also viewing the items scheduled to be auctioned in a little over an hour. Once the auction started, the room would be closed to viewing so that the auction employees could safely and carefully transport the items to the auction room as each lot was called.

Maggie and Nicole were interested in some Victorian china sets, but Sarah made her way through the crowd of people toward three quilts which were being sold today. Two were from the early twentieth century, one from the late nineteenth century.

The oldest quilt was of "unknown" pattern, a lovely geometric design with squares of yellow and white calico and short rectangular strips of dark blue that had been pieced to create the illusion of stars shining through a lattice.

One of the others was completely covered with flowers and birds cut from a toile fabric and painstakingly appliquéd onto a pale cotton background. Even the border was made of appliquéd toile rosebushes, with embroidered leaves and vines threaded through them. Around and on the appliquéd toile, a masterly hand had quilted a complex repeating wave pattern.

The third quilt was a riot of color. Sarah recognized it as a Chimney Sweep pattern, with colorful blocky diamonds encased in a lattice of blue calico. The lattice was edged by triangles that must have once been a lovely russet brown, but which had faded to a rather sickly ocher color.

The quilts, while well made, had not been preserved well and there were imperfections and stains. A couple were also frayed on the bottom edges, some spots worse than others. Sarah mentally priced them at about one thousand dollars each.

Maggie and Nicole appeared beside her. "Time for the auction to start," Maggie said.

"Already?"

"They're about to close the viewing room so they can start moving the items," Nicole said.

Sarah noticed a Lowther employee in a uniform politely directing people out. In the back of the room, a second door marked "Employees Only" opened and a trio of Lowther employees entered the room. They stopped just outside the door, obviously waiting for people to leave so they could collect the items for auction.

Sarah, Maggie, and Nicole exited the lot viewing room. They found the auction room's double doors flung wide open, revealing a room with chairs in neat rows and the auctioneer's podium at the front of the room. To the side of the podium was a raised stage with a cloth-covered table in the center. Behind the podium and the stage hung thick blue drapes.

On the left side of the room was a long table set up with computers and telephone stations. Each computer already had a Lowther employee manning it, and some employees were already on the telephone.

Sarah hadn't been to an auction as large and well funded as this one, and she had never before seen employees responsible for signaling the intentions of Internet and telephone bidders for the various lots. Lowther's auction house charged a higher "buyer's premium" percentage that was added to each lot's "hammer price," or the price affirmed by the auctioneer when the lot was won.

Maggie saw the line of computers too. "If I had to, I'd go online and bid on a lot, but I'd much rather be at the auction in person, so I can view the items before I bid on them. Plus there's something exciting about being in the room when the bidding gets heated."

"I hope the bidding doesn't get too heated," Nicole said as they took their seats. "I don't want to pay too much for the items I'm interested in."

"So what's your maximum for that sugar and creamer set?" Maggie asked her.

While they talked, Sarah looked around the room at the people slowly filling the seats. One woman in a yellow hat who sat by herself seemed to keep sneaking glances at another woman, large and serious-looking, sitting a few rows away and wearing a dark purple jacket and matching skirt, and also sitting alone. The yellow-hat woman glanced at her several times, but the purple-suited woman ignored her, if she noticed the woman's glances at all. Instead she eyed the empty table on stage with a gimlet eye. Goodness, Sarah thought, the purple-suited woman looked as if she were going to war.

Perhaps she was. Sarah swallowed a giggle. Each competitive bidder was, sort of, her enemy. Sarah hoped she wouldn't be bidding against the purple-suited woman for the Stifflemire quilt.

If it was authentic. She had to find a way to talk to a manager about examining the quilt more closely.

Finally, the auctioneer entered the room from a break in the blue drapes behind the podium. Sarah caught a glimpse of a very large open doorway in the wall, covered by the drape, before the blue folds swung shut again. The auctioneer stepped up to the podium. Bald but with dark bushy eyebrows, he was a bit rotund but light on his feet. He cleared his throat delicately, and the din in the room gradually quieted.

"Good morning," he said, his voice deep and rich, rolling his r's and enunciating his vowels like an opera singer. "Welcome to the first collectors auction of the year, put on by the Lowther Auction House. I am Blaise Cameron, your auctioneer."

The excitement of the opening of an auction made a pleasant buzz start in Sarah's stomach. She had been to several smaller auctions and she had loved them, all the wonderful possibilities of winning lovely antiques, the uncertainties of what prices would be paid, the competition of different bidders. Other people in the room also seemed excited, shifting in their seats, lifting their heads from their catalogs, straightening their backs, and sitting on the edges of their chairs as they waited for the first item.

"Let's begin," Blaise said. "The first lot up for auction is a late nineteenth-century quilt."

The blue drape was held aside by an unseen hand, and two Lowther employees entered with the latticework quilt in their arms. They had carefully protected the quilt by laying it on a white cloth and they both wore gloves and long-sleeved shirts. They laid the quilt on the table so that the pattern draped over the edge, and they held up opposite corners so the entire quilt could be seen by the audience.

"An unknown quilt pattern," Blaise was saying, "worked in a masterly hand. All pieced cotton and hand-quilting. Estimated date is 1889. We start the bidding at four hundred dollars."

A man in a dark green jacket immediately raised his bidding paddle.

"We have a bid for four hundred," Blaise said. "Do I have four twenty-five?"

A woman sitting behind a computer along the side raised her paddle.

"I have an Internet bid for four twenty-five," Blaise said.

Before he could say anything else, the man in the green jacket raised his paddle again.

"Four fifty," Blaise acknowledged.

The bidding continued. Sarah wasn't surprised the price went to eight hundred dollars, but when it rose above $1,200, she turned in her seat to see who was bidding.

It was between the man in the green jacket and a red-headed woman. Both continued against each other until the bidding rose higher and higher. Finally, the woman bid four thousand dollars.

"I have four thousand," Blaise said, and looked at the man in the green jacket.

The man subtly shook his head.

"Last chance," he said. "Four thousand dollars." After several seconds of silence, he struck his hammer on the wooden podium, saying, "Sold for four thousand dollars."

There was polite applause. Sarah looked around, but no one seemed particularly surprised at the hammer price.

"What's wrong?" Maggie whispered to her.

"Nothing," Sarah said. "I'm just curious. That quilt went for quite a lot of money, but no one seems to be surprised except me."

"What was the estimated range?"

"Eight hundred to fifteen hundred dollars." The same as the Stifflemire quilt. Sarah hadn't looked, but she wondered if the appraiser had been the same person for all the quilts being auctioned. "But I estimated it as no more than a thousand."

"Sometimes those appraisal values are a bit low to encourage people to bid. These people probably thought that was the case here and the actual value is higher."

"You're right," Sarah said. "And it *is* an auction. Everyone knows that an item can be sold for several times its appraisal value if there are two people bidding who really want it."

The auction continued. A Japanese teapot went up for auction that Nicole wanted. It was an antique, hand-cast iron pot with a decorative dotted design sweeping along the side, twisting around the delicately tipped spout.

Nicole bid, but had to drop out when the pot, estimated at two hundred dollars to three hundred dollars, soared past five hundred dollars. The woman who won gave a little squeal of glee and hugged the man next to her.

The second of the three quilts to be auctioned that morning finally came up. It was the beautiful appliquéd quilt, although on the carefully lit stage, Sarah could clearly see the deep fraying along one side. The quilt also draped awkwardly in the hands of the Lowther employees who held it up, an indication that the quilt had been stored in one position for too long and was stiffening along the fold lines.

"Lot twenty-two," Blaise said. "A beautiful quilt with appliquéd cotton toile, hand-quilted, estimated to have been made in the 1920s. Opening bid is five hundred dollars. Do I have five hundred?"

"Five thousand!" shouted a man in the back of the room.

There was a soft collective gasp from the room.

Sarah turned in her chair to look at who had bid, and saw a short, thin man in a rumpled suit lounging in a chair in the back. While his body language seemed to imply he had other places he would rather be, his leg bounced up and down in nervousness.

Well, Sarah would be nervous, too, if she bid five thousand dollars on a poorly preserved quilt worth one-fifth that amount.

Blaise took the bid in stride, and didn't betray by even a slight raising of his dark eyebrows that it surprised him. "Five thousand, last call."

It seemed the room held its breath before he said, "Sold for five thousand."

There was scattered applause, more confused than impressed by the win.

"Lot twenty-six is another quilt, this one in a Chimney Sweep pattern," Blaise said. "Estimated date is 1931. Opening bid is five hundred dollars."

The man in the green jacket opened the bidding. Sarah paid closer attention to the people bidding, wondering if any of them would bid against her for the Stifflemire quilt. Sarah watched in curiosity as the lone woman in the yellow hat bid a few times, while again glancing at the woman in the purple suit every so often.

Sarah noticed that one of the other bidders did the same. A woman in a blue silk scarf bid against the man in the green jacket, then cast a quick glance at the woman in the purple suit and the woman in the yellow hat.

What was even stranger was that the two women glanced back at her, and at each other.

Also bidding was a woman with glasses with thick, fire-engine red frames. She bid against the woman with the blue scarf, but didn't look at anyone else.

The amount was over two thousand dollars now.

Again, Yellow Hat glanced at Purple Suit and Blue Scarf and then bid.

The woman in the red-framed glasses bid.

Blue Scarf glanced at Yellow Hat and Purple Suit, who both eyed her as well, then Blue Scarf bid against the woman in the red-framed glasses.

How strange, Sarah thought. She didn't know about the woman in the red-framed glasses or the man in the green jacket, but Purple Suit, Yellow Hat, and Blue Scarf all seemed to know each other or were trying to communicate silently in the crowded hall. If they were friends, why hadn't they sat together like other women in the crowd?

At last, the man in the green jacket bid four thousand dollars, and the trio of silent communicators bowed out. The man and the other woman bid against each other until the woman won with a bid of five thousand dollars. Five thousand again! For a quilt Sarah had estimated at one thousand dollars? Just like the other two quilts, this one went for several times its actual value.

Sarah clapped with the rest of the audience, but in reality she was dismayed and suspicious. This was almost too much for coincidence. Why had the three quilts gone for so much? And if these quilts had, would the Stifflemire quilt go for just as much, or even more?

She intended to find out exactly why those quilts had sold for so much. Otherwise, she might not be able to acquire the quilt for the historical society after all.

A NOTE FROM THE EDITORS

We hope you enjoy Patchwork Mysteries, created by the Books and Inspirational Media Division of Guideposts, a nonprofit organization that touches millions of lives every day through products and services that inspire, encourage, help you grow in your faith, and celebrate God's love in every aspect of your daily life.

Thank you for making a difference with your purchase of this book, which helps fund our many outreach programs to military personnel, prisons, hospitals, nursing homes, and educational institutions. To learn more, visit GuidepostsFoundation.org.

We also maintain many useful and uplifting online resources. Visit Guideposts.org to read true stories of hope and inspiration, access OurPrayer network, sign up for free newsletters, download free e-books, join our Facebook community, and follow our stimulating blogs.

To learn about other Guideposts publications, including the best-selling devotional *Daily Guideposts*, go to ShopGuideposts.org, call (800) 932-2145, or write to Guideposts, PO Box 5815, Harlan, Iowa 51593.